"On par with *Olive Kitteridge*! But where Olive woos, Eva Gordon captures. MacKillop's characters landed in my bones, guts, heart—and took up residence. A poignant, utterly beautiful story of perspective and hope."

—**CHERYL GREY BOSTROM**, award-winning author of
Sugar Birds: A Novel

"A story about aging, caregiving, friendship, parenting, nostalgia, and dementia—and a delightfully memorable and flawed character who has made her fair share of mistakes in life. There is the kind of patience in the plot development and character disclosure reminiscent of the writings of Marilynne Robinson."

—**JIM HEYNEN**, author of *The Fall of Alice K.*

"Splendid! A novel full of life and transformation, as charming as a New England cottage by the sea. You can't help but fall in love with spunky, hard-edged Eva Gordon and the others connected to Try Again Farm. Anyone living with regrets will appreciate the gentleness and grace of this story, and the permeating sense of love will stay with you long after the final page."

—**CHRISTINE KINDBERG**, author of *The Means That Make Us Strangers*,
Christy Award winner for YA

"A stirring story of both great sorrow and great love . . . that reminds us that love is indeed redemptive. Much like Elizabeth Strout's *Olive Kitteridge*, *The Forgotten Life of Eva Gordon* gives us a woman who begs to be hated but who, page by page, we find ourselves unable not to love."

—**KATHERINE JAMES**, author of *A Prayer for Orion* and
Can You See Anything Now?

"With lyrical and heartwarming prose, *The Forgotten Life of Eva Gordon* masterfully captures themes of redemption and renewal in person, home, and land. Prepare to be endeared to the unlovable and contemplate the profundity of the grace of memory."

—**KATHERINE ELIZABETH CLARK**, author of *Where I End: A Story of
Tragedy, Truth, and Rebellious Hope*

"*The Forgotten Life of Eva Gordon* is an engaging and timely novel. Well-written with a dose of humor and poignancy, you will fall in love with this cast of characters who create a misfit community. MacKillop tackles the difficult issue of aging, regret, and memory loss, with hope for second chances."

—**ANGELA CORRELL**, author of *Grounded*

"Her memory may be rapidly failing, but seventy-five-year-old Eva Gordon's sharp-tongued wit is ever-intact as she navigates nagging regrets and unspoken desires. Readers of all ages will recognize the enduring challenges of living with difficult childhood memories in an increasingly inscrutable present and will root for Eva, even in her harshest moments. Linda McKillop's *The Forgotten Life of Eva Gordon* is a big-hearted family saga, suffused with grace and kindness, featuring a cast of appealing characters who would be right at home in Jon Hassler's *Staggerford* or Richard Russo's *Empire Falls*. A quiet triumph of goodness."

—**ADRIANNE HARUN**, author of *A Man Came Out of a Door in the Mountain*

"A gently acerbic, absorbing, and deeply compassionate look at the disorientation and dislocation the elderly often face in their last years, and at those who face it with them. Eva is a captivating heroine, both prickly and poignant, and MacKillop is a wise and canny writer."

—**SUZANNE BERNE**, author of *The Dogs of Littlefield*

"Linda MacKillop has created a cast of endearing characters that will touch your heart. She captures the essence of what dealing with memory loss looks like, but with hope and humor. I relished her beautiful writing style and ability to elegantly convey Eva's thoughts and emotions. A gem of a book."

—**TERRI KRAUS**, author of The Project Restoration series and *Farmhouse Retreat: Life-Giving Inspirations from a Rustic Countryside*

THE FORGOTTEN LIFE OF EVA GORDON

THE FORGOTTEN LIFE OF EVA GORDON

LINDA MacKILLOP

KREGEL
PUBLICATIONS

The Forgotten Life of Eva Gordon
© 2022 by Linda MacKillop

Published by Kregel Publications, a division of Kregel Inc., 2450 Oak Industrial Dr. NE, Grand Rapids, MI 49505. www.kregel.com.

Linda MacKillop is represented by and this book is published in association with the literary agency of WordServe Literary Group, Ltd., www.wordserveliterary.com.

Cataloging-in-Publication Data is available from the Library of Congress.

ISBN 978-0-8254-4732-7, print
ISBN 978-0-8254-7785-0, epub
ISBN 978-0-8254-6938-1, Kindle

Printed in the United States of America
22 23 24 25 26 27 28 29 30 31 / 5 4 3 2 1

To Bill,
my love

One

ON THE MORNING OF EVA Gordon's escape, the sun sat crisply in the New England spring sky like a promising sign.

She tilted her head as her granddaughter's Jeep whined through the shifting gears on its way up the street, carrying Breezy to her teaching job at Hingham High School. When the sound of the engine faded farther into the distance, Eva quickly stripped off her pajamas, then donned a long-sleeved blouse, plaid skirt, a sweater, and a light spring jacket, with her winter coat over the entire ensemble. After she pulled a suitcase from underneath the bed, she stuffed pre-folded clothes into it, packing the leftovers into plastic grocery bags. There, her closet would be emptied inconspicuously. She would need her medications, hygiene items, a little snack for the bus, and definitely her glasses.

Her heart pulsed with the anticipation of it all. She gave her well-endowed chest a good tap to get her heart back into rhythm, ran a comb through her short gray curls, then tied the bags to her luggage, dangling them hither and thither off the sides. The excitement actually made her mind feel clear.

She lugged the baggage to the front hall and left it by the door. In the kitchen, she positioned a goodbye note to Breezy propped against the coffeepot on the kitchen counter where her granddaughter would be sure to see it. After making sure the dog was inside, she gazed outside at Breezy's garage, where her granddaughter had helped her set up her furniture refinishing shop after moving all the tools and supplies from Cape Cod. Eva would be leaving unfinished work, but Breezy could bring it to her later, once Eva got settled at home.

Ah, so many good things to come—warm days and time spent in the outdoors with hands in the soil once again, tending roses and hydrangeas, maybe planting a few tomato and pepper plants after she arrived back on Cape Cod. And walking the beach. How could she forget walks on the underpopulated beach? She didn't exactly have a place to stay on Cape Cod—yet—but she would work that out when the bus arrived in her old town.

At least there'd be no more city noise or knocks on the front door at all hours of the night by Breezy's needy students. Eva tiptoed out the front door and peered at the driveway. Mabel Maguire's car wasn't there. Mabel, the nosy, meddling upstairs tenant who attended church with Breezy. With no sign of Mabel today, Eva thumped her overstuffed roller suitcase down the concrete front steps of Breezy's two-family home, down the walkway, and out to the sidewalk, hurrying as quickly as possible—as much as a seventy-five-year-old woman could hurry. She wanted to get to the Cape before the planting season ended. She sketched a rough garden plot in her mind.

But then, right there at the beginning of her journey, the bursitis in her hip decided to kick up with an achy, nagging pain, arriving like a reprimand that old people shouldn't be traipsing around on long journeys. Eva hesitated. She could turn back and grab aspirin from the bathroom medicine cabinet, but she was in a rush and didn't want to be caught if Mabel returned home from her morning errands. Once Eva got going, surely the exhilaration of the escape would act as an anti-inflammatory and dull the ache.

At the edge of the sidewalk, she leaned toward the street, scanning beyond the aged maples and elms that lined the road, on the lookout for Breezy's Jeep or Mabel's huge Buick. A small sedan car turned the corner at the end of the congested city block, but no one else. Breezy should be halfway to school by now and soon engrossed in teaching the troubled lot of her theater students. Only a few more weeks, and summer vacation would arrive.

A young mom, wearing yoga pants and sweatshirt over her tank top, turned from her home onto the sidewalk, probably to walk the young children trailing behind her to school just a few blocks away. She pushed one of those gigantic strollers big enough to fit an entire family. Even a small terrier sat in one of the seats. Farther down the street, a male commuter walked through his front gate, lugging a work bag for the train trip into the city.

The only cars on the street sat bumper to bumper along the sidewalk, as if kissing, leaving little room for Eva to squeeze through. She stayed on Breezy's side of the street, heading in the direction of the main thoroughfare where she would turn left, go straight, and eventually get to the bus station. She had practiced the trip over and over in her mind. Her neighbor, Mr. Cho, glanced at her briefly without speaking, then returned to watering his plants.

She had unintentionally offended him once, or so Breezy told her, when Eva barked out some command about his mangy, yappy little dog. There may have been a comment about "taking him on a one-way trip to the farm" when his yipping irritated her to death. But when she turned back to look again at Mr. Cho, he was leaning at a drastic angle, his ambling gaze taking in her attire, appearing to puzzle over some question.

Eva shrugged. She needed to focus on her trip. She took off at what would be just the perfect pace. Not too fast to look like someone running from a captor, yet not too slow to be seen by Mabel or anyone else who might recognize her and call her granddaughter. She tried to blend in with the morning commuters by slipping into their fluid lockstep to the train station. No one would confuse her with a businesswoman on her way into the city to work in a high rise. Instead, people could confuse her with a homeless person leaving the shelter for the night, what with the way she'd tied the Stop and Shop grocery bags to her one large roller suitcase, the crinkling plastic sounding like a hearty bonfire when a gust whipped in from the side.

As she rushed, the wind suddenly blew the bags and they slapped against a tall man wearing some kind of security uniform. "Watch it!" he said over his shoulder while still walking in the opposite direction.

Eva ignored his scolding and continued on her way. No need to let any unnecessary attention interrupt her morning plans.

Maybe because of her rushing, this was a memory morning. Some mornings were empty mornings, offering only a blank mind with familiar words vanquished, memories scattered. On those days, her gaze passed over so-called familiar objects in her granddaughter's house but their names escaped her. Not only that, sometimes she found herself thinking about *nothing at all*. She'd simply settle into an awareness that her mind was blank, the day was warm or cold or rainy. She was hungry. People were around her. But these thoughts never appeared as words.

Other mornings, like this one, were filled with a rush of memories, a consistent flow of stories and people playing like a video of her past, complete with a soundtrack of familiar voices returning with the good *and* the bad. As she rushed down the sidewalk, the memory of a tossed suitcase and spilled contents, including her favorite teddy bear, overwhelmed her mind. She let the memory come, its sounds and textures filling her consciousness and blocking out the present moment, taking her back to her earliest memory—one that had haunted her repeatedly over the past seven decades.

Three-year-old Eva watched her impoverished parents prepare to leave on the day of their move to New York City. Left to remain with her grandmother on Cape Cod, she shivered as cold air swept over her skin as she hid behind the Windsor chair, staring at the open front door. It looked like a mouth waiting to gobble up her weeping mother and angry-faced father.

"Holy Moses. No time to drag this out. Give her a hug and let's get going," her gruff father's voice had boomed.

She rubbed her arm where her father had grabbed it all those years ago, yanking her in front of the Windsor chair, grabbing her small suitcase and tossing it across the room, breaking the latch.

Instinctively Eva looked down at her roller bag as she hurried to the bus station. A strap held her suitcase together along with a zipper. No latch or stuffed bear. Right. She reoriented herself to the present moment. Stopping at the next intersection, though, she stepped into the street then jumped back on the sidewalk. How would she cross such a busy street with the whooshing of cars and trucks, with horns blaring and music busting out of radios then fading as the vehicles passed by? Stores lined the street with signs screaming *Bring a friend for a free dessert, Cash checks here,* or *Stop in and let us meet your insurance needs.*

After several false starts, she stepped in behind other folks crossing the street on their way to the train. On the other side of the crosswalk, Eva glanced down at her bags to be sure her contents weren't about to spill.

Her panties lay there on the top of her shopping bag, working their way toward the opening. Mortifying! She could only shove them further into the bag. No time for a permanent fix or she'd be caught by Breezy or Mabel.

With one stolen look down the street, she kept on toward the station but stumbled over a man's knapsacks and stuffed trash bags strewn across the sidewalk where he sat in front of ACE Hardware.

He jumped to help her before she fell, steadying her by clasping her arm, steering her luggage over to a wooden bench as though she'd be staying awhile. He gestured with his hand, offering her a seat. "You okay, ma'am?" He peered at her more closely. "Did I see you last night at Sheltering Arms?"

"No, you did not!" Eva huffed at the mention of the homeless shelter. Did he mistake her appearance to be on a par with his? "I'm just going on a trip, taking a lot of stuff."

He released her arm, nodded, and half smiled, holding his eyes shut for just a second longer than a normal blink, an expression that revealed his own knowing and seemed to narrow the distance between their two stations in life. One of his eyes focused farther down the street and one on her. He wore a fluorescent-orange ski coat on this warm spring day, with a thick sweater underneath, carrying the contents of his closet on his back and in worn bags, the same as Eva. His outfit seemed in need of a good laundering.

"I'm in a hurry, sir," she said, retrieving her bags. "Thank you for steadying me."

He glanced down, taking a good, long look at her nicely pressed skirt and newish sneakers. "You don't happen to have money for a cup of coffee, do you?" He blocked her way, moving to the left as she did so, moving to the right when she moved.

When a police officer came out of a nearby store carrying a cup of coffee, the man sat back down and pulled his belongings in close.

Eva took the opportunity to make her escape, dodging other people on the sidewalk, huffing loudly when she found herself stuck behind a slow walker. Glances over her shoulder said she was safe—no one on her trail. Her spirits rallied, buoyed to be saying goodbye to the noisy Boston suburb that couldn't even provide salty sea air without mixing it with the fumes of buses and delivery trucks. She picked up her pace a bit, rubbing her hip as she walked.

Bumping her suitcase over each split in the concrete, she gripped the handle more tightly to offset an increased wobble in one of the wheels. Hopefully the wheel would make the trip, as it was likely some careless bus driver would throw the bag into the bus's luggage compartment with little to no concern. She paused. Examining the wheel gave her a chance to steal a quick peek behind her. Had anyone spotted her? There were joggers and mothers with jogging strollers, and men dressed in black pants with white, pressed shirts, those computer bag things flung over their shoulders. Many walked while looking at their phones. Eva would trip on the sidewalk if she read her phone while walking. Of course, she could barely read anything on her phone without Breezy's help. She had hardly mastered making calls.

She approached a Dunkin' Donuts, and the coffee smell permeated the air, sparking a sudden craving for the warm beverage and the jolt it offered. But she didn't have time. She reached another intersection and stood next to one of the contraptions that changed the light to read "walk." She reached to press the button, but a child's eager hand beat her to it. When the moment came for her to cross the street, a strong memory of walking to school with her snakelike cousins invaded her mind.

Suddenly Eva was crossing Old Main Street near her grandmother's house. Daily she walked to school, crossing a street like this one with those hard-hearted relatives taunting her.

"You're just an orphan, Eva," her cousin Jake whispered just as a car sped through the intersection, preventing her from fleeing the abuse. "Nobody wants you to live with them. Not even your own parents."

She only stole a glance at him, enough to see his yellowed teeth stuffed with the morning's cereal.

She brushed the distressing memory away, focusing on the promising day ahead, taking a gander to the left and right and behind herself. No sign of Breezy's familiar Jeep or Breezy's boyfriend, Ian, in his police car. She kept on her straight path. The bus station *should* be located at the corner just after the chain drugstore.

The farther she walked, the more convoluted the route back to Breezy's house became. What if Eva never found the bus station? Each side street with their shaded sidewalks and snug yards and houses looked exactly the same.

She could always ask directions.

Taylor Street?

Yes, Breezy lived on Taylor Street.

And then, just a ways down on her right, the giant Greyhound Bus sign hung like a great, welcoming beacon from the sky. She almost gave it a wave. She switched her suitcase to her other hand for some muscle relief and pushed on for the last distance to the station, then rummaged through her purse for money. But when she arrived, a dark, empty building met her—and a completely empty parking lot without any buses. The glass window out front had a sign saying Greyhound had moved over to Central Street.

A tall young woman wearing cowboy boots and straight, tight slacks leaned against the glass, head down, hair pulled sideways over one

THE FORGOTTEN LIFE OF EVA GORDON

shoulder, purse strap crossing over her chest as she scrolled through a phone. Looking up, she said, "Good morning, Gram."

Breezy.

"Well . . . how did you, why aren't you . . . ?" Eva let go of her suitcase, hope and excitement exiting her body like a balloon deflating after a puncture.

Her luggage toppled awkwardly to the ground from the heavy, off-balance load.

"I told the principal I'd be late."

"How did you *know*?" Eva asked.

"I can follow you by your cell phone, remember?" Breezy held up her own phone and showed her grandmother the phone screen with a map of the area and a little circle with the initials EG. *Eva Gordon.* "An app called *Find My Friends.*" Breezy picked up the luggage from the ground. "Mabel is going to have to stay with you for the rest of the day."

"I don't want a babysitter anymore, Breezy."

"I'm parked over here." She started walking, motioning for Eva to follow as if assuming her grandmother would fall obediently into step with her. "Gram, this building was closed last week when you ran away, and it will be closed next week too. We need to talk."

~

After that, the memory day slipped away, silencing the flow of voices and faces in Eva's mind. Still a crisp New England day, but no longer as bright and promising. Breezy navigating her Jeep through the city to Taylor Street, singing along to the radio . . . country music. Mabel, with her puff of white hair and sky-blue smiling eyes, waiting outside the house, rubbing her hands, a slight bounce on her heels, a shimmer to her waiting petite body like a racer anticipating the firing of the starting gun. Breezy's engine cutting off. Mabel hurrying to retrieve Eva from the Jeep. Mabel and Breezy exchanging pleasantries. Breezy pulling luggage from the back. Eva shooing her away. The heavy luggage thumping up the front steps one at a time, retracing in reverse the earlier getaway.

Breezy and Mabel outside, heads close together, a whisper passing between them in the driveway, gazing up as Eva entered the house with her heavy burden. Inside, Eva opening the hall closet, yanking out the vacuum cleaner Breezy never used, stuffing the suitcase way in the back of the closet after untying the grocery bags and dropping them in the hallway. Pushing the vacuum to hide her suitcase. Breezy and Mabel coming inside as Eva carried the plastic bags back to her bedroom.

The rest of the day automatically flowed past Eva in the same manner. She observed the blur of images without engaging, attaching very little meaning to their arrival. Mabel following Eva for the rest of the day, sitting on the sofa across from her friend as Eva held a closed magazine on her lap. Mabel blathering on about something as Eva just nodded. Mabel banging pots and pans in the kitchen as she cooked dinner and kept up light chatter.

Breezy after work, sitting at the kitchen table, eating a meal of beef stew prepared by Mabel. Eva breaking crusty bread and dipping it into her stew, the crunching food echoing so loud and deafening inside her head, blocking the voice of the other person at the dinner table who showed concern by furrowing her brow, then quickly adjusted to a tense smile. Breezy moving her mouth and swooping her hands, offering the rising pitch of someone asking question after question with attempted calm. Eva struggling to hear her granddaughter over the crunch of bread inside her head.

Breezy's pitch flattening out as she offered reason after reason why Eva needed to stay and live with her.

Eva sitting back with her hands on her lap, staring at her beautiful granddaughter's face, seeing her own daughter's looks reflected in the dark lashes lining beautiful wide eyes filled with suppressed irritation but mixed with concern. Her mouth forming, over and over, into sentences and phrases Eva couldn't respond to with words. Over and over, her blank mind simply clung to the word *home*.

Two

THE NEXT MORNING, A SHIMMERING, clean May day, felt as welcome as the rare good night's sleep she enjoyed last night. And for whatever reason—possibly the new nutritional supplements Breezy insisted Eva take, handing her handfuls of pills with breakfast and dinner to be swallowed two by two with water—she could remember the fact that the bus station had moved. The next time she headed for Cape Cod, she needed to leave her phone behind to knock Breezy off her trail. Eva pulled a piece of scrap paper from a desk drawer and wrote herself a note, hiding the paper in a pocket in her leather purse to remember those details when her mind dulled. Hopefully she would remember writing the note.

Her plan today was to find that new bus station and make a practice run to it, the events of the previous day now just a lesson in perseverance. In the face of sunshine and rest, resolve didn't feel as desperately needed as on the other days when words failed to form in her mind. Sure, a quiet nagging haunted her about her mysterious foibles and how they weren't normal, but today she would push away that worry, feeling firm and strong, her mind crisp.

Maybe it would stay that way.

Eva opened the window shade and looked down at the crowded neighborhood outside Breezy's home, houses lined up tight like sardines, all pressed together with only a driveway separating them. No stone borders. Way too close for Eva's liking.

Summers in the city were especially challenging to someone who preferred whispering fields and wildlife over the noise from her neighbors' lives shared through open windows. Televisions blared soap operas or twenty-four-hour television news. Squabbles erupted between parents and kids over broken curfews and uncompleted chores—yelling about not helping with dinner, never picking up after the dog, not doing an equal share of the work. Radios resounded from garages where young men gathered in groups to work on old cars or motorcycles. Basketballs bounced on pavement or against the rims of nets at all hours, beating like an unwelcome drum in her ears. So she schemed about finding somewhere else to live, making that secret trip back to the Cape.

As a person who had lived alone for so many years, Eva missed her privacy. She missed the gentle curves in the roads of Cape Cod, the way the sea air wove through the treetops even from miles away, the antique shops selling their wares, the timeless antique homes with their twelve-over-twelve windowpanes, stone walls providing a nice border between neighbors.

Eva dropped the shade with a sigh and headed to the kitchen to make her morning coffee. Then she could find the new bus station and prepare to leave.

In the living room, as she reached to open the two front window shades, a small voice wafted up from the couch.

"Good morning."

Startled, Eva released the blind to *phit, phit, phit* in on itself, flapping in circles around its rod. "Who are *you*?" Eva protected her chest with trembling hands as she backed away from the couch. "I thought I was the only one here."

"Sorry." The girl's face slowly came into focus, looking alarmingly familiar as it peeked out from beneath a blanket on the couch.

Eva stared at her, unable to remember her name or whether or not she *should* remember her name. And then a closer look at the girl's sunken cheekbones and sharp shoulders poking through blankets said it all. "Sarah," Eva whispered.

Just uttering her daughter's name urged her to suddenly distract herself with straightening the house or making breakfast to avoid the feeling of grief.

"No, we haven't met." The girl pulled herself up on one elbow. "I'm Isabella, one of—"

"My granddaughter's strays," Eva finished for her, releasing the tension from her shoulders.

"Actually, I go to church with Breezy."

Eva introduced herself as the girl hunted around for a pair of glasses that made her eyes suddenly magnify when she found them and propped them on her delicate nose. Something about her strong jaw made her look as if she would make a great boxer in another life. Jet-black hair in one of those ratty messes on her head—dreadlocks, according to Breezy—framed her pale skin like a contrasting checkerboard.

"Well, I should be used to it by now," Eva said, gathering herself. "Breezy practically rents out this couch by the week. Folks from church, broken-down students. Anyone who needs a place to sleep."

The girl didn't move an inch while Eva straightened books and magazines on the coffee table and stacked a dirty mug on a plate to return to the kitchen. Amber, Breezy's golden retriever, lumbered into the room for a morning greeting but Eva ignored her. "Shouldn't you be in school by now?"

A long, thin hand emerged from beneath the blankets. The girl rummaged around until she held up a cell phone. "Yup. Missed my English Composition class at the community college. Oh well. Breezy woke me up, but I must've fallen back asleep."

Eva waited, but the child still didn't move. "Well, for heaven's sake," she finally snapped. "Get up. I'll make you something to eat."

Mary or Bella or whatever her name was jumped up with the blanket twisted around her body and tripped as she tried to untangle herself. In a clumsy tumble, she hit the coffee table, then headed to the bathroom.

"Be careful!" Eva marched toward the kitchen with Amber following at her heels in need of water or food. Looking in the hall mirror, she adjusted her hair and smoothed a few loose silver wisps back from her ashen skin. Each year, as decades passed and Christmas cards and letters arrived from old neighbors or her clients, Eva noticed other people fading from view, too, with lightened or invisible eyebrows and lashes and cloud-colored hair. As they grayed and turned sallow, they looked lighter in each photograph, as though they'd been underexposed. One day they might vanish completely, and the Christmas photo would arrive with only white paper.

In the kitchen, she gave the dog some food and water but halted in front of the coffeepot as the unwanted blankness washed over her mind, probably from being startled by the girl. With great effort, she puzzled over adding the filter or the coffee first. The coffee or the water first? She studied the diagram Breezy had drawn, arrows pointing in the direction of pouring like a flow chart. She hated to ask the girl for help. She read some Post-it notes marked up with instructions and finally put the filter in the top, added water, then coffee on top of the filter. Her mind cleared. She put bread in the toaster, which was simple enough. How long would the girl stay? Was she a babysitter? Eva didn't want to give up her plans for the day, but she could always lure the girl into driving her to find the new bus station . . . if Isabella—that was her name!—didn't have to go to school.

When she opened the refrigerator door, once again Eva's bafflement returned. So many food items she could never recognize as food. If it were just her and Breezy, she might be able to keep track. But who wouldn't be confused by the sudden appearance of almond milk (how does one milk a nut?), leftovers from meals she'd never cooked, vegetarian sausage, and something that looked like a stick of butter but wasn't butter at all? She had no idea what was inside the plastic bowl blocking her from getting the orange juice. She hoisted the unknown container in the trash.

"They've made me lose my mind," she said, giving the refrigerator door a slam.

"Who has?" The girl had lugged her disheveled self to the table and rested her head on her hands after setting her phone and some type of book on the placemat. Obviously, she had slept in her clothes—and had a restless, sleepless night by the look of her mess of a hairdo tangled around her face and those dark circles under her otherwise young eyes.

Eva threw her a clarifying look.

"Oh." The girl pointed to her own chest with a light touch of her finger. "Me?"

Eva's look didn't waver, but she made no response.

"Sorry to startle you in there. I forgot Breezy lives with her grandmother."

"Actually, I live with her." *But not for much longer.* When the bread popped from the toaster, Eva buttered a piece for herself and for the girl. She set it down along with two glasses of orange juice. Was that a moistness appearing in the girl's eyes? Not wanting to get involved, she refrained from questioning it.

"You're so lucky to live with Breezy. She's the best. She doesn't know it, but I targeted her at church. I wanted to get to know her . . . especially because she wears cool cowboy boots." The girl picked up the toast, examining it closely before turning her eyes to examine Eva with equal concentration. "You remind me of someone—my grandmother, who died five years ago." She took a bite of the crunchy bread. "Grandma used to make me breakfast when I visited." Water filled her eyes, and the girl brushed her cheeks with a wave of her hand. "Oh, brother. I don't know why I'm being so emotional. I'm just going through a hard time lately. My mom's life is very full. New boyfriend. New job. Yoga. New friends. And my father, well, he's a piece of work. Always butting into my life but couldn't keep his own marriage together. I'm actually used to those two, but now that Brad dumped me—he *was* my boyfriend—I'm feeling a little rudderless." She picked up her phone from the placemat and scrolled for some sort of information. "*Rudderless—to lack a clear sense of one's aims or principles.* That's me." She put the phone back on the placemat and looked to Eva as if for comment.

Eva simply cleared her throat and offered a faux cough.

The girl rattled on and on with details of her life.

When the coffeepot finished gurgling, Eva got up and poured two cups of coffee, then poured milk into a pitcher and sat down across from the girl. Her mind stuck on Isabella's words about being "lucky to live with Breezy." The good, warm coffee offered a welcome comfort. Eva could feel her mind calming.

The girl's mouth moved as she formed words about her family and her problems. She reached for the pitcher to add cream to her coffee, then pulled and twisted her hair until it magically tied itself in some sort of knot in the back, no pins required, loose braids spiraling around her face.

How could Breezy listen attentively to this blather on a regular basis? Her granddaughter was certainly a master at finding the neediest ones. The girl might've talked until lunchtime, if Eva hadn't interrupted her. "I'm not much good in the advice department, but I have learned I'm happiest if I don't depend on others for my well-being. 'God helps those who help themselves.' My parents always taught me that principle."

The toast stopped midway between the girl's plate and mouth. Finally, she said, "Breezy taught me a different principle. 'God helps the helpless—if they look to Him.'"

"How's that working for you?" Eva asked.

"Let's just say I haven't mastered the principle yet." She put down her toast and scraped off the butter down to the plain bread.

"So are you spending the day here or going to school?" Eva asked.

"School."

Remembering her plan, she just wanted to end the talk and send the girl on her way so she could take advantage of a rare day with a thinking mind. If only Eva could just hand her those things . . . whatever they're called . . . to start her car and get on her way. She sorted through her memory for the name of those things that jangled.

The back door rattled with someone's knock, and in walked Mabel.

"It's like Grand Central Station this morning," Eva mumbled. She gave Mabel a look over the top of her glasses before getting up to pour her neighbor a cup of coffee.

As was her custom most mornings lately, Mabel arrived armed with side-of-the-road weeds in an empty concentrated orange juice container. Dandelions, Queen Anne's lace, and itty-bitty clover. Her social security check would never allow for the extravagance of store-bought flowers, but Mabel was a gift giver. She'd been arriving in the apartment lately like a spontaneous visitor, as if she was checking in on Eva, spying on her with instructions to call Breezy with any suspicious moves.

"Good morning, ladies." She turned her attention on the girl. "Who do we have here? You look familiar. Have we met?" Mabel gently cupped Isabella's tearstained face in her hand for a closer examination from several different angles.

Eva started to introduce her as another of Breezy's strays, but the girl introduced herself as Isabella Barrington. "We attend the same church. That's why I look familiar. But you sit on the right side of the congregation, and I sit behind Breezy on the left side."

Mabel offered her age-spotted, vein-covered hand for a shake, which Isabella accepted heartily with Mabel clasping the girl's arm with her other hand. "Well, now we've officially met." They appeared to be instant friends. "Isabella Barrington. Are you George Barrington's daughter from Wollaston?"

"Nope. No relation."

"Or David Barrington, the pediatrician?"

"No. I'm the daughter of 'Lord' Thomas Barrington from Hanover, owner of Barrington and Todd Real Estate and builder of McMansions. You've probably seen all his beautiful masterpieces all over the South Shore."

Eva's mind was clear enough to detect the sarcasm.

"I don't know him," Mabel said, "but I'm glad to meet you, Isabella Barrington." She set her weeds down in front of Isabella. "I like to bring Eva flowers in the morning to get her day off to a good start, but if my hunch is right, you could use a little cheer this morning."

Isabella wistfully picked up the container and sniffed the weeds.

Eva busied herself with kitchen clutter, wiping down the counter. *Spoons,* she thought. *No, clips. She needs her car clips to start her car and leave? No, that's not right either.* Eva looked out the kitchen window at the girl's SUV in the driveway, blocking the door to the garage workshop. If she could find the girl's things, she'd send her on her way in that huge monstrosity of a vehicle. She finished at the sink and joined the ladies at the table to eat her breakfast.

Mabel opened the *Daily Times* as she did most days, moving the flowers, butter, salt, and pepper out of the way to spread the newspaper open on the table, then positioning so that both she and the girl could read it. "Eva and I like to have coffee and read the newspaper together. And offer our weighty opinions."

Isabella sat up straight, squaring her shoulders and sipping her orange juice. "You like politics? What do you think of this crazy president? He's going to destroy our country."

"Oh, we hate politics." Eva joined them to glance over the newspaper. "I just like to see all the lamebrain things people do in this world, like people working for the mob claiming they didn't know those people were criminals, or people trying to break into a house, not knowing a detective owned the place."

Isabella leaned across the table. "Ahh. There's a nice story." She pointed to a headline. *New Life for Old Throwaways.* "A local teenager started a business collecting old throwaway electronics and refurbishing them for the poor. Good idea. Kids'll never get by in this world if they don't have a computer or computer skills." She wiped her mouth with her paper napkin and turned over her upside-down cell phone, presumably to steal a glimpse of the time.

"Probably trying to get his parents' approval," said Eva.

"Who? That boy?" Mabel pursed her lips. "Oh Eva, that's a special young man to care about others," she said as a quiet scolding, her white hair puffing around her head like a cloud wanting to rain on an otherwise sunny morning. She removed her glare from Eva, flipped to the back section, and smoothed down the paper's creasing on the table. "And we like to check out the obituaries. At our age, we know lots of people on these pages." She tapped on someone's picture. "Like this gentleman. *Davies, Matthew. Departed this life May 7. Memorial service at 2 p.m. in the funeral chapel on May 13. Condolences may be registered on our website.* Can you believe it? A funeral website?"

Eva leaned closer to read the entries over Mabel's arm. *"Remains resting?* Does he need a nap or something?"

"Appears no one survived him." Mabel skimmed her knobby finger over the paper on her way through the obituary. "No loving words written by his family about being a devoted dad or husband. We'll have to go support him."

"Isn't he dead?" Isabella's gaze passed back and forth between the two ladies.

"Mabel likes to go to the funerals of the 'lonelies' in case no one else shows up. And you'd be surprised how often no one shows up." Eva raised her eyebrows for emphasis. Funerals with Mabel accounted for much of Eva's adult church attendance. More times than Eva could count, the two women had slipped into plastic, cushioned, or wooden seats, dressed in their most somber clothes, and listened to the eulogies and farewell words from families, pastors, and friends.

"You knew him, too?" Isabella asked Eva.

"Never laid eyes on him," she answered.

"Eva needs to get out of the house sometimes," Mabel said, "and I just hate traveling around all alone, so she joins me. You know, in case my car breaks down."

"She travels around town all alone all the time. She just likes to coerce me to cross the doorway of a church," Eva explained. "She claims she only wants to go to the funerals of the lonelies, but Mabel's been known to slip me into some packed services."

"And someday she's going to grace the doorway of our church. Aren't you, Eva?"

"Nothing on the other side of the door I can't find on this side, Mabel."

"I believe you're wrong." Mabel tapped the table before speaking again. "I've been overwhelmed by God's surprises over the decades. I might ask for something—beg even—only to receive something completely unexpected and find it's better than my pea-sized brain could've imagined. You can't possibly know everything about a limitless God, Eva."

Ignoring Mabel's comment, Eva silently recounted the many

surprises in her own life and their unwelcome arrivals. Finally, she returned her glance to the obituary, pointing to the page. "Not one loving relative? What'd he do to tick everyone off?"

"He wasn't the kindest of men. Made folks angry." Mabel dropped her head as if regretting speaking ill of someone.

"Was he a murderer?" Eva asked Mabel in between bites of her toast. "Did he work for the mob?"

"You don't have to work for the mob or murder someone to be bad. Scripture says if you say unkind things . . ."

"Unkind things have that much power?" She had been stirring sugar into her coffee, noting the tinny sound of the spoon against the porcelain, splashing liquid over the sides. She fell into the splashes, thinking of waves crashing over the side of a boat when they sailed on a Cape Cod summer day with her bossy cousins.

"You're just an orphan. An orphan with a doll instead of parents."

"Can you hear us, Eva? I'm talking to you." Mabel's voice came from some faraway place.

Eva shook her head, slowly exiting her waterlogged memory, refocusing her attention. She didn't like the concerned way the women looked at her. Eva stood and abruptly took the dirty cups from breakfast to stow in the dishwasher. She read instructions from the Post-it note on the front of the dishwasher.

Fill with dishes, add soap in dispenser on door, close door, hit start.

A gentle hand pressed on her upper back. "It's not full, Eva. I don't think we need to start it yet." Mabel quietly closed the door. "It saves water if we just run it when it's full. Now, let's take a look at your calendar." Mabel put on her glasses, adjusting them on her nose.

Eva found her own on the table and put them on.

They walked over to the wall calendar and stood side by side. "Oh, it's a big night for you tonight. You're going to the farm for dinner."

Eva squinted at the little squares that ordered her days. "I am?" She looked out the window.

The neighbor lugged his trash down the driveway to the street. How could he remember which day the garbage trucks came?

"A birthday party. For the old uncle who lives with Breezy's boyfriend."

The memory appeared slowly, like a gradually opening bud transforming into a full blossom. Breezy had behaved strangely about the birthday party, mentioning it way too often, earning Eva's suspicion.

"What's the uncle like?" Mabel asked.

"Haven't met him yet. Ian inherited him along with the farm." Eva recalled Ian's intrusion into their lives—especially now that he'd grown serious about Breezy. He added to the overcrowding of an already busy home and became as frequent a guest as the students and Mabel. Often his presence forced Eva to stay in her bedroom in the evening, even if she'd like a cup of warm milk to get to sleep or to watch a television program with Breezy. She didn't want him to see her in her pajamas or be a third wheel to his and Breezy's relationship. She could hear them down there discussing their day, like an old married couple, giving Eva concerns about what lay ahead. Often, they'd expand their discussion to include the old uncle Ian lived with and cared for. They didn't seem to know Eva overheard them comparing notes about caring for the elderly, like how to make conversation with people who didn't always have a lot to talk about or make meals that fit both their tastes. But their talk never moved to complaining about either her or the uncle.

"I'm sure he's a fine, interesting gentleman." Mabel accepted Eva's offer of a napkin from the counter to wipe some leftover breakfast off her chin. "Well, at least you're free on Monday so you can join me at Matthew Davies's memorial service. Would you like to come, Isabella?"

"School." The girl finished her coffee with a long gulp.

"Stop trying to rescue me, Mabel." Eva positioned her hands on her hips. "I can take care of my own 'inner life' without being slipped into a church under false pretenses. Or babysat."

"What do you need to be rescued from?" Isabella paused in the doorway to the living room.

Well, there was her inability to drive, her forgetfulness, her financial episodes, self-imposed isolation, and the Post-it note parade. "Myself."

The first time Mabel had asked Eva to join her at a funeral a couple of years ago, the woman appeared to have lost her mind. "Let me straighten out this question," Eva had said then. "Lay it flat on the table so we can be sure we're talking about one and the same thing. You're asking *me* to attend the funeral of a total stranger with *you*? Someone *you* know, but that I've never laid my eyes on?"

Mabel's eyes grew wide and she nodded.

It was the craziest invitation Eva had ever received. But afternoons usually looked a lot like mornings. Straightening the apartment. Painting a set of dresser drawers for a client. Taking out a piece of meat to thaw. Trying to come to terms with her new, overcrowded living arrangement.

Eva had agreed to go. By now, she'd said goodbye to dozens of people she had never said hello to in life.

"I'm glad that's settled." Mabel now penciled Mr. Davies's funeral on the calendar. "Monday morning it is."

"Mabel just has this natural ability to influence people to go somewhere they have no desire to go." Eva grabbed Amber's collar and pulled the dog to the back door and out onto the back steps, where she clipped the collar to a rope so the dog could relieve herself without escaping the property.

Amber lumbered down the back stairs, then onto the meager grassy area while Eva watched from the back steps, hearing her father again bellow about getting "this show on the road."

"Eva, I was just saying that I think that's the nicest compliment you've ever paid me," said Mabel from the table. "Did you hear me?"

"What's the nicest compliment?" Eva asked as her father's voice faded out.

"That I influence you to go places where you have no desire to go. Because I only influence you to go to *good* places. Like Mr. Davies's funeral." Her arthritic finger pointed to the open newspaper.

Like church. Eva came back inside, letting the door slam behind her. She and Mabel sat in those pews and listened to all sorts of ministers of the gospel—male and female, educated and uneducated, silly and substantive, and probably a few imposters—and Eva thought of the existence of God. When she was a child occasionally visiting a church with Grandmother before she died, she used to stare at the stained glass windows and make up stories about the pictures there to avoid the preacher's description of a terrifying God—someone who existed *everywhere* and knew *everything*.

"But it's not even a *funeral*. It's a memorial service at the funeral home. How about this one instead?" Eva pointed to a distinguished-looking man on the page. "Don't you know *him* too? Charles Fletcher Sr., seventy-eight, who went home to be with the Lord, leaving a widow and a million children and grandchildren and a much-loved church and job." Smaller crowds made her nervous.

"Oh, I do know him too. A fine man. Served on many boards and built a new exhibit at the zoo. Great family, but Matthew Davies *needs* us."

Once again, the pressure made her acquiesce to someone else's lead. Just like when as a child she sat next to her strong grandmother as her parents left her behind, her little girl's coat still accidentally worn upside down because she had hurriedly tried to leave with them as they moved away. Ever since that day, Eva had mimicked her grandmother's stance, reflecting a sternness toward people and toward life, standing with feet together, legs straight, back tall, no tears, no emotions. Just resolve.

"Eva, you're not listening again, dear," Mabel said. "I have some errands to do today, and you're welcome to come with me."

A drive around the city would allow her the opportunity to spy the new bus station. "Might as well." Eva walked outside to where her father's old ship's bell hung by the back door. Reaching for the bell with *The Eleanor* still visibly etched into the brass, she rang the gong three times.

Amber dashed around the side of the yard in response.

Isabella had returned from the living room where she apparently had gone to retrieve her shoes and sweater. "You call the dog in with a ship's bell?"

"Doesn't everyone?" Eva smiled.

Mabel filled in the blanks. "The bell was a special gift in Eva's childhood when she went through a separation from her parents for a time.

Ship's bells always announced the whereabouts of one ship to another on foggy nights."

Wistfully, Eva looked outside at the bell. "'If you ring it for us, we'll always know where to find you when we're on our way home.'" Abruptly she turned and gathered the girl in her sights. "Mother gave me those words—and the bell. Then they left me." And they gave her one other item—a Bible with her name monogramed on the front, which Eva never read anymore, only using it to prop up other books on her shelf.

"Huh," Isabella said, looking to Mabel as if needing an explanation. Mabel just smiled.

"I think I should be going now." A nervous titter suddenly appeared in Isabella's voice. She collected her book and phone from the table.

Mabel gave her a warm embrace, then reached for her ever-present purse. "I almost forgot. Where is that rent check of mine?" She rummaged through her purse pockets. "I don't want Breezy evicting me. Please tell her I apologize that it's a day late. I wanted to walk downtown and get a cashier's check for her."

"For heaven's sake, she told you not to bother with cashier's checks, Mabel," Eva said.

Mabel stuffed the cashier's check in Eva's hand, leaning in as if a swift wind pushed her from behind, closer and closer, and then wrapping her fingers over Eva's, giving her a good firm pat.

"Do you know how jealous this makes me each month?" Eva pulled her hands away, waving the check in the air. "When you get to pay rent on your *own* place where you *choose* to live and can nap without anyone knowing, or stay in your nightgown till noon if you want to, or make your *own* plans for the day?"

Isabella paused by the back door, watching the two women.

"Is it really so awful living with Breezy?" Mabel said. "Living with a beautiful granddaughter who loves you? Some people have no one."

"Yeah. At least you *have* family who loves you." A deep sadness appeared on Isabella's face.

At least I have family? If only they knew how many unwanted goodbyes had inserted themselves into Eva's life, how powerless she'd been to prevent them.

Isabella pulled out keys from her purse and jingled them.

"Keys!" Eva yelled. "You needed keys!"

"No, I have them right here." The girl raised an eyebrow questioningly. "Well, thanks for everything. Sorry for scaring you, Mrs. Gordon." The girl who looked just like Eva's Sarah left.

The memories came. The soft feel of Sarah's pudgy hand on Eva's arm when her daughter was a child, the sound of Sarah's gravelly teenage voice echoing in Eva's ear. A failing memory served as Eva's only connection to her daughter, making it her most prized but ailing possession. What if she forgot her daughter scampering up trees, then sitting on branches while singing "The Sound of Music" lyrics to an invisible audience? Or the way the memory of peeking in on Sarah's sleeping body in her small bedroom recalibrated Eva as a parent, allowing her to fall in love again with the quiet, unobtrusive child so that—just maybe—she would make it through one more day with children in tow.

"Mabel, where are you going on your errands?"

"To Claire Abernathy's to drop off a meal, and a few other places."

"Isn't Claire Abernathy somewhere near Central Street?" Eva asked.

"As a matter of fact, she is. See, you can still remember some things."

Eva would join Mabel on the errand of mercy. They would drive by the new bus station, and Eva would see it firsthand, gathering information about her next attempt to get home—like a reconnaissance mission.

Mabel tended to many people. Diabetic Willy Martin, who needed to be driven weekly to dialysis. Marge Hamilton, across town, who used a walker, so peanut-sized Mabel helped her with grocery shopping and errands.

Then there was Eva.

What made Mabel want to rescue Eva? Eva, who *at least had family*, but felt alone and desperate to make her escape from the encroaching changes.

Three

AFTER A FULL MORNING OF errands with Mabel as she delivered food and medicines to people like the shut-in, lonely Claire Abernathy, who had nothing to say for the hour they all sat awkwardly together in her living room, Eva spotted the new bus station on their way back to Breezy's. The sighting of that building with its full parking lot of buses made the entire morning and that insipid conversation with Claire feel worth it. Eva tried to commit the route to memory, noticing the drugstore they passed, the direction of the sun, the proximity from the water, the butcher shop, all leaving her feeling exhausted and in need of a nap.

As they pulled into Breezy's driveway, Eva announced her afternoon plans to Mabel: "Lunch, a nap, then some refinishing time in my workshop."

"I think I might actually put my own head down for just a minute too." Mabel slipped the car into park.

Eva wasn't fooled. Mabel always seemed to have an ear out for her every move, probably peeking often out the window from behind her drapes, checking for Eva and any possible escape. They may not be in the same room, but Mabel seemed aware of Eva's every footstep, commenting on how her friend had been restless on certain days, or walked in and out of the back door multiple times, or slept with a fan on.

Eva went back to her room but couldn't sleep. She lay flat on her back on the bed, arms crossed over her chest like a corpse in a coffin, eyes shut and resting. She'd heard that hikers who couldn't sleep while on a long hiking trip just attempted to quiet their bodies at night, allowing for the stillness to provide the needed rejuvenation. Eva took deep breaths, exercising techniques Breezy's students talked about as attempts to manage their stress. But her mind rushed through escape scenarios and the accompanying embarrassment over yesterday's failed attempt. If only she had just one confidant in the world, someone who would brainstorm with her but not divulge Eva's plans to Breezy.

No one came to mind.

When she gave up the attempt to nap and pulled herself from the bed, the fog of her mind dispersed, leaving her with talking memories, a collection of chattering people crossing the decades, some not knowing each other in life. She took all those thoughts with her as she went out to the garage-turned-workshop and hunched over a dresser to sand off the old finish of a thrift store find. Her refinishing work often helped her mind to operate on several different levels. She could be buffing a desk while exploring solutions to get to Cape Cod while relishing a memory from sixty-five years ago. Her mind didn't always work correctly, but functioned in many ways like a congested highway in need of a traffic cop. She worked best alone, but Mabel seemed to appear the minute Eva started any project, as if Breezy had made an arrangement with her.

Post-it notes lined the peg board on the wall to remind her to *apply polyurethane after sanding, shake the cans, wash the brushes, unplug the sander.* With the garage door flung wide open, sawdust flew out while fresh spring warmth filed in. The welcomed quiet and solitary work felt almost as good as an afternoon alone on Cape Cod. The smells of raw wood, fresh paint, and outdoor air—like home. Not exactly the tantalizing aroma of cookies in the oven but homey nevertheless. The monotonous sanding, and later, the gentle smattering of a brush smoothing on a gurgling mixture would provide a calming backdrop for all her private thoughts.

She felt a kinship with the particular dresser she worked on today. Years of serving a family had left scrapes and water marks on its surface.

Life had roughed up its surface, marring the finish. Her job was to erase the damage of years. While Benny Goodman music blared from the radio on her workbench, she rhythmically sanded with coarse paper, then finer and finer paper. Her legs and lower back began the usual ache as the ancient finish vanished one smooth layer at a time, one speck of sawdust at a time, allowing an hour to pass by in peace. At last, bare, fresh wood appeared underneath, unaware of all the damage the world could inflict on its poor, exposed surface.

Give me your tired, weary, and worn desks, chairs, and cabinets, and I'll make them like new, read the brochure Breezy had helped her create to be passed out to acquaintances. For decades, Eva had been covering over flaws in people's furniture or buying pieces to fix up and sell. She knew how to hide and smooth out defects. Back on Cape Cod, she had regular customers.

Breezy humored her with "customers" by having her friends bring their worn furniture to Eva for refreshing. The work occupied and distracted Eva, and she would take the customers any way she could get them. Most often, she found old pieces at Goodwill and refinished them for Breezy's friends to purchase. Sometimes she and Breezy put the piece out at the street with a sign that read $75. People came and knocked at the front door and offered crisp, green bills for the item.

When she restarted the sander, letting it hum along loudly to remove dirt and grime from the wood, she looked up to see a small woman's image floating through the haze of the rising debris. Her grandmother, who used to take Eva's hand for a walk to the mailbox at the end of her driveway to collect letters from Eva's parents.

I'm working as a nanny for a well-to-do family. Make sure Grandma reads to you each night from the Bible we gave you.

Eva's mother's letters described life in New York while disguising the news of her father's flight through odd jobs as he searched for something that fit him best. Eva recognized her mother's ploy in hindsight only. Her father had begun in the Sears warehouse, hoping for advancement—until the boss man got under his thin skin and he quit. Then he eyed those skyscrapers, wanting to join the ranks of the brave workers constructing structures like the Empire State Building. Instead, he landed a job as a hotel janitor, eventually becoming a painter on a skyscraper.

No shame in work of any kind, Eva's mother wrote often. He finally settled on carpentry, beginning as an apprentice and eventually learning to make the most beautiful furniture . . . and teaching Eva, once they reunited, to use his tools and skills.

The vision waved to Eva through the sawdust, and Eva merely nodded back, still angry that Mother and Father never did send for her. And that interminable wait until they returned!

Oh Eva, her mother wrote in another letter, *It seems our visit passed too quickly. I will never forget arriving to hear you ringing the ship's bell!*

Then the vision spoke.

"Eva, can you hear me? I'm asking what you're working on." Mabel's voice dispersed the memory.

Eva released the button, allowing the sander to *wing, wing, wing* down to silence, at which time she gave Mabel a piece of her mind for startling and sneaking up on her. "Could you please announce your arrival next time, Mabel? I thought I was imagining things."

"I'm sorry, dear. I didn't know how to get your attention with that sander running. You up for giving me a lesson today?"

"A short one," said Eva. "Grab yourself a smock from that hook on the wall. I'm almost ready for the final coating on this project." Eva's favorite and satisfying stage of refinishing furniture was adding a thick layer of protection.

Mabel donned the smock and together they cleaned up the sandy, dusty surfaces and pulled out the shop vac to suck up the debris from the floor. "Your father actually taught his *daughter* to do woodworking? He was a man before his time."

"That's one way to describe him."

"Can't you listen?"

"This is how you use the vise."

"Make sure you clamp the wood or you'll make one more mess."

Her father's voice traveled through time with his harsh words meant to weatherproof her from life's unexpected calamities, as she had tried to do with her own children.

"Good thing you can work alone, Eva, since you can't get along with a soul with that mean mouth of yours."

"From what you've told me, I know he was a bit hard on you, Eva. And he had no right to predict your future the way he did. A parent's words are powerful—especially when children believe the negative ones. I don't understand why any parent would wish trouble on their own offspring."

Eva pretended to admire the dresser's lines while catching her breath.

Her father offering a snort of approval over her handiwork.

Her father chiding her about her clothing.

Arguments with her husband, Wallace, about misunderstood motives and words.

The car engine as her kids drove away from her house to start their own lives and leave her behind.

She brushed dust from the dresser top. "It's over and done with now."

The phone rang inside the house.

"You go grab the phone, Eva. It might be important." Mabel grabbed a stirrer and began mixing. "I can even start brushing on the finish."

Eva hustled inside to catch the caller before they hung up, chest heaving by the time she answered.

"This is Sheila from Cedarwood Nursing Home. Is Breezy home?" the caller asked.

"No, Breezy isn't here. Did you say . . . did you say you're calling from *a nursing home*? Why are you looking for Breezy?" She felt a rude spell come on. "It would be best if you try another time."

"Actually, I'd rather leave a message."

"Of all the bother. I don't have a pen right here." She rubbed her finger over the ballpoint pen sitting next to the phone on top of a message pad.

"I'll wait while you get one." The Cedarwood woman spoke in a professional tone.

Eva set down the phone and counted to thirty while remaining in place. She opened a drawer, shut it, then waited some more. Finally, she picked up the pen and the phone. "Okay. I'm ready. What's the number?" she asked, then scribbled it on the pad as the lady repeated it several times. Eva's body stiffened after she hung up, and her jaw clenched. She stared at the phone, resting in its cradle, then crumpled the paper and threw it in the trash.

So Breezy was talking to a nursing home. One more reason to find a new place to live.

Four

WHEN THE CLOCK IN THE front hall chimed, the back door opened and Breezy entered as if on cue, like someone living her life by the directions of a stage manager. She flung her work bag on a kitchen chair.

In her recliner, Eva shut her eyes and feigned sleep, waiting until her granddaughter lightly shook her before slowly opening them with a blank look for the sneaky granddaughter who was having secret conversations with nursing homes.

Still dressed in nice black slacks and a blouse from her day of teaching, Breezy seemed to assess her grandmother's appearance with a slow move of her eyes from the oversized work T-shirt down to Eva's stain-covered sneakers, where a hole allowed a couple of toes to peek out. Her expression said it all, silently chiding Eva for not being ready for the birthday dinner out on Ian's family farm. A lingering look at her watch said Breezy expected her grandmother to get a move on.

"Gram, I said you could be casual . . . but I did expect you to clean up from your shop. I see the sawdust in your hair. This is what I'm wearing." She waved her hands past her work attire.

Eva ran her fingers through messy curls, feeling the grit of sawdust on the strands and scratching against her scalp. As the hall cuckoo clock came into focus, slowly she pushed aside the distraction caused by the nursing home call. She should've showered. She locked eyes with her granddaughter, who squinted as if trying to appraise her grandmother's state of mental clarity. Breezy had learned to decipher Eva's memory days, or foggy days, or blank days, offering a different Breezy for each day. Soft Breezy, insistent Breezy, nurse Breezy.

Silently, Eva defiantly stared back, offering no hints of her state of mind. She had so little privacy left, and keeping her thoughts to herself remained one of the few barricades she could erect. She wouldn't talk about the call until she felt good and ready. She would give Breezy a blank day even though it was a memory day.

As Eva rallied, pushing herself up out of the chair by the arms, hard Breezy turned into soft Breezy, gently lifting her grandmother by the arm to assist her up, placing one hand on Eva's back to balance her.

"We have time for you to take a quick shower, Gram. And put on some clean clothes. It's a big night."

Eva froze, then turned toward Breezy. "Why's it a big night?" Suspicion tingled through her bones, coupled with just a hint of fear. Would they announce sending her to Cedarwood Nursing Home?

Breezy averted her eyes. "Just a special night. Your first trip to the farm and all." Her words sounded unconvincing.

When they met up again in the front hall, Eva felt refreshed and clean even though anger simmered below the surface. Or was it hurt? She preferred being the only one making secret plans for her life. Couldn't life pause for a moment, giving her time to catch up and make sense of all the events?

Eva spotted the stamped letter she had meant to drop in the mail earlier on the hallway table.

Breezy picked it up, jingling keys in one hand. She had put on her Boston Red Sox cap, which she wore while driving to hold her hair captive, just a ponytail poking out the back. The cap made her look so young, yet she held so much authority over Eva's life, determining where Eva would live—in an apartment, a nursing home, or somewhere else.

So much authority . . . That last rear-end collision had been the beginning of the end, landing Eva in Breezy's house.

A couple of years ago during one of their weekly phone chats, after filling Eva in on her teaching, the return of an old boyfriend—Ian

Ward—into her life, and the lovable lady from church renting her upstairs apartment, Breezy had asked how Eva was doing.

Eva had broken the news about the collision of her car. "I had a little accident and decided to get rid of my car. But I can walk around this village just fine."

"Not again, Gram. Another accident?"

Eva pictured Breezy dramatically dropping her face into her hand, rolling her forehead back and forth as her hair fell across her face. When she finally looked up again, she'd probably reach her slender hands toward the ceiling and silently mouth the words: *Not again, Lord!*

But Breezy's voice continued as if feigning calm, dropping in volume, as if nothing could ruffle her feathers. "You can't walk around Cape Cod for all your errands. Everything's so far apart."

Underneath Breezy's words, determination and frustration.

"I hate to broach this subject again, but I wish you'd consider living with me. You'd do better living with family . . . and I think you'd enjoy the company instead of living alone. You know they say people who live with other people have a longer lifespan. I'm serious. It's science. And, on top of a longer lifespan, I'm not a bad roommate," Breezy said. "You'd have lots of community with my friends, neighbors, and church family."

"I don't want to leave my home."

"It's not practical to walk everywhere on the Cape, especially not in winter."

"I've lived here forever," Eva had said. Even as she uttered the words, she felt her resolve weakening as Breezy's argument hit its target, raising the question of all the what-ifs. And Eva's daughter, Sarah—Breezy's mom—would never take her in after all they'd been through, their rocky relationship, the split from Sarah's father. Oh, how messy—and not a memory she liked to revisit. And her son, Rob, lived overseas. Not a chance of moving there. Besides, he never kept in touch. Breezy was likely the only family member who would be so generous.

Eva agreed to a trial run, and a week later, with a mumbled agreement between them, Breezy appeared at Eva's house, letting herself in just as the bells chimed at the church down the road, as if announcing the arrival of someone of importance, someone in authority, someone about to bring change to one's life. "You need to live where I can help you," her granddaughter said. Then she picked up the phone to call a real estate agent.

Eva should've given her a piece of her mind. She thought she'd be keeping the house, like a comfortable family member waiting for her to return someday when all the health crises passed. While Eva remained childlike and silent, this granddaughter who once played with her dolls in Eva's sunroom dialed the numbers one rotary dial at a time on Eva's old phone—the number 8 and release, the number 7 and release . . .

"Hello, Mr. Orelong? I'm calling about listing my grandmother's house for sale . . . over at 739 Pinecone Dr." She covered the mouthpiece with her hand. "We're going to head this thing off at the pass."

They had become roommates since no one else wanted Eva—not her son across the pond or her daughter. And all the other relatives had passed on.

If she had just kept the accident and her loss of a driver's license to herself, maybe she'd still be living in a salty place surrounded by unobtrusive, private people amidst sand dunes and tidal pools.

Now Breezy carefully studied the front and back of that envelope, her face looking heavier than it had looked that morning. At the moment, creases between her eyes replaced the usually smooth, taut skin below her dark, thick eyebrows. Most days, she wore an expression of determined and intentional joy for others to see, standing tall and throwing back her shoulders, voice ringing loud and confident like a performer. She offered a thousand expressions through the movements of her face and eyes, like a thousand characters telling a myriad of stories covering all range of emotions.

Eva could smile, remain expressionless, and frown.

But Breezy?

All with the most subtle adjustment of her eyes and face muscles, Breezy mixed surprise with knowing, self-deprecation sprinkled with assurance, anger dotted with justice, and subtle suspicion masked as interest.

Breezy held up the envelope. "Does he ever write you back?"

Eva didn't answer Breezy, still clamped shut inside her pretend blank mind day. If she answered, she would've said, *"Well, maybe I had the wrong address. I'll check before I write him again."* Instead, Eva moved toward the door as her father echoed, *"I said, let's get this show on the road."*

Breezy dropped the letter on the table and rushed to open the door for her grandmother. "Doesn't that hurt you?" Without waiting for an answer, she pulled the door open wide, directing her grandmother onto the porch with a respectful arm wave and a half bow. When she whistled for Amber to join them, the dog bulldozed past them and trampled down the front steps sounding like a carrier suitcase on wheels. "Maybe you weren't a perfect mother, but who is?"

Outside the house, they loaded into the Jeep with Amber crowding and drooling over Eva from her spot standing on the backseat.

Eva gave the dog a shove and turned her face toward the window. Why should she converse with a granddaughter who was making secret plans?

They wove through the city streets, leaving Quincy behind for quieter, smaller towns where shadows elongated and yards widened. "It's a perfect summer night to be out on a farm, Gram. You'll love the place."

Eva offered only silence in return, even when Breezy tried to pry out answers to a few small-talk questions. Breezy apparently gave up trying to engage Eva and raced into a monologue of her day, students' successes and challenges, and end of the year events, eventually landing on one pointed question. "Gram, do you like Ian?"

Eva had been watching scenery go by, fighting images of drooling patients in a nursing home, but suddenly jolted back against the seat before looking with surprise at Breezy. "Of course I like Ian. What sort of a silly question is that? Don't I act as if I like Ian?"

The lift of Breezy's eyebrows and the pinch of her lips said it all.

"He's a far cry better than your past boyfriends."

Breezy offered a whooping laugh. "Agreed. And all that time while I dated losers, Ian waited in the wings since we were kids. Not sure how we didn't figure out this relationship sooner. I guess I just needed to go through my 'bad boy' stage."

"Yeah, I never figured out how you ended up with some of those guys dressed all in black with surly attitudes."

Breezy smirked, then reached over to scratch Amber behind the ear when the dog leaned in the front seat. "I just always looked for the best in people when others write them off. And with the surly guys, I thought I could cheer them up with my . . . magnetic personality." She waggled her head for emphasis.

Breezy had always been the family optimist, dancing through her days as if beckoning her family to substitute their bickering for love and fun. As a child, she changed her name numerous times before morphing into the family manager of forgetful grandmothers and the high school student rescuer. Named Breann MacPherson at birth, she became Emily Grace in middle school so she could have two separate names *like girls down South*, then Rose in high school, like the flower, not the color. Sarah finally nicknamed her Breezy, like the wind, because whenever she appeared, things began to move and change.

Ian was the perfect match for Breezy. He was a police officer impersonating a farmer, and she impersonated someone with no burdens to shoulder. Together, the air would always swirl with life around them.

Eva's life certainly moved at Breezy's presence—sometimes for the good, sometimes not so much. What would Breezy be like if Eva had raised her? Probably far less of a healing wind. Eva never would've been as obliging as Sarah if her own children had wanted to change their names. Of course, Eva hadn't seemed to win any of the battles that came along, especially considering the outcome of her relationships with her kids. She had tried to control Sarah's behavior, eating habits, her dress—and even more unrealistically, her feelings toward her mother, which seemed to fade out more and more, like an underexposed photo, until in her adult years they went kaput altogether.

"How long is it going to take to get us to Try Something New Farm?" Eva asked.

"Try Again Farm, Gram. Try Again. Ian's grandfather bought it after World War II when everyone was *trying again* to get back on track. Maybe you can remember it that way. He had a rough time overseas, getting shot, losing a bunch of friends, and thought a farm would be a place of healing. Wait 'til you see it! Ian and I think of him every time we wander the fields, listening to the birds chatter and the wind whistle. Ian says the farm saved his grandfather from all sorts of inner turmoil. Unpopulated places allow you to hear God over the whir of life's noise. Some of Ian's best memories are of working in the garden, picking herbs with his grandmother to be dried, and selling produce at their farm stand."

Eva softened slightly, staring at her granddaughter's face. What kind of horses had they boarded? How many acres surrounded the farm? She softened more. How compassionately this granddaughter of hers leaned into the Ward family story, offering her listening face tilted in their direction with empathy. Breezy would be the person to tend all their wounds.

"And here we are!" Breezy announced their arrival in the giant metropolis of Pemberton. Strip malls and small businesses dotted the center of town, which consisted of just two main roads intersecting like a cross. An attorney's office put an old Cape Cod–style house to good use. A couple of humdrum side roads spidered off the main street. Past the intersection, subdivisions looked as if they'd been dropped from the sky into fresh farmland, naked without trees. A large wooden sign with letters etched in gold appeared:

PEMBERTON
ESTABLISHED 1750

"Well, isn't this just charming." Without any sidewalks where neighbors could meet up with each other and missing a village green where folks could picnic, the town grew up around an intersection, nothing more—a place where people could collide but never engage.

They turned down a quiet road onto rough asphalt, worn and gray and bumpy, passing woods, a cranberry bog, and cornfields. At last they pulled into a dirt driveway marked by an open white wooden gate and a swinging black sign proclaiming *Try Again Farm* in painted silver letters.

The Jeep halted, and the engine cut out. Country sounds appeared: the creaking of the sign, the rustling leaves, and the hammering of a new house being built in the distance.

Eva's unease drifted away with her exhaled breath.

She had imagined the house differently, more like her childhood home, a warm Cape Cod–style house with its narrowed second floor. But this simple L-shaped farmhouse had a central chimney jutting out the middle and a red front door with white clapboard siding begging for a fresh coat of paint. The roof shingles needed to be replaced, and black shutters waited on the ground for some type of attention. The weed-infested lawn encroached into the shrubbery, erasing the demarcation line between garden and grass. A truck sat in the wide driveway that separated the house from the barn by about one hundred yards.

Behind the house, an orchard remained, but with long grass growing up around the tree trunks and down what used to be a path between the trees. Despite its disheveled appearance, the house seemed to open its arms and welcome her with an unexplainable familiarity, as if she had eaten breakfast there with loved ones for years. As if the back door would fling open and she would leave dressed for school, swinging a lunch sack, headed to the village, maybe with her mother sending her off with a wave, only to have Eva arrive home years later with a beau on her teen arm, ready to make a lifelong pledge. The farm felt like a place that homed and welcomed all, creating a vision of people inside the kitchen window, steaming up the glass from cooking on a winter's night, with warm lamplight coming from the living room where others sat and read in front of a fire.

Breezy exited the Jeep and let Amber out the back door. The dog took off like a missile. Then Breezy assisted Eva, who already had swung her legs around and searched for sure footing to get out. "A little different than living near the city, huh? I love how the wind in the tree-tops sounds as though someone's applauding our arrival." She released her grandmother's arm in response to Eva's tug of independence. "Just needs a woman's touch to be absolutely perfect." Breezy winked at her grandmother.

The winds of change blowing across her body caused a sudden shudder deep within Eva.

The fields and gardens and orchard must've been enchanting once upon a time. Eva loved the herbs lemon balm, chive, peppermint, and sage. Were those plants now hiding behind weeds, thistles, and dandelions? The grass around the property bent and waved with the wind as to an unseen hand, almost like waves on Cape Cod. She sized up the place, feeling an urge to get her hands dirty in those gardens.

The sound of a whirring saw drew their attention to the open barn doors, where a large German shepherd emerged and lunged at Amber.

Breezy ran across the yard and jumped between the dogs. "Be nice to her, Buck! She's your guest!" She stomped with great authority, clapping her hands until the dogs separated. She could control students, dogs, and her grandmother.

A window shade on the first floor slapped against a glass pane where an old man peered out at them, then disappeared. Next to the house, a gray flagstone walkway led to an overgrown herb garden where spiky lavender leaves with a hint of purple flowers poked out.

Breezy had claimed the property just needed a little care. A *little* care? Weeds and leaves partially hid pottery containers that looked as if they'd been empty and tipped over for years. Someone had made the good choice of confining the peppermint plant so it didn't rule the roost. Roses needed tending and a plant from her childhood, comfrey, dominated a large corner spot. Eva's father knew enough to slap comfrey on his skin every time he cut himself in the workshop.

The buzzing saw in the barn silenced, giving Breezy the opportunity to yell, "We're here! How's dinner coming?"

"Maybe someone should 'try again' to make this place look alive," Eva said, turning to find she had just spoken into the elderly uncle's face.

His smile evaporated and a suspicious, resentful look replaced the welcoming expression. "You think so?"

"Gram, this is George. Ian's uncle."

The man looked partly straight and partly crooked with arthritis. He'd missed patches of silver whiskers in his attempt at shaving, and his thinning flyaway salt-and-pepper hair looked like he'd just woken from a nap. "Breezy's grandmother, huh?" He offered her his clawlike hand with bent, arthritic knuckles forming his hand into a C.

She shook his hand. For a small guy, he was deceptively strong. Eva towered over him and probably outweighed George by forty percent. She could tuck him under her arm and sneak him into a movie theater without anyone noticing. But his handshake said not to mess with him.

Breezy had told Eva the man had some sort of sordid past, spending time in prison once but "not for murder or anything."

Eva wasn't sure she trusted him, but something in his eyes—a peculiar childlike enthusiasm that softened the unkempt appearance, complete with chest hairs peeking through a dime-sized hole in the breast of his shirt—dared her not to like him, holes, flaws, and all.

"Nice to meet you, George. I hear you live with a member of the younger generation, like I do."

He seemed to soften and gave Eva a smile and a nod toward the barn. "I keep the kid in line."

Ian sauntered over from the barn holding a wooden sign, then lifted it above his head with one hand and swept up Breezy from behind with the other arm to gently kiss her neck. He boasted a five-o'clock shadow on his face and looked disheveled, sweaty, and dusty.

He was neither attractive nor unattractive but appealing all the same—a little like the place he called home.

A head taller than Eva, he brushed her cheek with an unappreciated kiss, his musky sweat mixed with wood and some sort of sautéed food lingering after he backed away. Despite his height, nothing about him seemed intimidating, only quietly, approvingly pensive. He was always listening intently, chewing one side of his mouth or scratching his lip absentmindedly.

"Changing the name?" Eva quipped to Ian, nodding at the sign. "Something that fits better, like Trying Times Farm?"

Breezy's jaw jutted forward in annoyance. "Gram, please."

But Ian accepted the comment with a subtle knowing and a one-sided smile as if acquiescing. "In a way." He turned the sign for Eva to read. *No Developers. Property Not for Sale.* "Another pushy guy came around earlier trying to get me to sell, saying everyone's making a mint with all the new subdivisions popping up. He said in five years we won't recognize this town. Not a big selling point for me." His voice turned annoyed, his eyebrows pointing like mountain ranges while Breezy patted his arm. "The sleazebag had the nerve to call my house a 'teardown.' This is no teardown. We'll show him, won't we, Shorty?" he said to his uncle before picking up a hammer and some nails from the back steps and heading toward the street.

"You bet we will." George kept up with his nephew at a pace that suggested he could outrun the younger man.

At the road Ian hammered the sign into a tree next to the Try Again Farm sign. Then he steered everyone toward that dilapidated wonder he called *home.*

"How about a quick tour of the property before dinner?" Breezy tugged Ian toward the back fields.

"Sure, sure. Then we'll have a nice meal and celebrate this old guy." Ian pulled his short uncle into a side hug.

The uncle gave Eva a look that seemed to silently challenge her idea that someone should "try again" with their farm. As Breezy and Ian walked ahead and George dropped back beside Eva, he muttered, "We don't want no trouble around here."

Eva's mouth dropped at the indignation of his comment.

Ian collected Breezy's hand and held it even while pointing to the far field. They were always touching or reaching toward each other, closing in to be sure the other one's presence wasn't a mirage. After a long time apart post-breakup, they'd bumped into each other one night in the North End of Boston, eating Italian food with friends, and had been inseparable ever since.

The group now began the tour out by the small apple orchard. Ian talked about his grandfather buying the farm, getting married, and starting a family, growing produce in the now overgrown field. "The horses were kept over there." He pointed to a field behind the barn. "My grandparents had a couple of horses of their own and boarded for other people. But Gramps had these bad ghost pains in his leg from the war."

"Really bad pain." George's face dropped at the mention of it. "Before the war, he was the strongest person I knew. Played football. Could swim across the lake, work in the fields with our Pops and never get tired. Then when he came back and one of those pains tormented him, he'd be right back to Europe in his mind. Saddest thing I'd ever seen." George shook his head as if trying to rid himself of the memory. "He'd need to sit for hours on the back porch, breathing in the farm. The only thing that helped him."

Ian swept his arm over some overgrown gardens. "My grandmother loved picking fresh herbs and fruits, making homemade jams and jellies to sell at a farm stand. The farm's been in our family ever since." He smiled at Eva with eyes that shone with both peace and hard life experience. "Enough of the farm's history. Let's get some dinner." Ian turned and led them toward the house, taking them all in the side door near the driveway. "My uncle lives in there." Ian pointed to an addition off the back, which formed the L-shape of the house.

They trudged up the well-worn stairs, where decades of footsteps had worn away the white paint leaving only weathered treads and a smattering of paint along the edges. George walked in front of Eva, chatting about when they would eat. His pants hung loosely enough at his hips that his cuffs puddled at his feet. Would he trip?

Ian opened the door and stood back to allow them all to pass inside, but Eva's own footsteps slowed as she approached whatever news awaited her inside. Why did they want her at this party?

After stepping over the back door threshold, she froze. Ian had to gently move her out of the way to come inside. The room's chaos stunned Eva into silence.

Breezy seemed oblivious, hanging her purse on a chair back and examining some freshly painted wood trim on the door leading into the dining room. "Hey, nice work getting this trim finished, hon!"

"Holy Moly, what a mess," Eva's father would've said about the

Wards' kitchen. The cabinets looked ancient and banged up, the ceiling yellowed with splotches of water stains in some places. A porcelain sink overlooking the yard overflowed with dirty dishes, while pots clamored for a spot on the stove. In the doorless pantry, sprigs of cut herbs covered in a layer of dust hung upside down tied by the stem to dry.

She wouldn't be eating any food or drinking any tea that included those herbs.

The windows were smudged with grease, giving a blurred view of the outdoors, as if she had suddenly taken off her glasses. An outdated calendar was pinned to the gold-and-avocado plaid wallpaper just outside the cluttered pantry. On the refrigerator hung a magnet with the Bible verse, *But small is the gate and narrow the road that leads to life, and only a few find it.* Newspaper clippings of local events, including an ancient article about Try Again Farm owners winning a Best Apple Contest, hung next to the Bible verse.

At least a delicious aroma came from the oven, like meat roasting.

"Do we have enough food for everyone, kid?" George washed and scrubbed his hands under the faucet of a giant porcelain sink, large enough to bathe a baby.

"Stop worrying, Shorty. Have I ever let you go hungry?" Ian stuffed the hammer and nails he had been carrying into a wobbly drawer, then turned to Eva. "Welcome to our palace." He swept his arms out in a house introduction. "Glad you finally made it out to the country."

Eva responded with a smile and a glance around. Did he see something she didn't?

Ian pulled out a plate of cut-up vegetables from the refrigerator and set them down on the table. He motioned with his hand. "Help yourself."

While Breezy and Eva picked up pieces of celery to chomp, Ian went to the sink and scrubbed potatoes and carrots.

Eva rummaged in her giant leather purse for a birthday card she brought. After finding it, she offered the card to George. "Happy birthday. You made it to another year."

George dried his hands on a towel. "For me? You shouldn't have." He accepted the card, examined the envelope, then set it on the table.

"What do you need me to do, hon?" Breezy gave a ladder-back chair a good shake before directing her grandmother to sit down at the pine table. "You relax, Gram. Let the guys get dinner ready."

Eva sat down and immediately straightened her posture in the rigid chair, as if the chair demanded perfect behavior while they prepared dinner. She looked around the house, orienting herself. In the adjacent dining room, ladders, tarps, and paint containers took up residence. A house under restoration. Through the dining room and into the living room, she could see all the way to the street out the front windows by the front door and stairway. The living room appeared a little more organized.

Breezy noticed her grandmother's gaze. "Want a tour of the inside while dinner cooks?"

The obstacle course of equipment offered a tripping risk. "I'll just sit and watch dinner preparations."

"Hey, Shorty, can you help me cut these up and get them in the pots to boil? I'm going to chop up some herbs."

George took up a spot next to his nephew, collecting a cutting board and sharp knife. He worked on the vegetable prep while Breezy rummaged through the cabinets for the right size pans to fill with water.

Beyond all the chatter and clatter of dinner preparations, voices reverberated—generations of people eating dinner, talking about the upcoming fair, the apples that needed to be canned into pie filling, the pie crusts that needed rolling. They came and went from the room, changing from work clothes to night clothes, to work clothes again, checking the weather outside, reading a newspaper, whispering by the sink to prevent the kids from hearing any troublesome news about bankruptcy or bad business deals, or broken-down vehicles.

"The floor's the first thing to go," said Ian, who turned around and caught Eva staring at the holes in the fake brick floor covering. "I'm working on new subflooring pieces in the barn. I didn't realize how rundown the old place had gotten until I saw it through new eyes." He looked at Breezy, who brushed his arm as she passed him on her way to the fridge.

Breezy pulled candles out of the pantry and placed them on the table. While she took her time lighting each wick, a cool evening breeze rippled the lace curtains, beginning at the top and flowing toward the bottom. The scent of lilac perfumed the air through the window just as it had in Eva's grandmother's house. For years, Eva and her grandmother would read Eva's mother's letters over their morning eggs together at a table like this one . . . the same table where neighbors would sit one day with family, listening as Eva's parents planned Grandmother's funeral.

That horrible day, when she couldn't wake her grandmother, running outside to ring the bell, gonging loudly until neighbors came to help her. And then her parents appearing from New York, as if responding to the ring of the bell.

Music materialized out of small speakers in the corner of the ceiling, shaking Eva from the memory. But the volume set her nerves on edge. Normally music, especially Breezy's singing, delighted and calmed Eva, but combined with the men's voices and the opening and closing of the oven and pan tops, Eva's breathing quickened. To make matters worse, Breezy raised her voice to sing along loudly while she worked, but she didn't recall the words and only hit every third word in a verse. "Hold her . . . hmm . . . hmm . . . don't you . . . hum hmm . . . say so."

After lighting the candles and setting the pots to boil on the stove, George took Breezy's hand in the middle of the kitchen floor, giving her a spin to the music. They laughed and invited Ian to dance with Eva but he declined, continuing with his herb concoction, using a paper towel to dry the freshly rinsed herbs.

Dancing and fooling around in the middle of dinner preparations always invited disaster in Eva's experience with young kids underfoot. Glasses knocked off the table to shatter on the floor. Milk spilled. Plates upended onto the table. Eva squirmed in her chair, looking around the room for a volume button to turn down the music.

Throughout the dancing, a pan sat precariously on the stove's front burner. When George lifted Breezy's hand for another spin, sending her backward, her elbow bumped the handle, which clattered onto the floor, splattering some sort of leftover food across the fake brick linoleum.

Eva jumped from her chair. "I knew this was going to happen!"

For a minute all motion ceased. All eyes landed on her.

Breezy's mouth dropped open. "Not necessary, Gram. Do you think you're overreacting?"

Eva rubbed her hands together. "You were being wild. Something always happens when you get wild."

"*Wild* is if we invited thirty people over," said Ian, "turned up the music, and everyone's had a few drinks and things start to break. Lots of things. This isn't wild, Mrs. Gordon." He turned to his uncle. "No harm done, Shorty. At least you just spilled the grilled cheese pan from lunch. Not our dinner." He winked at his uncle, then walked over to Eva and gently squeezed her shoulder as she sat back down in her rigid chair.

Tension seemed to flee the room for the others as quickly as it arrived but Eva's knee bounced furiously.

Breezy handed a paper towel to Ian, who passed it to George, who wiped up the mess, then threw it away. Why was Eva the only one who had raised her voice?

Ian returned to cooking and pulled a delicious looking roast from the oven. He and George offered an impressed whistle.

"Looks like your best one so far, kid." George continued to eye the roast while he drained the cooked potatoes. Afterward, he pulled out a masher, butter, and cream, and set to whipping them up. Then he drained the carrots and smothered them in butter. Everyone moved on from the accident as if nothing had happened.

Eva watched, her knee finally stilling.

"I'll let the roast rest a few minutes." Ian pulled out a set of laminated placemats designed with a Boston map, each placemat sticking to the one beneath it as if they hadn't been wiped down in months. Following behind, Breezy swept away the vinyl placemats, then replaced them with a lovely pale-green linen tablecloth she had retrieved from the dining room.

Eventually they sat down to dinner. Ian, Breezy, and George automatically bowed their heads to pray for the meal, something that happened at every meal whether Eva joined in or not. Out of respect, Eva had developed the habit of bowing her head along with Breezy and slowly followed their lead now. Ian prayed for all who grew the ingredients for the food, prepared it, delivered it, and cooked it. But, as usual, Eva's eyes remained open and she stole glances at the others.

What drew them to say these words each night? Didn't they earn a paycheck, buy their own food, and cook it?

When she glanced over at George, his eyes were as wide open as her own, staring down at his claw hands. She snapped her eyes shut before he caught her.

The meal looked like something out of a Dr. Seuss book—pork roast with green mashed potatoes and bright orange carrots. Ian explained they were his grandmother's specialty. "Herbed mashed potatoes. Loaded with thyme, chive, and parsley."

Eva glanced toward the dusty herbs hanging in the pantry and took a hesitant forkful. Fortunately, everything tasted fresh from the A&P.

George ate like an adolescent, holding his fork incorrectly, talking with his mouth full about how he hoped Ian bought him a new set of "wheels" for his birthday. He had never learned to drive or got his license, so he just rode a bicycle around town. There had been an old Murray bike outside, red with metal baskets hanging over the back tires.

Hmm, a bicycle might give Eva some independence.

"He's a regular fixture around Pemberton, pedaling up to the center for groceries or over to the neighbor's farm stand for milk and eggs." Ian took a bite and chewed before continuing. "And he works part-time. Right, Shorty?"

"At the thrift store in town." He scraped the dregs of potatoes off his plate.

"He brings home broken things no one wants and repairs them for resale at the store. Makes for a better bargain for people."

"We're in the same line of work, George. I've refinished furniture for years." Eva adjusted the napkin on her lap.

"Ain't that a 'coincident.'" He eyed her but kept eating.

Outside, the sun settled in for the evening, the sky turning into a striped backdrop of blues and reds, casting a rich hue over the kitchen as they ate around the kitchen table. Dusk blurred the clutter like the forgotten background in a photograph, focusing instead on the four-some eating a delicious and colorful meal—a meal cooked for Eva by other people.

They finished dinner and Ian announced a trip to George's favorite ice-cream stand up the street in place of cake. "But first, let's do presents." Ian retrieved a large package out of the hallway closet. Breezy plucked Eva's card from the counter where George had left it earlier. He flashed Eva a smile when he accepted it from her.

George ripped the newsprint wrapping paper off the package to find a collection of old baseball memorabilia. He bounded out of his seat and slapped Ian's hand, thanking his nephew profusely.

Next George slipped Eva's card out of the envelope. He nodded politely at the photograph of a mountain scene and a deserted cabin and seemed to skim the caption and her inscription. His mouth dropped, though, as he counted out the bright green bills falling into his lap.

What to give a near stranger? Money was best.

"Mrs. Gordon, you shouldn't have," he said.

Breezy stood up and walked behind him, watching the shuffling bills. "How much money did you give him, Gram?"

"I didn't have time to buy anything, and money was the easiest thing." She smoothed her skirt wrinkles.

"These are twenties, Gram." Breezy held up the bills for everyone to see. Ian suddenly sat upright, the chair legs banging on the floor. "Whoa."

The conversation ceased, their faces focused on the bills.

Even the crickets outside silenced their chirping.

Eva looked back into her purse. There was the bank envelope where she stashed her withdrawal money for her trip. Empty. But . . . why would she give the bulk of her savings to a man she hardly knew?

The ticking of the hall clock and Amber's and Buck's wheezing from underneath the table filled each inch of the room.

Breezy spotted the bank envelope in her purse. "I think you made a mistake. You were probably doing two things at once and got confused." She leaned over George's shoulder and collected the money from his claw.

He frowned.

Breezy handed him back one twenty-dollar bill. "But we'd better check with the bank tomorrow and see what you've done. This is an awful lot of cash for you to be carrying around."

A flush of embarrassment—and fear—raced to Eva's cheeks. She didn't want Breezy checking out her account. *Write out a birthday card. Include some cash.* How had she confused that process?

"Hey, we all make mistakes," said Ian. He and George gave some piddly examples of getting lost on the way to work or leaving groceries at the store and having to ride the wheels all the way back to town to pick them up.

"It's the thought that counts. And the thought says you think I'm worth bundles." George grinned as if warming up to Eva, then opened a few more cards and well-wishes from distant relatives, none with as generous a gift as hers.

Ian took to reading the inscriptions out loud.

Finally, two more envelopes appeared on the table and Ian slid one to Eva and one to George.

Eva's mind turned to its all too familiar shade of darkness. Why was she getting an envelope? Do all guests at birthday parties get cards? Was it her birthday? She looked at George and followed his action as he pulled out a gray, speckled notecard with a penciled sketch of Try Again Farm drawn as it should be before the roof shingles fell off and the shrubs became unwieldy in the front yard. Eva found the same card and a key inside her envelope.

George looked at the cover, opened the card, then closed it immediately. "You read it for us both, Mrs. Gordon."

"I'll pass," she said.

"We'd like you to read it, Eva," Ian insisted, his expression looking more serious than a birthday party required.

"Well. Let me see here." She rummaged for her glasses.

You are cordially invited to life at Try Again Farm
as Breann MacPherson and Ian Ward
join their lives together August 10

to celebrate their second chance.
May two become four.

"Well again," Eva said, sitting the card on her lap and fighting the urge to weep with anguish over yet another surprise in her life. *You're right, Mabel. Life is filled with the unexpected—and the wrong kind of surprises.* The invitation announced the ending of her days alone with her granddaughter. Turning the cold metal key over and over in her hand, she shook her head. How did Cedarwood Nursing Home fit into the plan? "You're getting married. My little Breezy," Eva said. "I wish you all the best, but don't worry about me. I'll find my own place." She slipped the key back across the table toward Ian.

"Just remain strong, Eva. No need for emotion," said Grandmother.

At least her suitcase was already packed at home. A great comfort, like an escape train waiting at the station.

"Gram, do you understand what the invitation means?"

Ian pointed around the table. "One, two, three, four. All of us." He pushed the key back to Eva.

"Congratulations, kid." Ian and George high-fived.

"I should be able to find something soon."

"Eva, we're asking you to live with us—right here on the farm after we get married," said Ian. "We *want* you to live with us. No need to find something else. This can work."

"Oh, no. *No,*" Eva asserted, shaking her head like she did as a child until her curls flew. "I've had a hard enough time adjusting to living with Breezy and her parade of students and friends. But living with two men? No, just plain *no.* Besides, marriage is hard enough without adding a couple of old relatives with dentures and arthritis living with you. I'll come up with an alternative."

"I wouldn't cause no troubles, kid," said George.

Ian shook his head.

Breezy leaned in on her elbows, rubbing her grandmother's arm and speaking close to Eva's ear. "I think you know you can't live alone anymore, Gram."

"And I don't wear no *dentures*," George added, scraping the last of his green mashed potatoes off his plate.

"You can be like our older stepkids," Ian winked at Breezy as he slouched in his chair as if tickled at his own benevolence.

Eva was not comforted by this comment. By the sound of it, they would all be like Breezy's students and troubled youth group kids from "blended" families, with strange combinations of people making up households: mothers with boyfriends, parents with stepkids, and mothers with kids fathered by several different men.

"I don't know anyone out here," she said. If she still lived alone on the Cape, no one else's marriage decisions would affect her. She stared at her granddaughter's face bathed in evening light. A severed marriage caused devastating results for everyone. And now marriage had the potential of painting new lines while severing Eva's line to her past. They were four adults being swept along by one couple's romance and sent off into a new direction.

But Eva didn't want a secondhand life where she lived with *their* wallpaper, *their* kitchen dishes, and *their* scratchy tweed couch and family photos on the wall. Later in the week she would go to the new bus station, the one near the Walgreens on Central Street, or Center Street. She would buy a ticket, and she would leave.

"I guess old folks just float along on other people's wakes," Eva said glumly.

The May air came in the window, rustling papers and curtains.

"So when is the big day?"

The breeze flipped the pages on the calendar through May, June, July . . .

"August. Right here on the farm," said Ian.

~

On the way back to Quincy, Eva brought up Breezy's engagement. "When did it happen? Why didn't you tell me?"

"I wanted to find the right way to let you know. Ian and I knew we needed to work out some details before we mentioned it to you." Breezy brought up the subject of Eva's marriage. "You were young when you married Grandpa Wallace, weren't you?"

"Eighteen. And parents by nineteen. Family life came earlier back then." How could she explain to Breezy how she'd once felt Wallace was an answer to a girlhood prayer yet she let him slip away? She wanted to warn her granddaughter about all the ways the feelings in a marriage can peter out and die of neglect. When folks weren't careful, all the responsibilities snuffed out the love in a relationship.

A year into their marriage, when she held her son for the first time, she thought he looked exactly like Aunt Agnes, who had died a couple of years before, his hair swirling over his forehead just like hers. He had an unrecognizable nose and sleepy blue eyes that stared above Eva's head as if they were seeing angels until they finally focused on Eva's face.

"Let me introduce myself," she had said. "I'm your one and only mother." When Wallace arrived in the hospital room, her large husband surprised Eva by crying at the sight of his newborn child, displaying a great amount of weeping, wiping his tears from his eyes on the back of his hand.

They took Rob home to their small apartment, where he joined them in the single bedroom. And even though he was an easy child, his demands for Eva's arms and attention grew to be too much, making her feel she'd always been a parent and never someone's child. During nap time, most days she just sat stunned in a chair, looking out the window at the downtown area overlooking the pharmacy, gas station, and family-run Italian restaurant as neighbors ran about doing errands.

Breezy interrupted Eva's reverie. "We're thinking Isabella will be a good chaperone for you when we go on our honeymoon—so you won't have to be alone with a man. She needs a little spare cash, and gets along well with everyone. I've found her to be resourceful in challenging situations. We would've asked Mabel—"

"But you wanted someone under the three-quarters of a century mark?"

"Well, yes. There's that." Breezy offered a nervous smile. "There's plenty of room at the house. Three bedrooms upstairs, plus the addition where George lives off the kitchen. I'll give you some time, Gram, to consider our offer. But if you don't come to the farm, we'll need to make other arrangements. Our first choice would be to have you join us, but if you refuse, we'll have to put our heads together and figure out something else."

Amber leaned over the seat and licked Eva's hand. Only the dog offered her sympathy.

Five

On Wednesday, after hearing Breezy drive away slowly up the street, Eva rolled out of bed to an unusually warm New England spring day. She dressed earlier than usual, throwing on a black denim skirt and a checkered blouse. She wanted to double-check her packed suitcase and add a few more items from the medicine cabinet before leaving with Mabel for the service. After pulling Q-tips from the cabinet, she opened a Ziploc bag and dropped a few inside. As she hurried around the apartment, the purposeful sounds of her footsteps on the floor built her optimism about the day. Going to a funeral with Mabel hopefully would throw the woman off her trail and let her think all of Eva's plans to escape were gone.

Mabel tapped at the back door right on schedule, stirring Amber from her slumber. Once they had settled the dog down with a rawhide bone and the radio tuned to Amber's favorite station, the ladies embarked on their excursion. In her boat-sized Buick parked in the driveway, Mabel adjusted her cushion to be able to see over the steering wheel. She fiddled with the rearview mirror for what felt like an hour, all the while chattering about her tasks for the day. For almost the entire trip to the funeral, her blinker clicked in perfect rhythm like a metronome setting the day's rhythm.

Eva never bothered telling her to turn it off.

"Okay, let's play our game. We're going to a funeral home, so what kind of songs or hymns will they sing?" She insisted they make music predictions based on the church building or the denomination.

"You go first." Eva hated the game at first but never mentioned to Mabel the songs were becoming familiar to her. Some she even liked.

Mabel finally noticed the blinker and turned it off. "Take a stab, Eva. Last week, you guessed 'Rock of Ages' and we sang it at the service. That was a good guess!" She took her eyes off the road briefly to steal a quick look at Eva. "If we were going to a Baptist church, we'd likely sing . . ." She let her voice trail off so Eva could fill in the blank.

Eva remained silent.

"We'd likely sing stirring songs, like 'Blessed Assurance' or 'Leaning on the Everlasting Arms.' Presbyterians love order. Remember? And being serious. What if we were going to a Catholic church today?"

"A Mighty Fortress Is Our God." Eva spoke with her own assurance. Their cathedral-like stone buildings filled Eva with awe—even fear. She rubbed the age spots on her hand and studied the neighborhood through the car window. Why would one church celebrate God differently than other churches? Wasn't He the same to everyone? Distant and displeased? But this God of Mabel's seemed to offer many different faces to the world.

"That's right! And how about today?"

"We're going to a funeral home, huh?" Eva tapped her fingertips together. "Maybe contemporary songs with a guitar player."

"Oh, you know I hate it when family or friends choose a song *they* like but that the deceased would despise." Mabel's voice held uncharacteristic irritation. "Matthew Davies wouldn't want a contemporary song sung at his funeral. Remember Eva, funerals and memorial services should be something with meaning for the deceased. Not just to tickle the fancy of those left behind." She finally pulled her car into the nearly empty parking lot with its newly paved asphalt surface, parking next to a hearse.

They had their choice of empty spaces behind the one-story brick building displaying a sign by the back door reading *Munroe Funeral Home.*

"Where is everyone? Are we early?" Eva checked the clock on the dashboard for the time. They tended to visit funerals with low attendance, but this took the cake.

"This is Mr. Davies's memorial service," Mabel said matter-of-factly. She put the car in park, stepped on the emergency brake, and turned off the engine. "We just talked about him, Eva. He doesn't have many people to send him off."

Eva faced her friend squarely from the passenger seat. "We were going to Mr. Fletcher's funeral. You said that: 'We are going to Mr. Fletcher's funeral.'"

"I'm sorry, but you are mistaken, Eva." Her eyes never left Eva's face as she primly put her keys into her purse and snapped it shut. "We talked about this at breakfast with Isabella. You agreed to come. We wrote it on your calendar." Mabel emphasized each word with a nod like a kindergarten teacher would. "I wrote the words on the space for today. *Matthew Davies's memorial service.*"

"I'll wait outside." Eva faced front and crossed her arms determinedly to stare out the windshield.

"You'll do no such thing, Eva."

"Oh, yes I will. I didn't agree to come here. I'm tired of people making me go places I don't want to go. Look at this parking lot! Nobody is here. We'll stick out like a prickly plant in a funeral arrangement. People will offer condolences to us again like that other time, apologizing for our grief when we don't even know this man! Just leave me."

An ambulance screamed by, causing the passing traffic on the busy main street to pull over before rushing once again to their demanding lives, everyone heading to something more important and pressing than the funeral of a stranger.

"You'll roast. Just last week, we read that article in the newspaper about the father who left his son in the car—"

"Leave me, Mabel." Eva focused straight ahead. Mabel would be back in a minute and give in to her demands. She wouldn't really leave Eva in a hot car.

Mabel lowered the windows, gave Eva a pat on the arm, and got out.

"Suit yourself, dear. But sometimes attending a funeral is a gift in disguise. Helps us remember our mortality and get our priorities straight." She shut the door, leaving silence and heat to wrap around Eva.

Sitting in her own sweat never really bothered her. She had a high tolerance for hot weather. She stole another glance at the funeral home door with her hands calmly folded on her lap.

That poor, lonely soul inside being eulogized. Something about his existence did make her curious.

Mabel said he was a real cad in life, so what would his last moments above ground look like?

Her underarms perspired through her dress as two cars arrived and a couple of mourners entered the funeral home over the next ten minutes. Where would he be in the afterlife?

Eva cracked open her door since she didn't have the keys to put down the electronic windows the rest of the way. She retrieved a tissue from her purse to wipe off the drops forming again and again on her forehead and above her lips. Ten, eleven drops. After what seemed an hour, she turned again and scanned the parking lot and the funeral home door through the back window to see if Mabel was on her way out yet.

No sign of the little fireball.

She wiped more sweat away, closed her purse, and pushed the door all the way open to lug herself out of the car.

A minute later, Eva stepped into the hushed carpeted funeral home. Immediately the cool air-conditioning and smells of perfumes mixed with flower arrangements met her in the entranceway. A sign in front of a small room announced *Celebration of the life of Matthew Davies.* The room held twenty or thirty cushioned chairs. Most were unoccupied.

Mabel sat in the second row, hands folded in her lap and her head held high as if she were gazing toward the heavens. She patted her hand when Eva slipped into the pew next to her.

Eva had come of her own accord, making her the victor. She tugged her hand away.

Three pitiful bouquets perched on the white wrought iron stand near the casket.

Eva stared at the flower petals. Were those carnations or roses? It didn't really matter except to say that some mourners spent more money than others.

The vibrancy of the colors clashed loudly with each other, one orange-and-yellow arrangement next to a pink and red. Over a loudspeaker, Frank Sinatra's "My Way" played for the group.

The music ended and a man stood at the front of the room, likely the funeral home director, reading a poem to those assembled about a ship setting out to sea and "please don't cry for me," which none of the eight mourners were doing. Dressed in a conservative dark suit with hands folded in front of his groin, he formed his face into a practiced series of expressions designed to express grief and empathy as he spoke.

The small size of the gathering made Eva's stomach tighten nervously and her breakfast toast make its presence known. She had often wondered what would happen if anyone discovered she and Mabel were fake mourners, attending the memorial service of a stranger. Certainly no one would issue them a fine, make a scene, or call the police. They were just observing someone else's misfortune and trying to offer support in the person's last hours before burial.

After all, the events were open to the public or else they wouldn't be announced in the newspaper obituary column. And Eva felt comfortable with grief—but not morbidly so. At one funeral, the minister even read a Scripture passage about Jesus being "a man of sorrows, acquainted with grief."

Eva looked around the room. Mr. Davies won the award for having the smallest ceremony they had ever attended.

At that moment, Mabel took out a pen and a scrap of paper from her purse and jotted something down. When she finished writing, she discretely passed a note to Eva asking which charity they should make their contribution to in the deceased's name, as was their custom. Eva always chose one recommended by the family—just a few dollars here and there.

She accepted Mabel's pen and wrote *The Salvation Army Food Pantry*. Underneath, *Are we staying for the reception? I'm hungry.*

Mabel accepted the note and read Eva's words. She shook her head and wrote another back. *It's a funeral home. They don't serve food.*

At funeral homes, there was no reception in the church fellowship hall afterward, where they'd hunker down with donuts and coffee in the corner or over egg salad sandwiches where someone had cut off the crust on the white bread. Of course, it was a relief not to be meeting the other mourners and having to nod politely, pretending to feel sorrow for the loss of Mr. Hildaegger or Edna Morrison whom Eva had never met. Those encounters made her anxious.

After reading his poem, the funeral director invited attendees to share memories or thoughts of Mr. Davies by coming up front to where the poor soul lay in his closed coffin, resting his remains.

Mabel fidgeted next to Eva, as if itching to get up and comfort the mourners.

Eva held her skirt in place, but Mabel finally broke free and stood to address the group.

"Could we just take a moment to sing in honor of Mr. Davies? How about we all join in on 'Amazing Grace'? Does everyone know the words?"

Two heads nodded.

Mabel began the song in her vibrating soprano voice, and the group awkwardly joined in.

Eva remained silent, listening to the words, dissecting their meaning. She grew up hearing her father use the deity as a threat to execute punishment whenever Eva misbehaved. And God didn't bother to assist or come close during Eva's most pained hours. But recently, she heard many ministers present different sides to God, often implying He cared for weak humans, despite knowing *everything* they'd ever done. Eva never had a fondness for people's weaknesses but felt a simmering comfort knowing that the Maker of all the earth might have a patience for people's foibles. Suddenly, Eva found herself whispering her first little prayer in a very long time, although her prayer request was impossible.

She needed Him to fix her past.

Mabel continued singing and Eva remained silent while the song stirred a mysterious feeling of despair . . .

"*Mrs. Gordon? Would you like help back to the limousine?*" *A strange man in a suit extended his arm for her to clasp while her son walked ahead with her ex-husband, Wallace.*

After Mabel sat back down, a baby-faced thirtyish-looking woman with half-purple hair stood and introduced herself as Amanda. Probably she recycled electronics for the poor like that boy from the paper the other day. "I lived next door to Mr. Davies for about two years, and I was the one who found him. We rarely spoke, so I didn't know him. But his cat had been meandering around the yard meowing and meowing at all times of the day and night, and finally it struck me that something must be wrong with Mr. Davies. It's my belief that we should all care about our neighbors because our shared humanity matters most in life, so I went over and knocked on his door, but he didn't answer. Then I peeked in his window and I saw his dinner sitting on the plate at his kitchen table—a couple of pieces of chicken and some mashed potatoes. Since it was nine o'clock in the morning, I tried the back door."

In addition to his poorly attended funeral, the poor man didn't even get to finish his dinner. And no one found him until morning?

"It was unlocked, so I went inside," the girl continued. "That cat rushed in behind me. The place smelled badly. Then I saw poor Mr. Davies on the bathroom floor and called 911." She rattled on, using way too many words to describe a neighbor she hardly knew.

Eva created a fictitious mental account of what Matthew Davies might've done to push everyone away and even prayed God would forgive all his sins. Her own troubled relationships tried to rise to the surface, but instead Eva let the deceased speak to her from the dead. Who would come to Eva's own funeral or make donations in her name? What charities would people associate with her after all her years living in isolation? Would she be welcome or unwelcome in God's sight?

She searched her purse for a tissue.

Six

INSIDE THE CLOSED COFFIN, EVA pounded on the velvety padded walls and lid, then kicked to get someone's attention. She desperately needed them to know they had made a mistake—she wasn't dead after all. They needed to let her out.

But the pillowed walls silenced her efforts and suffocated her. Sweat drops trickled down her face—ten, eleven, twelve—and the cramped quarters prevented her from moving her hand to her face to wipe them off, nearly driving her mad with the frustrating tickling sensation. Would this be how she spent forever?

A muffled voice spoke from the outside the coffin. The funeral director called around, trying to find someone to attend her service, but by the sound of it everyone was previously engaged—including Breezy, who had an end-of-the-year play at school and felt too busy to come. After he hung up from talking to Breezy, he moved around the outside of the coffin singing an unfamiliar tune.

Choking for much-needed air, Eva sat up in bed gasping and pulled herself out of the dream, throwing off the blanket. The feel of dripping sweat remained on her cheeks, but at least it was only a dream. With a trembling hand, she reached for the glass on her bedside table, then sipped some water. When she laid back down, her mind wouldn't rest. After a long effort to return to sleep, she gave up. She was too jarred. Instead, she waited for the rest of the neighborhood to rise and face the day.

This was the day she would make her escape, returning to Cape Cod. But surprisingly a hollow feeling settled inside her chest as she thought of leaving the familiarity of Breezy's home, this room looking out over the neighborhood, Breezy's form all curled up on the couch reading one of her favorite Flannery O'Connor stories. The sadness arrived unexpectedly, accompanied by a quiet doubt that maybe she shouldn't be living alone.

Maybe she needed Breezy.

No, she missed desolate beaches and the privacy of her old town.

The tiniest hint of light seeped through her window.

She sat up, swung her stocky, veiny legs and square ankles over the side of the bed, and adjusted herself to the upright position before moving any further. She began planning ways to carry out her getaway that day. *Phyllis, Rob, Nicole. Phyllis, Nicole, Rob.* She recited the names over and over in her mind, exercising her memory. But who was the best option for helping her? Who would offer her a place to live?

Most people in her address book were deceased or lost to Eva. Her best hopes were those names she kept repeating. Phyllis, her high school friend with whom she had words years ago. Nicole, her niece who never stayed in touch. Rob, her son in Europe. Sarah.

Her mind struggled to dip into the memory of Sarah.

It would be easiest to make up with Phyllis. Who even remembered the nature of their spat anymore? Surely it was minor.

Suddenly the dreariness of the heavy gray morning and the earlier nightmare vanished, replaced by the light of a plan. Phyllis still lived on Cape Cod, and if Eva moved in with Phyllis, she could live once again surrounded by dunes and water and very private people.

Eva hunted in the drawers of her desk for her thin, tattered address book, then flipped through pages looking for her old friend's phone number. This interlude in her life with Breezy could be over, banishing all the dreadful threats of moving to Ian's farm. Oh, she might go and visit Breezy and the gang on occasion, but she wouldn't have to *live* there.

Eva scurried past certain addresses that pained her, like Wallace's former apartment address blacked out with a marker. Despite lines drawn through the street listings, the remnants of the handwriting underneath still showed through, the marks like asphalt roads that drove her family further away from her.

She flipped the page to forget.

What was Phyllis's last name? She couldn't conjure it up. Even the image of her face failed to come to mind except for a smooth fullness on a person of short stature with wavy, red hair, often pinned back with a bobby pin or two. Eva assumed she could recognize her old friend on the street; it just had been so long.

She read each entry in the address book one at a time, very slowly, through the Andersons and Appletons, the Baxters and Browns . . . all the way up to the Ss, where she recognized it. *Stevenson.*

Phyllis Stevenson.

She picked up the phone, holding it in her shaky hand for several moments. What if Phyllis had memory problems of her own and couldn't place the name *Eva Gordon*, couldn't recall *her* face? Well, Eva wouldn't know unless she tried. Slowly she dialed Phyllis's number, excitement and possibility building as the phone rang.

Soon she'd be back in the Cape—she could practically smell the fried clams—enjoying restaurant water views, once again able to find her favorite smoked paprika in the grocery store without having to ask for someone to point out the correct aisle.

The phone rang and rang.

After about the tenth ring, her excitement drooped. Even Phyllis's voicemail failed to respond. Where would an old woman be at this hour of the day?

After pulling on her cotton bathrobe, Eva snapped up the window shade as *The Boston Globe* delivery truck came down the street, inching its way between the narrow pass of parked cars. The neighborhood slept in heavy morning darkness with the exception of the Strongs' house across the way, where a crack of light shone beneath the bottom of the drawn window shade in their upstairs bedroom. As if blown by a fan, the shade slowly fluttered, like a person winking at her, encouraging her to dial someone else.

Eva winked back. A setback couldn't stop her from persevering with her moving plans. She would try Nicole, daughter of her long-deceased brother, Daniel, even though they hadn't spoken in years. Maybe Nicole would enjoy the company if she still lived alone.

Nicole answered but sounded very irritated to be woken up. "Eva. Gordon. I don't believe it. And at this time of day." She shifted the phone, maybe stretching to see a clock.

"Oh. Yes. Sorry about the early hour. But I'm coming back to the Cape later. And I wondered if I could come by to see you."

"Haven't you been living with Breezy? And now you're coming back here?" Nicole made rustling sounds as if she was pulling on some clothing.

"Yes. Today."

"Aunt Eva, who hasn't been in touch since my own father's funeral. Tell me again why you're calling?"

"Well, I wondered if I could see you." Had Eva said something that offended the girl? A memory struggled to the surface. Eva tried peppering the woman with kindness. "Oh, and I wanted to tell you Breezy's getting married. Just got engaged."

"That so?"

"Yup. I'm sure she'd love to see you at the wedding."

"Sure. So that's the reason you're calling at the crack of dawn? I worked a late shift at the hospital. A little tired over here."

A nurse. The memory returned to Eva. "Sorry. Sorry. Yes, I was wondering . . . well, I'm coming back to the Cape and I'll get my own place, but until I do—"

"I think we're skipping a beat here. Last time I saw you, while I was still grieving my father's death, you ranted about his mismanagement of family finances and inability to contribute to the care of your ailing father. And you're wanting to live with me?"

A bed frame squeaked.

Nicole seemed to be preparing to end the call, but first listed ways Eva had neglected to be in touch. No Christmas cards, no visits, no politely apologetic phone calls for years.

Eva's jaw clamped shut at the attack.

"Nothing to say? Well . . . maybe with some sleep I might feel better about having a conversation." Then she hung up.

Nicole had looked like Eva's brother. Eva and Daniel used to bike along the canal together when they were young.

For a good long while, she stood holding the receiver in her hand. Didn't Nicole know Wallace and Eva always tried to take good care of Daniel when he was young? For the love of Pete, they were practically his parents. Even after the way that child appeared in Eva's life like a little prince when her parents finally returned from New York City. Seven years without her mother and father and they return with Daniel in their arms?

Your father has many new skills to put to work up there. And you have a new brother! I hope you are as happy as I am, her mother had written.

The window shade across the street gave a gentler wink of empathy, as if understanding why Eva didn't feel as happy as her mother about Daniel's arrival. Before her parents returned home, the news turned darker. Her mother wrote of not bouncing back from the delivery very quickly and having to postpone the move back to Cape Cod.

It seems giving birth has taken a toll on me and the doctor would like me to remain here for a time. When I'm feeling better, we'll be there and introduce you to your brother. Be ready to ring that bell!

Eva had to persevere in her own efforts. *Home matters. Home calls us.* She would lug that suitcase to the front door, show up at Phyllis's small, neat Cape Cod home with its extra bedroom upstairs, and work things out with her. Phyllis's last name etched itself in Eva's mind, her face finally appearing, as did Phyllis's house, large enough for two elderly women who didn't take up much space to share. Widowed for many years even before the spat with Eva, surely Phyllis would appreciate some company. And Eva could be closer to Sarah on the Cape.

After decades, things had changed on the Cape, yes. But there were breadcrumbs to help her think back to a time before leaving. A brick house on the corner, where she once played rummy for hours with classmates. The place that's now a Tae Kwon Do school used to be the best bakery in town. The building where her children attended elementary school remained but became the administrative building. Eva so clearly remembered her children coming out the door there at the end of a day to meet her, Sarah's arms filled with a stack of books, her hair all undone on her shoulders, and Rob with his large group of friends making afternoon plans. Eva needed to find her way back there.

She pulled herself away from the darkened window and turned on the light to make her bed. After breakfast, she would try Phyllis again, but if the woman didn't answer, Eva would just *go*. Just slip away unnoticed before Breezy returned from her school day. Her insides tingled the way they once felt before a movie date with Wallace when they were teenagers or how she felt the week when she finally had solid plans to move out of her father's dreadful house.

After deciding to make Breezy a nice farewell breakfast, Eva experienced a pang of sadness conjured up when she imagined not seeing her granddaughter's face daily. After all, she wasn't leaving because she didn't love her granddaughter. She would never want anyone to think this of her. Breezy had been a godsend in so many ways, a friend really. A roommate and a friend.

She had provided many moments of levity for Eva, the way she imitated runway models, always falling off her heels, or newscasters, flubbing her teleprompter reading by mispronouncing words and losing her place and having to backtrack. The way she abruptly switched from stir frying chicken to impersonating Faith Hill with passionate singing when one of Faith's songs came on the radio. Breezy didn't need to mimic, really. She had a very good voice.

And the way she tenderly sat curled up in one corner of her living room couch with a mug of hot tea cupped in her hands, listening to any of her confused students—or Eva herself. It wasn't just the fact that she listened well to everyone, it was the way she listened, barely blinking, all concentration, as if absorbing every word so closely she could fall forward into their story if she wasn't careful, likely creating a recipe for aid in her mind.

Breezy was beautiful to look at, though many people might see the slight crookedness of her front teeth, which never had the benefit of braces, or her heavy, unplucked brows and think the opposite.

If only her granddaughter hadn't pressured her to move away from Cape Cod. And if only Breezy's life wasn't so full of *people*. Dozens of students seemed to take up residence on the worn, velvet couch in Breezy's living room, talking about Shakespeare and musicians Eva had never heard of. Or their parents. Oh, they loved to talk about their parents—how those poor folks seemed to be letting them down, never available, only interested in themselves, cheap with their money, having outdated values like still believing in organized religion and fidelity in relationships. They threw around words Eva could never define even on the good brain days, like existential-something-or-other, irony, surrealism, so Eva would slip into the kitchen to make herself useful trying to expand her recipes to feed ten people, all the while thinking how these other people were never part of the arrangement.

Dinner time was *surreal*, to quote many of the young people who used the word as if they'd been forming it in their mouths since grade school. Eva had never used it in a sentence in her life, but once she learned the definition, it aptly described her new living situation. Many nights she found herself at a dinner table with a group of teens and twenty-somethings, current and former students or church friends, trying to make sense of a confusing world.

Eva skimmed their faces with her gaze, their odd hairstyles with clipped or bushy manes, unshaven skin, good and bad table manners, crazy T-shirts with logos she barely understood (ironic, they liked to say), and the rude way they talked enthusiastically with a mouth full of food. And speaking of food—they cooked the oddest meals: pizza with figs, lavender flavor in their coffee, eggs on top of their hamburgers.

Although she never let on to Breezy, some nights she marveled at how much her life had expanded from the quiet Cape Cod days—and it didn't always seem that bad. Not *always*. But she should have been forewarned about all the people—and given the option to go home.

Where was all the sentimentality coming from now? Best to make her way back to the Cape. With a determined brush of her hands, Eva headed to the kitchen, tiptoeing around the corner of the living room, half-expecting one of Breezy's rescue projects to be sleeping on the couch.

Miraculously, the couch held no one. Instead, just Amber slept on her dog bed in the corner, ears standing at attention when Breezy's shower shut off in the bathroom.

In the kitchen, she set out two coffee cups, hoping to coax Breezy to stay an extra minute before pushing off into the dark morning so they could enjoy their last breakfast as roommates. Her sentimentality continued to surprise her as she pulled food out of the cabinets and refrigerator. Cereal, milk, a bowl and spoon. She stared at the toaster, wiggling the knob for a moment before slipping a bagel from a basket on the counter inside and pushing down the handle. Sitting at the table, Eva waited for what felt like hours for her granddaughter to get ready for the day, do her hair and makeup, and finally come into the kitchen. In the meantime, all the faces of Breezy played before Eva—her irritation, her grief over her parents' struggles, her wide smile gifted to her students and friends who filled the chairs around her dining room table.

When Breezy finally entered the kitchen, she backed up as if in surprise at the sight of her grandmother's early rising and breakfast but smothered any words. Visibly she collected herself, grabbing one of those car cups or hot cups for travel from the cabinet.

"Oh, Breeze. Can't you use the mug I set out for you and spend a few moments with me?"

Breezy's wide brown eyes expanded even more than usual and remained open, her eyebrows arching uncharacteristically for a sleepy teacher. Reluctantly she put the car cup on the counter and scraped the kitchen chair back to sit down at the table without saying a word to her grandmother, as if it was either too early for company or a blank-mind time of day for her. She reached down and gave Amber a scratch behind the ears, then accepted the poured coffee from Eva, adding some cream before stirring. She took a sip, then stood to let out the dog before turning the radio on to Amber's station—smooth jazz. When she finally took a seat again, Breezy waited expectantly for Eva to say something.

What could get her talking? "A penny for your thoughts," Eva said. "Only accept large bills. Sorry." She wasn't quite awake yet.

"Well, there's some of that crunchy stuff you like and a bagel there for you." Eva pointed to a box on the table.

"Granola."

"Yes, that crunchy stuff." *Granola, bagel, coffee. Bagel, coffee, granola.* She collected a bagel from the toaster and buttered it for Breezy. "You know . . . I've been wondering . . . What's been your most memorable time of us living together?"

Breezy stopped pouring her granola and looked at her grandmother with the milk carton poised in the air. "Where did that come from, Gram?" she asked, her voice rising higher before she continued to pour. She added two-percent milk on top, narrowing her eyes to wait for words Eva had no intention of speaking. "My favorite time living together." She stirred her milk and granola together. "My favorite time . . ."

"Is it that hard to think of something?"

Breezy pushed the milk to the center of the gateleg table, picked up her spoon again, and shoveled a small bite into her mouth. She spoke with her head tilted back, keeping milk from dribbling down her chin, placing a hand in front of her mouth to hide her chewing. "The night I got you to lay out on the front lawn and watch shooting stars. You complained the whole time about the dew on your nightgown, but I know you secretly loved it."

"Not the dew. I didn't love the dew. You could've at least put a blanket down first."

Wallace laid down the blanket in the field beyond their woods, and Eva stretched out, arms folded behind her head to study the stars. Wallace suddenly appeared above her, his strawberry-blond curls hanging down as he studied her face, blocking her view.

"Wallace and I used to watch stars when we were kids growing up together."

Breezy put down her spoon. "You never told me that, Gram." The creases of her smile lines appeared lightly around her eyes. *All the lines have fallen to her in the right places.*

Where had Eva heard that sentence before? "Probably not." Pushing away the thought of their life ending in ruins, she stood and moved over to the toaster before realizing she had already buttered the bagel. She filled Breezy's travel cup with coffee so her granddaughter wouldn't get halfway out of town and return for it, catching Eva in her escape.

"Well, I'd love to hear more when I get home from work today." Breezy scraped her cereal bowl empty and guzzled her coffee before dropping the cup in the sink. "It's salmon night tonight. Are you up for that?"

"I'm not sure. We'll see what the day brings."

Again she looked at Eva quizzically and spoke slowly. "What the *day* brings?"

"Never mind." Eva walked over and kissed Breezy on the cheek and rubbed her arm before handing her granddaughter the coffee. She would miss the dear young woman, but Breezy would come visit on the Cape.

Breezy didn't say a word but tapped her fingers on the counter by the back door, studying her grandmother.

In the driveway, Mabel's car engine started. Probably pulling out for some early morning coffee date, making it the perfect moment for a getaway. Eva would take advantage. She handed Breezy her purse. As they said their goodbyes, Eva might've been a little more affectionate than normal.

Eva watched from the living room window as the Jeep backed down the driveway and paused longer than usual, then maneuvered into the street and chugged through the parked, sleeping cars, up and around the street corner, and out of sight. She quickly pulled together her things, including a couple of sandwiches, a bagel, an orange, and some nuts to munch on during her travels. Could she stay in her old house, even though new owners lived there now? Why hadn't she thought of that option before?

Maybe they'd all get along just fine. Eva certainly knew the ins and outs of the place, the way that downstairs bathroom toilet needed an extra jiggle to stop running, how the basement walls became wet with rainwater after a deluge.

But as quickly as the thought entered her mind, it vanished, causing brain strain as she tried to remember what she was just thinking about. Giving up, she hurried off to try one last call to Phyllis. When no one answered, she grabbed a few items from her dresser and bathroom, stuffing them again into plastic bags, then pulled the vacuum out of the hall closet to get to her packed suitcase. She tied the crinkling bags on tight and dragged the heavy bag to the front door after checking to be sure Mabel hadn't returned. She had a brief window of opportunity and needed to get away quickly.

When she determined where she'd be living, Breezy could bring her other belongings. Mabel could finish the dresser project in the garage. Eva would share the payment. She checked her wallet for cash so she could reopen her bank account on the Cape and decided against leaving Breezy a note, since she'd written so many notes already only to have them tossed in the trash. But she did leave her cell phone behind on the counter before she left the house, repeating the directions over and over in her mind, remembering the Walgreens on Central Street.

Hustling along the sidewalk, she confirmed her directions with a young mom jogging with her gigantic stroller.

"Yes, you're headed in the right direction. Straight that way." The young, healthy woman pointed with her sculpted arm in the direction of the bus station.

"The new one. Not the one that's shut down?" Eva needed to be certain she was going to the correct station.

"Yup. The new one. Just walk two more blocks . . ." The young woman's voice slowed down as if speaking to the child in the stroller. "Then go right and take your first left. Simple."

Simple. Eva kept walking. *Straight this way. Go right, then first or second left?*

Standing at a stop sign before crossing a main thoroughfare, she watched cars come from all directions, some stopping while others whizzed past. She stomped her foot and looked around. If only someone was here to help her. Noticing a small break in traffic, she stepped into the street to cross, but a car appeared from around a corner, just missing her. She hurried back onto the sidewalk, breathless. *Don't these foolish drivers know pedestrians have the right of way?* She tried again after the cars passed her on the left, but another car appeared honking from the right, sending her back up onto the sidewalk. Should she wait until a stranger joined her so she could take their arm and cross?

Finally, the cars seemed to space themselves out enough for her to get to the other side.

She *went*, holding her head high and keeping her eyes focused on the crossing signal on the other side of the street. That car horn and shrieking driver needed to learn patience. Once on the other side of the road, she clasped the signal pole and waited a moment before continuing.

A man dressed in a suit, walking with a quick pace, approached her.

Eva grabbed his arm. "Could you tell me if the bus station is there?" She pointed down the road.

"Yes. One more block, behind the apartment building. See?" They both looked. "Turn right and you'll see it." He took off walking at his purposeful clip once again.

When she turned at the final block, there it was. The bus station—with buses parked out front and customers coming and going. *Joy!*

At the counter, Eva waited in line while a few other people bought their tickets in front of her, heading on trips to New Hampshire and into Boston. Finally, it was her turn to stand up to the counter, where she counted out a few dollar bills and passed them through the window toward the ticket person. "I'd like to go to Cape Cod, please."

"Cape Cod's a long strip of land, lady. Where exactly you wanna go on Cape Cod?" The bearded clerk never looked up at her as he continued tapping on a computer screen, his hands slightly stained either from ink or a lack of cleanliness, his shirt cuff soiled and worn to the point of fraying.

Eva straightened her shoulders, trying to retrieve her dignity after the faux pas. "Of course." She scavenged through her memory for the town's name. "Hyannis, please."

While staring over Eva's shoulder at the next patron, he offered her the instructions. "You have about forty-five minutes, leaving from that door over there." He nodded to Eva's right, sounding like an automated message on a telephone rather than a human being with an active blood stream.

The details rushed from Eva's mind just as quickly as they entered.

In response to her silence, he dropped his eyes to her face, stopped talking, and focused on Eva for the first time. He took an inventory of the situation, maybe seeing an old woman standing before him with many layers of clothing, seemingly confused about a simple bus ride. With a silent, purposeful nod, he scribbled a little note on a piece of yellow paper with all the needed information and instructions written out clearly for Eva to follow. He even lowered his voice so other patrons couldn't hear.

Eva thanked him, accepting the ticket that would take her home and to freedom. She held that slip of paper tightly to her chest, closing her eyes briefly and smiling. When she opened her eyes again, the man looked bemused. She turned away from the counter to find a seat in the crowded lobby to wait for her bus and chose one next to a man reading on his phone, then settled in to wait.

When she heard that loudspeaker announce the arrival of Bus 200, she practically sprinted outside.

Eva handed the driver her luggage as he stowed passenger bags underneath. "Just want to confirm this is Bus Number Two Hundred?"

"You're in the right place." He scanned her ticket. "This bag'll be easy for you to find when you get off. The only red bag with this sea of black suitcases." He hefted her luggage onto the bus. "Sets you apart from the crowd." Then he smiled at her.

Her mood shifted. She had her ticket, her luggage was stowed, and the driver was friendly. She climbed up the bus stairs and found a good aisle seat. Then she untangled her seat belt from her seatmates' to buckle it.

Outside on the street, her granddaughter was nowhere in sight.

The exhilaration of a successful escape arrived. As the bus driver closed his door and checked his mirror to confirm that everyone was seated properly, Eva grinned at him, then at the lovely girl seated next to her holding an interesting book.

The girl smiled back before returning to her reading.

After they pulled out into the congested street, Eva leaned back against the headrest, lulled by the gentle back-and-forth swaying of the warm bus and the stop-and-go motion, almost as if she was in a rowboat with Wallace at the helm.

Eva studied her seatmate. "And where are you heading?"

The girl put a bookmark in between her pages and shut the book before meeting Eva's gaze. "I'm starting a summer job on Cape Cod at a camp. I'll be a counselor, teaching arts and crafts." She looked off into the distance, as if enjoying the image of working with kids.

"What's that you're reading?" Eva aimed her pointer finger at the book on the girl's lap.

The girl turned the book over in her hand. "I love to read about health issues." She showed Eva the cover. "I'm reading how deadly polyunsaturated vegetable oils are created by a toxic process, but everyone uses these substances for cooking, thinking they are a healthy alternative to animal fat. We eat them at an average of seventy pounds per person per year."

The words were clear, but what was the girl saying?

The girl opened her travel bag and took out a couple of protein bars. "Want one? They're made with healthy oils."

Eva hesitated but finally accepted the offering, slowly peeling off the wrapper. She took a tentative bite.

"Chicken and sriracha." The girl contentedly munched on the odd mixture. "And are you returning to Cape Cod or going there to visit someone?" She wiped her hand on her pants before offering it to Eva as an introduction. "Vanessa, by the way."

They shook hands. "Eva Gordon." Something about the sound-proofed atmosphere of the bus made Eva spill more details of her life than she normally shared with anyone. "I'm going home to Cape Cod. I've been away for a few years, staying with a family member. But I have roots on the Cape. Grew up there, met my husband there as a child, raised my kids there. I just can't get it out of my blood."

"I know how that is. My grandma went into a deep depression when my parents moved her out of her home and to a different city."

Those were scary words—*deep depression.* Why couldn't she have had her own grandmother's life, never moving from the place that housed her most important memories? The thought of her grandmother's home resurrected the memory of the night Eva's parents finally returned from New York after so many years away.

Wallace had been standing close enough to her in the field near her cousins' house that she kicked up dirt on him as she took off in a run when their taxicab pulled up.

They got out looking like two strangers. Her mother's clothes hung off her thin body as if they belonged to someone else. Her father's hair had thinned, and the lines around his eyes made him look like an aging, weary man.

Cancer, the cousins mumbled.

Eva found herself explaining to Vanessa how she had waited so patiently for her parents to return only to have them take seven long years. Her father couldn't find work on the Cape, so her parents moved to New York City, where he thought he'd have more opportunity in a huge place. "They couldn't afford to take me with them when they both needed to work, so they left me with my grandmother. And when they finally arrived home, my father pulls out a travel bed from the back seat and tells me the small, sleepy baby buried beneath a mound of warm blankets was my new brother. He told me say hello to 'his boy, Daniel,' saying the little tyke wouldn't bite me so I didn't need to keep backing away."

"Wow. They came home with a new baby but hadn't sent for you all that time?" Vanessa asked. "Did you feel replaced or something?"

"Yes. Or something." Eva grew quiet. Why was she telling this total stranger about her childhood?

The bus made regular stops along the way, once at a station and other times at side-of-the-road places, accepting new passengers and letting others get off. Travelers stashed their bags up above the seats and snapped seat belts on.

Eva recalled other Cape Cod memories for Vanessa, who happened to be a very good listener.

Eventually, the shifting sounds of the engine mixed with the muffled sounds of hushed voices and Eva's own exhaustion caused by a poor night's sleep made her eyes feel heavy. The more Eva struggled to stay awake, the quieter her seatmate grew, eventually returning to her book, but not before remarking to Eva that it's always good to come *home*.

Seven

AFTER A LONG, CONFUSING, AND painful dream about Wallace, Eva woke suffocating under hurt and panic. She pulled her face from the makeshift pillow of her wrinkled jacket, certain it left deep creases on her skin, additions to the other creases.

A voice announced something over a loudspeaker.

Who was talking? Why?

Eva looked around. Oh, she was on a bus.

She jumped from her seat and collected her items to get off.

How had she gotten on in the first place?

The girl seated by her laid a hand on her arm. "Mrs. Gordon, are you sure this is the correct stop?"

Eva speared the girl with her eyes for being a busybody.

"You were in a deep sleep, Mrs. Gordon. I didn't mean to scare you, but I think these are yours." The girl sheepishly handed Eva two grocery bags.

After looking at the bags and then at the earnest girl, Eva collected the belongings. They seemed familiar, but what did they hold? She forced a stiff smile while her mind sifted through memories, finally recalling the girl's name. "You're Vanessa." She patted the girl's shoulder. "I'm sorry. I'm a little disoriented and forgot where I was. A deep sleep and all, like you said. Thank you for my things." Eva held up the bags and exited the bus after Vanessa wished her well.

Outside, the driver opened the door to the underneath storage space.

Eva just stood there, watching him pull out bag after bag and line them up on the sidewalk before slamming the door. Should she ask for help? And what kind of help did she even need?

The driver pointed to a red suitcase. "I think that's the one you gave me when you got on."

"It is?" Eva hesitated before approaching the vaguely familiar-looking bag and slowly falling into the routine of tying the grocery bags on the handle as if she'd done it many times before.

The bus driver slammed the luggage compartment shut. "Yup. You had the only red one. Enjoy the rest of your trip." He climbed back on the bus and started the engine.

As the bus moved out toward the road, Eva stood alone in a large parking lot full of cars without any sort of building other than a shelter built over a bench. While she was getting her bearings, still rising from her deep sleep and even deeper confusion, she remembered she was on a trip to Cape Cod. She was going home.

Then alarm set in. The other folks who had gotten off the bus seemed so certain of where they were going.

Eva's mind simply felt empty. She looked from person to person, silently pleading for someone—anyone—to settle her confusion.

But one by one, they got into cars and departed, leaving Eva standing firmly in place with just a single other woman seated on a red bench.

The woman impatiently looked at her watch time and time again.

The passing remnants of someone's newspaper blew slowly across the lot. To be useful, Eva chased it a bit and took it to the nearest trash can.

Afterward, Eva approached the woman. "Excuse me, but where on earth are we?"

"It's the Park and Ride lot in Sagamore." The woman pulled her eyes off her watch. "The place where husbands leave their wives to wait in purgatory." She gave Eva a sideways glance as if to commiserate.

"What's a Park and Ride?"

"You didn't know where you were getting off?" She turned her full attention on Eva. "It's the lot where people leave their cars when they commute into Boston. Were you not expecting this?"

"No!" Eva said. "I want the station."

The woman looked out at the street and glanced down at her phone as if checking the time. "That's two stops down. In Hyannis. You got off too early. You'll have to wait 'til the next bus comes by in about an hour."

A small four-door car wove through the enormous parking lot and stopped.

She dropped her phone in her purse. "Ah . . . here's my timely husband now." The woman got in, greeting the man with a barrage of complaints, then leaving Eva alone with the sound of distant traffic.

"Oh, for heaven's sake," she grumbled, leaning her suitcase against the bench and dropping down to sit and simmer in fears about being alone. While she waited, she took out her wallet and counted her money. How much did she need before her next Social Security check arrived?

Her mind returned to the current worry. What would happen if the woman was wrong about a bus arriving in an hour? The terrifying vision of sitting on a glossy red bench when darkness arrived surfaced. Rummaging through her purse looking for her cell phone, she remembered she left it behind for some reason.

A large, dark, older-model car drove into the lot with a man in his thirties or forties behind the wheel. He slowly came closer and closer to the bench, coming to a full stop nearby and staring at her through his passenger window.

What a menacing, suspicious look—no hint of a smile! Was he possibly appraising how much money Eva held in her wallet? The street suddenly felt miles away.

The man turned off his engine and adjusted his rearview mirror.

Pulling her purse a little closer, she followed his gaze. Who would hear over all that street traffic if she screamed as he tried to drag her into his wreck of an automobile? Her mind fabricated all sorts of dangerous and brutal scenarios, all resulting in her abduction or death.

To settle her blood pressure, she imagined Breezy at school, probably at her lunch break or teaching a drama class. Safe in a sea of students and other teachers, where Eva wished she could suddenly descend.

Oh, Breezy would offer quite a lecture for her grandmother if she knew her current predicament. *"Seriously, Gram? Alone in a deserted parking lot with your purse and all your money . . . and no phone?"*

Just then another car pulled into the lot from the street, weaving through the pathways in the lot toward Eva. Fortunately, the new driver pulled into the spot adjoining the suspicious man, turned off his engine, and pulled out his phone to read. Both men remained in their cars.

Eva felt safer with two rather than one. She was starving, so pulled out a sandwich from her bag.

Back to waiting nervously for what seemed hours and hours, Eva distracted herself by checking her watch, searching through her purse for some sharp object—a lipstick tube, a comb, a broken pen—any potential weapon if she needed protection. In the distance, traffic continued its faraway background whir.

Finally, the rumble of a bus engine came from up the highway, the changing of its gears as it grew closer, and turned into the lot, heavy with its load of passengers safe and sheltered behind glass windows. The driver took an interminably long time winding through the parking lot and pulling up to the bench, where he let out passengers and climbed down to unpack luggage.

The suspicious man got out of his car, came near, waited for the passengers to get off, and warmly greeted an older woman about Eva's age and size, wrapping her in a hug.

Eva elbowed her way through the people, ready to get herself on that bus. She chided the driver for the lack of station out there in the wilderness as she handed off her suitcase, looped her bags over her forearms, and shouldered her purse.

His gaze passed over her face with such a short-lived glance he couldn't have even noticed if she was old or young. "Wait over by the door to board."

She leaned closer to him, whispering, "I have a ticket for Hyannis, but mistakenly got off too early. What do I do?"

"Just reboard, lady. It's not all that complicated." He motioned for her to follow, climbed up the bus steps, got situated in his seat, and asked for her ticket.

Once settled, she felt determined to stay alert and pay attention to the stops. *Hyannis, Hyannis, Hyannis,* she recited to herself. Her mind cooperated, allowing her a chance to push away the fog. She was traveling to Phyllis's house!

At the station a couple of stops later, Eva lingered by her seat. Could she fully trust herself to be at the right stop?

Finally, the bus driver cleared his throat. "Off we go. You've arrived at your destination."

She looked out the window at available cabs in the parking lot. "Just wanted to be sure I was at the right place." She collected her bags and moved awkwardly down the aisle toward the exit, clinging to each headrest as she walked. As she descended the bus stairs, she tightly gripped the handrails, careful to watch her footing.

She found a cab waiting by the curb, collected Phyllis's address from her purse, and approached the driver's side window. She handed the scruffy-haired driver the paper. "Can you take me here, sir?"

"Hop in." He flicked away the nub of a cigarette, splashing ashes across the asphalt before opening his door and loading Eva and her things into his cab.

Neither Eva nor the driver seemed in the mood for conversation as he pulled out onto crowded Route 6, so they drove in silence as she read sign after sign along the roadside advertising fried clams. She could practically taste them, their hot, crunchy goodness. *Sandy's Fried Clams. M & J's Seafood.* Just the clean salty smell of the Cape Cod air introduced a small smile to her lips. It was good to be home.

When they drove down one particular street, an old Cape Cod–style house with weathered shingles came up on the right.

Eva knew that place. "Stop!"

The cab driver slammed on the brakes as if avoiding a pedestrian in the road and pulled the car over before throwing it in park. "What was *that* about?"

"I need to get out here. For just a minute." Eva directed the driver to the house on their right.

With both hands on the wheel, he dropped his head in exasperation as she stepped onto the curb in front of the familiar residence. "This isn't the address you gave me, you know."

No, but it was her old home where she lived with Wallace and the kids.

She lifted one finger into the air to shush him. "I know, I know. Just give me a minute." As she walked a little closer to the property, images flooded her mind. The kids's coming and going through the front door, Wallace leaving with his fishing gear, wearing his work clothes, wearing his Sunday best, kids running in the sprinkler, passing out Halloween candy, hanging large-bulb Christmas lights around the door.

Those were the happier memories, but she also recalled the fights over the children, foul moods, and financial woes. Looking at the upstairs bedroom window, she remembered her final fight with him.

"You're expecting the impossible from me, Eva. I'm working as hard as I can, but you've become just like your father." He had stood an intimidating few inches from her, hands on hips, an unfamiliar anger stretched across his face, challenging the lines to form into unfamiliar patterns instead of his normal swirls of peace. "And I *don't* want to be married to *him*." The gears had seemingly shifted in his brain as his expression grew darker and darker. Finally, he threw up his hands, speaking in the quietest manner which evoked unspeakable power. "I'm done." And his hands flopped dejectedly to his sides. After marching over to his dresser drawer, he whipped open each individual drawer, emptying the contents, throwing underwear, shirts, and pants into the old trunk they kept at the end of their bed.

She sat on the bed dejectedly as he listed all his reasons for leaving, forming some perverted kind of shopping list. "You berate me for my job choice in front of others. You berate our kids when they make the smallest mistake. You make each mealtime a war zone. You even make fun of me when I try to say a prayer at a meal like my family used to do—to teach the kids about faith. I love you, but I can't live with you."

"You're exaggerating again, Wallace. Stop it. Put those clothes away."
She stood and followed him back and forth across the room and later
as he loaded his car, carrying box after box outside with Eva refusing
even to hold the door for him. She hounded him with all the impractical reasons for moving out, like the expense, his reputation, the kids'
well-being. But finally she hushed, seeing his tight jaw and the angle of
his eyebrows.

As he closed the door behind him for the last time, "Betcha By Golly
Wow" played on the radio in the kitchen. As a family, they heard it sometimes while they were driving, the kids singing along.

On those days, driving with the wind coming in the window and
whipping the children's hair and book pages in the back seat as they
tried to read, Eva had never imagined the tune would one day be the
backdrop to her marital breakup.

Wallace's voice now lingering in her memory, Eva dropped her head
and studied her hands a moment, while the cab driver reminded her his
meter was still running. Pushing Wallace away, she shook her head and
returned to the back seat of the car. "Please get me out of here. Take me
to that address I gave you." Eva heard the catch in her voice, the emotion
she rarely expressed. She needed to see a familiar face. Phyllis must be
home.

When they finally pulled up to Phyllis's house, the property looked
exactly like Eva recalled it from memory but with longer grass, as if
Phyllis had neglected her yard work—and her exterior painting, which
flaked off in mostly small swatches all over the house.

But Eva could offer to help her. She conjured up a conversation in her
mind where she greeted Phyllis at the door and pretended to be the new
live-in yard help.

The cabbie leaned down and studied the property through his window. "You sure someone lives here? This place looks a little deserted."

Eva studied the property as well. "Well, I'm not so sure, now that you
mention it."

"Want me to stick around?" He passed weary eyes between Eva and
the front door.

"No." She paused. "I don't think that will be necessary."

"Suit yourself." He got out of the car and helped her with the suitcase. As she started up the walkway toward the house, he called out, "Hey, I think you're forgetting something." He held out his open palm. "That's thirty-five dollars."

She turned back and apologized. "So much on my mind." She pulled some cash from her wallet and stuffed it in his hand.

While she was waiting for Phyllis to answer the door, he pulled his cab away from the curb.

Maybe she was too early or too late or chose a bad time to come? Eva abruptly waved him back. She didn't want to be left alone again, but he was turning the corner and driving out of sight.

"Hello there," a voice called from across the yard. A neighbor man peeked through the hedges, rake in hand. He separated the bushes, stepped through, and sauntered over in Eva's direction.

"Hello. I'm a friend of Phyllis's. Eva Gordon. She doesn't seem to be home and wasn't expecting me, so I don't know where she might be."

"No, I believe she wouldn't be expecting you." The gentleman pounded the end of his rake with a firmness like he was trying to hammer the tool into the ground. He looked up at the upstairs window, moving his lips as if struggling to find words.

"Why not?"

He stopped pounding his rake and met her eyes, his voice sounding like a funeral home director's searching for the perfect blend of empathy and fact. "I hate to break this to you, ma'am, but Phyllis passed away a few months back. Her house is going on the market soon."

"Oh no." Eva dropped down on the front step, shading her eyes from the sunlight to get a better view of the man.

"I was just coming over to do some yard work since the daughter seems to be falling behind." He reached out a hand. "Sam, by the way. We've lived here for decades and you look familiar."

Eva shook his hand, then scanned the overrun yard where their girls used to play. "We sort of . . . lost touch. Yes, you look familiar, too. I'm sure we've met. Years ago."

Sam waited as she adjusted to the news and watched as Eva stood and approached the living room window for a peek inside to see Phyllis's old, familiar belongings. Phyllis loved houseplants, the color blue, and her family. She talked with a slight lisp. Her nervous energy kept her in constant motion and incessantly talking, adjusting table decorations that had been adjusted only moments before, telling a story about an excursion earlier in the day while rushing around the living room trying to find a new spot to put the Swedish ivy. In the end, she'd just return the plant to its original home.

"Her daughter comes by every now and then, but hasn't been keeping up on the lawn much."

"So I see. Do you happen to have a key?"

"I do." He studied Eva for a moment. "Can't imagine you'd do any harm. We used to look in on Phyllis as she . . . well . . . aged. Let me go get it."

"We were very close once, but her daughter must not have my new number," she said. "I don't think she'd mind if I stepped inside for a look." In reality, they'd lost touch long ago over a spat Eva couldn't even remember.

Sam hurried across the yard, and Eva rested on the stoop while he was gone, looking around the neighborhood. The four young ones ran and screamed and competed out there in the street and in the yard, throwing balls and racing each other on bicycles, chasing childhood moments.

After ten minutes or so, the neighbor still hadn't returned, so Eva walked around back to see what she could find. The garage door and back door were locked, but when she shoved a screenless window situated just a few feet off the ground near Phyllis's eating area, it slid open. After setting a wrought iron chair underneath it, Eva cautiously climbed on the chair and slipped her hefty legs through the opening, gingerly pulling the rest of herself inside, aware of the need for a careful landing on her old bones, possibly porous with osteoporosis. Thankfully, no one witnessed the ungraceful landing.

Inside, she walked through the downstairs, reminded more and more of Phyllis as she took in the woman's belongings. In the living room,

Eva noted the Queen Anne–style chairs still gracing the living room. Eva had once restored them for her friend, spending oodles of time working on those shapely cabriole legs. Today, the chairs still wore the same upholstery. Not Eva's favorite style, but she could settle in and live with them as long as a few of her own things were sprinkled around the place. The chairs brought to mind the time meek and mild Phyllis took an uncharacteristically authoritative tone with Eva, pointing for Eva to take a seat so they could have a hard chat about something.

Deep resentment over her friend's bossiness had filled Eva, but she had sat down anyway.

After taking off her apron and draping it across the back of a chair, Phyllis had pulled up a seat next to Eva, forearms leaning on her thighs. As she spoke, her lisp lashed letters together. "This is hard for me, Eva. You know I hate conflict, but we need to have a serious conversation about Sarah. Something is wrong with her, and I'm very, very concerned. I've watched that girl count calories on the side of her napkin when Wendy invited her over for dinner and a . . ."

"What's the big deal?" Eva interrupted. The woman had no right to be criticizing her parenting, intruding into Eva's business. "It's not as if your kids are so picture perfect."

Phyllis ignored the insult. "She's gotten so small, Eva. She has the body of a ten-year-old. Sarah doesn't need to be counting calories. When I offer special after-school snacks, she just pushes them away. Most kids ask for seconds."

The pungent smell of coffee percolating in the kitchen swirled as she stood to leave the confrontation with Phyllis. As delicious as that hot goodness and some of Phyllis's treats would taste, she couldn't stay. She shook her head vigorously.

"Don't go, Eva. I know you want the best for Sarah. You never had your mother around to teach you how to parent."

"How dare you bring up my mother in this conversation? I'm *not* a negligent mother, Phyllis. Compared to my own parents, I'm pretty . . ."

"I know, Eva."

"I'm not perfect, but I'm trying my best. I don't know what else I can do to satisfy everyone! I put so much effort into giving those kids attention, never shipping them off to live with other relatives, keeping them fed, dragging them to Sunday school." Eva stormed over to the door. "It's my turn to pick up the girls after sewing club today." And she left with a loud slam. Phyllis had never brought up Sarah's weight again. Slowly their relationship had changed, growing into something resembling mere acquaintances without ever petering out altogether.

Eva stared at the empty chair where Phyllis had sat all those years ago just trying to show concern. The same anguished feeling returned.

Eva shrugged off the memory and stepped out onto the front porch to retrieve her luggage. She turned her face into the wind. She would get busy settling in and focusing on more pleasant thoughts, like finally being someplace familiar and quiet.

Across the yard, the neighbor was returning with a key.

Eva opened the front door. "Well, *you* took forever. But I found a way in through the back."

Sarah's thin face came to mind, and the sound of her doing jumping jacks in her room after eating two helpings of pasta at dinner.

Eva dropped her head in shame and muttered an apology.

"Don't mention it." He watched her with his kind and weathered face. "My wife stored the key, and it took me a while to find it. I had to call her at the grocery store." He held out the key for Eva, but didn't release it into her hand when she reached for it.

She gave him a confused look, as the two of them each held an edge.

A moment later, he let go of it but held her gaze for a moment before speaking. "I'm sure everything will still be familiar to you. Just tuck that under the doormat when you leave." He pointed to the key before turning to cross the yard to his home. "Let us know if you need anything."

Eva went inside, where she immediately set to work opening windows, front and back, to create a beautiful cross breeze to air out the house. She replaced the nagging memories with a mental list of errands. Calling her old doctor and dentist. Getting back into their practices to deal with a persistent back problem and a tooth that needed attention.

The phone rang several times, but she had no intention of answering it. In the kitchen, she drank a large glass of water and ate the fruit and nuts from her bag. She was too tired to call Sarah today. Talking to Sarah would require energy. Eva would call her in the morning.

She looked again around the living room. Apparently she and Phyllis shared the same propensity for keeping their décor unchanged for decades. Phyllis loved dusty blue, always had, and everything included that color in one shade or another, some striped, some plaid, some solid—her couch, chairs, draperies, and throw pillows. Eva might need to add some other colors. Even Phyllis's wardrobe used to consist mainly of blue clothing, or at least some spot of blue in every outfit.

On the coffee table sat one bowl filled with peanuts and another with hard candies, as if Phyllis expected visitors for tea. Eva sank onto the couch and unwrapped a peppermint candy, sucking on it while she renewed her energy.

Phyllis had implored her to stay that day, not run away from words that weren't meant as an affront. *Let's just put our heads together to help Sarah.* But criticism never felt like helpful advice—only as a weapon of war used against her.

She made her way to the kitchen and shook the enamel teakettle on the stove to check for water. While filling it to the top, she took stock of her situation. She would need groceries. A cab to get to the store. In the kitchen drawer, she found a paper and pen to begin her shopping list as the water came to a boil. While drinking her tea, she ate some crackers and peanut butter she found in the pantry. After going outside, she appraised the backyard garden. *What a mess.* The once manicured and perfect yard now looked weed filled and overcrowded with the lawn invading the flower beds.

A project or two would clear her mind of the past. She set her sights on the overgrown yard and the weeding that needed to be done. She decided to make peace with deceased Phyllis by cleaning up her garden after she finished her tea.

In the garage she collected a trowel, a bucket, a pair of gloves, a garden rake, pruning shears, and a pruning saw before setting to work in the back of the house. She would do one section at a time, little by little, until the whole big project was complete.

After thirty minutes or so, Eva stepped back, rubbing her sore hips and lower back, admiring her handiwork. She had done enough for one day. A large pile of weeds sat next to the roses and another pile of thinned out lilies waited for a new home. Phyllis would be pleased if she saw her plantings looking better. After lugging the weeds over to a compost pile near the garage, Eva felt weakened with exhaustion. She needed some sustenance and water.

The sun settled lower in the sky, so she'd have to rummage through Phyllis's kitchen to find something for dinner tonight. She could sleep in Wendy's room—certainly those sheets would be clean. Tomorrow she would contact Sarah and see if they could talk and work through their troubles.

After putting the trowel and equipment back in the garage, Eva made a meal of boxed pasta and a jar of red sauce she found in the pantry.

The phone continued to ring.

At least she wasn't the only person who didn't know Phyllis had passed.

Before long, temptation took over and she found herself snooping. Eva examined Phyllis's prescription medicines, lifting them one at a time from the counter by the sink, carefully reading each label, trying to recall if she had heard of the medicine before. *Toprol.* Mabel took that one for high blood pressure. And *Fosomax* for osteoporosis. The woman was falling apart. Most surprising of all was the *Lexapro.* In the sludge of her mind, that one rang familiar. Didn't one of Breezy's church friends take that for depression? What would have made Phyllis depressed?

Upstairs, Eva rummaged in Phyllis's bedroom, checking out the books on her bedside table—Jan Karon, Barbara Kingsolver. Eva slipped an Anne Tyler book off the shelf and under her arm to take back to her own bedroom. Then she concentrated on the dresser drawers. The woman was so *neat*, rolling each pair of underwear and socks into perfectly formed bundles and lining them up without an inch of wasted space.

A peek underneath Phyllis's bed revealed a tempting-looking shoebox. After straining to get down on her hands and knees after those hours in the garden, Eva finally managed to tug out the box and open the lid.

On top of a stack of pictures, childhood memorabilia, school awards, and notes written in a child's handwriting lay a death notice and a bulletin for a funeral. Phyllis had ghosts. Everyone did.

Her son, Timothy, had died a few years ago and Eva had never known. Why hadn't Phyllis called?

She struggled to get up off her knees and sat on the bed to steady herself from the shock, shoulders drooping with the weight of the news and the loss it stirred in her. She felt like swallowing the depression medicine on the counter as she read each little card he had ever written to his mother—a sweet child who loved sports and dressed daily in some athletic uniform, whether he had a sports practice or not. He often played with Rob when Sarah and Wendy played together.

How did he die? What did he grow up to be like? Did he and Rob ever keep in touch?

Phyllis probably had lots of people to console her when Timothy died.

After a while, Eva took her suitcase into Wendy's room, where she rummaged through the closet for some glimpse of the past, something from those days raising a family, commiserating with Phyllis about the stress of it all. On the top shelf in the closet, she found an old photo album from Wendy's high school years. She sat on the bed and flipped through the pages, remembering some faces, but not many. One thin and pale face pained her as Eva traced her fingers around the girl's cheek and smoothed her flyaway hair.

Sarah, in her freshman year.

Sarah had moved away from home shortly after that picture was taken.

Eva left the album open and laid it on the pillow next to where she would lay her head for the night.

Just getting ready for bed took great effort, Eva's body feeling as if a backpack of unwanted memories and regret weighed her down. She paused each step of the way to rest, thinking about what she'd read and remembered, pulling out her pajamas from the suitcase and hanging her clothes in the closet, unpacking her underwear and shirts in the dresser drawer. Before climbing into bed, she opened the window to let in the sounds of Cape Cod and smell the air, then anticipated how they both would lull her to sleep. After folding back the blanket covers and smoothing her hand over the sheets where Sarah often had slept, she slipped into the bed, comforted by the sheets and warm homemade quilt on her skin.

Tomorrow would be a good day. A better day. She would work in the yard, and while she was weeding, the drapes could be spinning in the washing machine, washing away years of dust and mustiness. She would look for any leftover paint cans in the garage; maybe paint those ugly kitchen cabinets. Or at least wipe them down for the time being. And mid-task, before she finished imagining cleaning out the knickknacks that cluttered up the china cabinet, Eva fell into a deep sleep.

≈

In the morning, she woke feeling as if someone had battered her with a fist or a baseball bat in the middle of the night. The muscles in her back ached, and her joints felt frozen with stiffness. She circled her foot under the covers to slowly wake up her body, then circled her wrists outside of the covers. Sitting at the edge of the bed, she raised her arms above her head for a slow stretch and leaned to the right, then to the left, circling her feet some more.

Now, where was she? In a comforting room with blue paint and an unfamiliar quilt. Reorienting herself, she wandered the rooms of the house, looking at each and every picture on the wall. *Ah, Phyllis's house.* And Eva had lots of plans for it.

Despite her good intentions to keep up the work around the house, she stayed in her pajamas, watching morning talk shows and sipping black coffee. She added to her shopping list to replace the perishables in the fridge: *butter, eggs, milk.* And some nice white paint. She needed to scrub the bathroom and work on the next section in the yard.

During a commercial, the doorbell rang.

Phyllis came to the door the next day after their disagreement about Sarah. She rang the bell.

Eva peeked out from behind the curtains and saw her standing there, holding a fancy tin with a bow on top. Likely her delicious brownies as a peace offering. Tempting.

"Eva, I hear you in there! Please don't push me away. Let's talk."

Eva turned up her program, "Truth or Consequences."

When Rob came downstairs, he looked at his mother watching the television and then at the door where Phyllis persistently rang the bell. He went to the door and answered it. When he came back into the living room after talking with Phyllis for a few minutes, he dropped the tin on the table. "Why would you ignore her? She's your friend—and the nicest lady in the whole town."

The doorbell rang again and again, and someone pounded on the door, calling her name.

Fine. Eva would answer the door, invite Phyllis in, and accept the brownies. But when she peeked through the curtain, expecting to see Phyllis, or maybe Sarah, she instead saw the unthinkable.

Breezy.

Eva leaned against the door. Should she ignore it? Let her in? She hesitated while her brain unscrambled. Finally, the persistent knocking forced Eva to unlock the dead bolt and turn the doorknob. She had barely moved out of the way of the door before Breezy rushed in like a tornado.

"Oh. My. Goodness, Gram. You're here!" She leaned against the wall as if for support with her face hidden in her hands. "Do you know how hard I've been trying to find you? I've been calling people. The police. Your doctor. The hospital. A million people are praying. Poor Mabel is beside herself—"

"Breezy. I didn't mean to upset everyone." Eva smoothed back curls from her moist forehead.

"What in the world are you doing here, and why didn't you call me? I don't know whether to smack you or hug you," she said, before throwing her arms around Eva's neck.

"You knew I wanted to come home, Breezy." Her granddaughter's arm across her mouth muffled the words.

Breezy pulled away. "You didn't leave any way for me to get in touch with you. Not even a note this time! And all I could think was you left because of what I said the other night coming back from the farm about making other arrangements if the farm didn't work out . . ."

"I don't even remember those words." Eva thought a moment. "Wait. What kind of 'other arrangements' did you mean?"

"Not now, Gram."

Was Breezy some sort of programmed homing pigeon, always set to locate her? "How did you find me, then?"

"I knew you were up to something yesterday morning. After I taught my first class, I left. My principal is going to have my neck if this doesn't get straightened out. I went home and you weren't there. I called the bus station. They were no help. Then I called the police. They were a little more help. I couldn't figure out where you'd be going. I searched the house for a note you never left. Then this morning in your room, I noticed your address book was open to Phyllis's page."

"I forgot to pack the dumb thing."

"I thought maybe you came to see her. But nobody would answer the stupid phone. It had to be her, since she was the only person still alive on those pages." Breezy paced the edges of the foyer, her long mane of wavy hair bouncing behind.

"Cheery thought." Eva fidgeted with the pewter bowl on the table. "But actually, she's not alive either." Eva glanced through the living room and out the back window.

The neighbor man was filling his bird feeder by his hedges.

Breezy halted, hair still swinging, hands thrown out as if stopping traffic. "Wait. What did you say? She's not alive? Who are you here with? Wendy?" She looked around the corner, into the kitchen.

"Just myself."

With a finger pointed at the door, Breezy asked, "You're here by your-self? Who let you in?"

"The neighbor. He gave me a key."

Breezy seemed to slip into her nurse persona, offering feigned calm as she spoke in a hushed voice, sounding like a soothing breeze coming off the bay. "Gram, are you telling me Phyllis isn't alive anymore and you're in her house, all alone, making yourself at home?"

Eva nodded nonchalantly, even though the words sounded like an indictment on her sanity. She beckoned Breezy to follow her into the kitchen, where Eva took a seat at the table.

Breezy dropped to her knees in front of her grandmother, gripping Eva's legs. "What are you thinking, Gram?"

"Can I make you a cup of tea, Breezy? I know you don't mind it plain."

"In *a dead woman's house*? You're drinking tea and making yourself at home in *a dead woman's house*?" Her head fell on Eva's knee. "I want to help you, Gram, but I don't know what you want from me."

"Right now, I want a cup of tea. Do you want a cup of tea or not, Breezy?"

She let out one of her weighty sighs. "Oh, if Phyllis doesn't mind."

Eva stood up and put on the kettle, then rummaged up some teacups and tea bags, which she set near the stove. "Sorry, no milk in the house."

"Squatters can't be choosers," Breezy said.

They both took a seat at the kitchen table while the water heated.

"I was just about to call Sarah, see if we could meet," Eva said with clear cheeriness. "I know it's been a long time, but I thought we could go out for coffee and have a good chat. A little heart to heart. Straighten things out. Smooth over the tensions. Then you arrived at the door. At first, I wondered if you were her ringing the bell." Eva chuckled.

"Sarah who?" Breezy tilted her head like a giant question mark.

"Don't tell me you've forgotten your own mother already."

"Mom? You're talking about *my* mom, Gram?" Her voice slipped into the concerned voice of nurse Breezy again.

"Who else would I be talking about? My daughter, Sarah. Your mother. For goodness' sake, Breezy."

When the teakettle whistled, Eva stood to pour the water, but Breezy motioned for her to stay put.

Silently the young woman stood, took the kettle off the stove, poured the water to the top of the mugs, and steeped the bags for several minutes without speaking. She turned and smiled sweetly while bringing the mugs to the table and setting them each down on top of a napkin she took from a basket in the center of the table.

After getting settled in her seat and rubbing her fingers a few moments on the wood, Breezy leaned in close to her grandmother with a tender determination in her eyes, like a teacher preparing to offer critical information to a student. "Gram, my mom has been dead for almost a decade. Do you remember that?"

"*Mrs. Gordon? Would you like help back to the limousine?*" *A strange man in a suit extended his arm while Rob walked ahead with Wallace, leaving Eva to fend for herself at the cemetery just after they laid Sarah's coffin in the ground.*

Eva's hand shook as she lifted her teacup for a sip, spilling the liquid on the table before setting it back down with a clamor. "She's gone?"

Breezy nodded, wiping up the spill as the digits on the stove clock made an adjustment for the hour, clicking ahead. Someone started a lawn mower. Birds chirped.

The women sat in silence, drinking an entire cup of tea as Eva brushed away her tears and wiped her nose with napkins.

"I think you know you need to live with someone." Breezy covered her grandmother's hand with her own. "And besides, do you really *want* to be all alone at this point in your life?"

After all the pitiful funerals, and the memories that either fled or haunted her, Eva had to admit she did want someone to know when she passed. She did want a gathering of family—but a gathering of her own choosing, comprised of actual relatives rather than strangers inserted into her life by Breezy's overgenerous heart. Wallace, Sarah, and Rob.

She'd never told a soul, but those were the people she wanted to gather together one last time for a meal or a conversation. "But my memories are here, Breezy. And I do *not* want to live with those men—or anyone. Except you, and you alone."

"You bring your memories wherever you go, Gram."

Like the memory of Wallace leaving, or the fight with Phyllis, or Sarah's battles with food. "It's less confusing for me if I live in a place where everything's familiar. If I shop in stores where I've bought groceries since I was young and can still find the mustard aisle. Make chitchat with the old bagging man who worked at the A&P since before you were born."

Breezy slowly got up and explored the kitchen, looking at the pictures and magnets on the refrigerator. "I remember Mom's friend Wendy. She used to send me a Christmas card."

"She's not doing a very good job taking care of the lawn."

"You don't know what she's shouldering."

"You sound like Mabel. 'Always offer people grace. You don't know their situation.'"

The refrigerator hummed. The house ran on, even without its owner.

"Ian and I know this isn't easy for you. We want to make your transition as smooth as possible. They'll be respectful of you . . ." Breezy stood next to Eva's chair, gently rubbing her grandmother's sore shoulder.

Eva flinched from the pain.

Breezy drew back. "Are you hurt?"

"I did lots of gardening yesterday."

"Well, I say when we get back to Quincy, let's call a doctor. Get you totally checked out. Your shoulder, those forgetful spells, everything. A good old-fashioned physical."

One more thing to dread—a doctor's appointment. All of the previous day's exhilaration vanished. How could Eva manage this new season of her life, or find a better living situation, if Sarah was gone?

Something would come to her. For the moment, she would return with Breezy, fall into step with her granddaughter's wishes, and wait for the perfect opportunity to leave. "Want to see Phyllis's house before we head back to Quincy?"

Breezy leaned down and twisted around to read her grandmother's face. "You'll come back without my dragging you?"

Eva nodded. "What other choice do I have?"

"First I need to send a few texts. Let everyone know I found you." Breezy took out her phone and punched in letters.

Afterward, the two women went outside and inspected Eva's gardening work. Then they took a tour of the house, walking upstairs to the bedrooms with Eva pointing out people in pictures on the wall, sharing memories of Wendy.

In the guestroom, Breezy picked up the high school album lying open on the bed next to where Eva slept.

A piece of paper fell out from between the pages. Eva picked it up and read the words.

MacPherson, Sarah
MacPherson, Sarah, nee Gordon, 46, passed away Jan 16, 2009, after a long illness. Beloved wife of Luke, loving mother of Breann of Quincy, MA, and sister to Robert Gordon of London. Loving daughter of Wallace and Eva Gordon. Will be sorely missed by many relatives and friends. Funeral to be held Monday at the Morris Funeral Home, 569 Ellis Avenue, Plymouth. In lieu of flowers, contributions can be made to the Sarah MacPherson Fund at Bellevue Treatment Center at 223 First Avenue, Boston, MA.

Why that shameful mention of the treatment center? She folded the paper back into squares and returned it to the pages of the book.

Breezy smoothed Sarah's young, unblemished skin in the picture the same way Eva had.

Eva pulled her folded shirts, pants, and underwear from the drawers, and took the hanging outfits from the closet. She made the bed and said goodbye to the once-manicured lawn and the rooms that had held the memory of Sarah's skinny little starving frame—and Phyllis's big, unheeded warning.

≈

On the way back to the city, Eva lost her words. Instead, her mind swam through memories the way she swam through her dreams, with one scene blending and overlapping into the next in a nonsensical way, filled with emotion. Voices long gone formed in her mind and the presence of people no longer alive surrounded her.

"I know. I know, Phyllis. She needed a doctor."

"What'd you say, Gram?"

Eva startled and turned to her granddaughter. "I don't think I said anything."

Breezy nodded and they continued their journey in silence.

Back at Breezy's house, her granddaughter carried Eva's luggage inside, then hunted for Amber, who surely needed a good run in the back yard. While she was gone, Eva pulled out the vacuum cleaner and stuffed the packed suitcase once again into the back of the closet, having removed only her needed medication.

She would be ready for the next time.

Eight

FOR DAYS AFTER HER RETURN to Breezy's house, Eva lived in a stupor, unable to make plans or see her way forward. She just sat in the back yard, watching the dog rollick and play, listening to the neighbors swim in their aboveground pools and call over fences to each other.

Eventually Mabel materialized, insisting Eva go with her to the coast for a memorial service on the beach. She listed all the usual reasons why a memorial service would be good for Eva's soul. Mabel knew the deceased from her volunteer work for an organization that served the poor and shut-ins. Hugh James was his name, Mabel had said. Or James Hugh. Either way, some neighbors decided that since he was a retired Navy guy, a service on the waterfront would be appropriate.

Mabel had never taken Eva to a beach service. Perhaps the familiar salty air would lift her out of resentments about having to be forced into a living arrangement with those men by her granddaughter.

They drove the fifteen minutes or so to the funeral, with the windows down and sea air blowing through the car. "Was it good to be home, Eva? Even if you couldn't stay? Did it help you just to know it's still there?"

"Where else would it be, Mabel? Blown out to sea?" Eva turned her face to the wind so it blew her hair back off her forehead rather than into her eyes. "Of course it was good to be back. I felt like wrapping my arms around a tree and never letting go, so Breezy couldn't pull me away again."

"I'd love a trip back to Indiana myself, to see all those flat cornfields and visit with my old acquaintances. Just don't know if any of my old circle still remains." Then she cleared her throat a bit. "You know, Eva, maintaining relationships is tricky. And most relationships introduce pain into our lives in one form or another. People's words hurt us. People leave. People die. But they're worth it."

"What would you know about pain in relationships, Mabel? Have you ever had any pain?" Eva shook her head, silently answering her own question.

"Of course I've had pain, Eva. Everyone experiences pain in this life. I've lost loved ones. I was married once and loved my husband, Richard, but he was no angel. And you don't work as a teacher for thirty years without having people speak sharply to you when you don't deserve it. Parents reamed me out more than once when I tried to do my best by their children. I needed to learn to let things go, to forgive, so I wasn't carrying an unnecessary burden. People are challenging. But please, don't push everyone from your life. Don't run away from people who care about you, no matter how uncomfortable it appears. Moving to the farm will be an adjustment for you, but the Wards will become family. No one had to invite you to live there, but those men are opening their house for you."

"We're not all saints like you, Mabel."

"I'm no saint, Eva. You shouldn't put me on a pedestal."

They drove in silence for a number of miles while Eva processed the idea of Mabel doing anything besides earning points toward sainthood. She just couldn't envision her friend snapping at anyone, slamming doors in anger, or using cuss words. "What have you ever done wrong, Mabel? A teensy-weensy little white lie, maybe?"

"Sometimes I'm exasperated by *you*, Eva—but I feel terrible about it. Did you know that? Did you?" A note of challenge appeared in Mabel's voice. "Like even during this conversation, you offer an abrupt answer to my well-intentioned question about your escape . . . and it makes me feel . . . well, it makes me a little upset!"

Eva shook her head at Mabel's sudden outburst. "You hide it well." Eva stared out the window but stole furtive glances at Mabel. She recalled the woman's footsteps upstairs at all hours of the night when she was unable to sleep. When asked in the morning why she was stomping above Eva's head and keeping her awake, Mabel would say she couldn't sleep because she kept thinking of people who needed notes of encouragement to know they weren't alone.

Why had she, Eva, been such a bad friend to Phyllis, never even offering an apology when the woman just wanted to help? Letting the relationship go cold despite all Phyllis's efforts to stay in touch? "I think my friend Phyllis took depression medicine."

"Some days I think it would be good for me to take."

Eva whirled in her seat to face Mabel, the wind now blowing from the back, pushing her hair over the top of her head into her face so that she had to hold it down. "Why would *you* be depressed, Mabel? Happy *you*—upstairs at three in the morning, writing to the entire world, passing out bowls of happiness to everyone who feels forgotten? Praying for every soul you meet in the course of a day?"

Mabel clasped her lips together in a rare show of feistiness, shoving her pointer finger in Eva's direction but keeping her eyes on the road. "And did you ever think I run around filling my days with other people's problems so I don't think about how *I've* been forgotten? Maybe you see me driving out to everyone else's house, but do you see people knocking on my door to come for a visit? Do you see people lined up to bring me meals when I'm down with a cold? Now do you, Eva Gordon? And sometimes I feel pretty resentful and hurt about it!" Mabel looked a little too long at Eva, who gestured toward the road as a reminder.

"Mabel, I didn't know you felt hurt like this." Eva studied her friend's face as tears ran down Mabel's cheeks. Eva let her have some privacy and looked back out the front window.

Eventually, Mabel pulled into a parking lot at the beach and put the car in park before turning off the engine.

Eva collected her purse from the floor and scooted to get out but stopped with one foot on the floorboard and the other planted outside her door on the gritty beach parking lot. Over a low dune, beachcombers collected their shells.

A couple of other folks arrived and parked their cars nearby, then walked down the boardwalk between two dunes.

Mabel finished blowing her nose and put away her hankie. Eva briefly placed her hand on Mabel's arm. Together they just sat in comfortable silence, listening to the crashing waves and distant music. Finally, Mabel decided they needed to get down there to support Hugh James, and the two ladies collected themselves and trudged over the sandy parking lot to the boardwalk leading down to the beach. Once they crested the dunes, they saw an awning covering a couple of dozen fold-up chairs on the beach. At the front sat an urn on a table next to a folded flag. A few viewers gathered in attendance while music escaped from a small speaker. But where was the casket?

The weather was perfect for an eternal send-off—puffy clouds, a warm but reserved ocean breeze, and bright sunlight making a funeral almost appealing, almost a *good* reason to gather on a summer day.

Mabel and Eva chose their seats, sharing a bemused glance at the paper boat held in place by a rock sitting on top of the program set on each chair. After picking up the papers, they sat down and adjusted themselves, causing their chairs to sink deeper and deeper into the sand with each shake of their bodies.

Eva read the program, noting the song now playing was "Anchors Aweigh." She also noted the deceased's name and tried to commit it to memory. *Hugh James.*

Mabel seemed to be weighing the paper boat in her hand, bouncing it up and down as if trying to gauge its purpose. Then she held it high in the air as though testing if it would catch the wind and suddenly sail away to the heavens.

In due time, a chaplain in uniform walked to the front carrying a Bible and welcomed the small group. "A beautiful day for a goodbye, isn't it? We'll have a little memorial here, honoring Mr. James, then Hugh's niece will take Hugh on his last boat ride out to sea, where they'll spread his ashes." He listed Hugh James's accomplishments in the Navy, including time on a sub. "He loved to tell stories. And he loved woodworking. In fact, he made wooden bowls to give away as gifts 'til the end."

Eva shared that skill with Hugh James. Wooden bowls once were her specialty. She always loved the way the bowls looked a little rough and banged up. Once, after a raging storm, the winds took down a large oak tree in the back yard. Eva decided it was about time to teach Sarah some woodworking skills. The girl had been hanging around, watching her mother mold, shape, and sand different projects. Eva hired someone to come out to the house to cut up the tree and move the logs near her shop. After examining one particular piece, Eva used her maul and wedge to knock the wood into two pieces. Rob helped her heave the wood onto the workbench, where she showed Sarah how to turn the piece on its side and shave off the bark to get down to the wood hiding beneath. They hunted for the flattest spot to serve as the bowl's base, shaving off wood until they were sure they had a good, solid foundation for the bowl. With the sharp adze Eva's father had long ago made by hand, they leveled off the sides before using an old bucket to trace a round pattern with a pencil that would form the bowl's mouth. They dug out the wood until they formed a hole—Sarah's favorite part.

"It's like scooping out the seeds and guts from our pumpkins."

Once they chiseled out the guts of the bowl, they turned it upside down and took a hatchet to the outside edges that still formed more of a square than a bowl shape. Sarah didn't complain about the hard work, just like Eva had never complained when her own father showed her his tools and how to make decorative boxes. They worked in silence with only the light-as-feather sounds of wood chips falling on the rough shop floor, the chisel hitting the wood surface again and again—the same background noises that made Eva feel safe in her own silent father's shop.

After carving the bowl into the desired shape, they took it outside and placed it upside down onto the rough asphalt driveway, rubbing the edges on the driveway to smooth the rough spots before sanding it thoroughly. Once the bowl had dried, Sarah applied stain and sanded it smooth one more time before applying shellac. Eva pointed out how the wood's imperfections became the bowl's charm and character. Both the bowl and the imperfections would remain in their family always.

The chaplain read a psalm:

> Some went out on the sea in ships; they were merchants on the mighty waters. They saw the works of the Lord, his wonderful deeds in the deep. For he spoke and stirred up a tempest that lifted high the waves. They mounted up to the heavens and went down to the depths; in their peril their courage melted away. They reeled and staggered like drunkards; they were at their wits' end. Then they cried out to the Lord in their trouble, and he brought them out of their distress. He stilled the storm to a whisper; the waves of the sea were hushed.

Next, the chaplain invited the group to share memories.

Of course, Mabel stood and slowly walked to the front clutching her handbag, pretending her polished pumps weren't getting scratched by the sand granules. "Hugh was such a gentleman, such a good-hearted man. I used to bring him meals with another volunteer, June, and, in the beginning, Hugh invited us in to share some tea and snacks." Her fingers drummed the front of her purse. "We realized that, more than needing a meal, he needed companionship, so June and I began taking the ingredients to his apartment, where we would prepare a meal together, being certain he had leftovers for the rest of the week. We usually fried some chicken, made some rice—his favorite. Whenever we left him, we always recited Psalm Twenty-Three. He didn't know the verses when we first started visiting him but had it memorized after a few months. I'd like to recite it for you now." And she did.

The gentleman beside Eva bounced his foot, causing his chair to sink lower and lower into the sand.

The chaplain replaced Mabel at the front. "And now I'd like to introduce Hugh's niece, Roberta. She has a special tribute planned."

A middle-aged woman sporting long salt-and-pepper hair tumbling down her back stood and walked up front. "Thank you for coming, everyone. I'm sure you've noticed the paper boats on your chairs." She held up a sample for everyone to see. "We're going to send my uncle's memory out to sea. We'd like everyone to take your boat, unfold it, and write a well-wish on it for Hugh. Then do your best to refold it, and place the boat in the basket up front." She pointed to a straw basket in the sand attached to balloons. "The helium will lift his boats to the sky, and the wind will take it out to sea."

Heaven balloon? Floating balloon? Helium balloon. After a brief pause, the sound of pens scratching out notes to the deceased could be heard, while Eva's pen remained still. She sat like a lump for a good long while. When was the last time she wished anyone well? And who was it?

Not Phyllis. Not poor Mabel, who sometimes felt alone and ignored.

Oh, Eva enjoyed being the recipient of well-wishes but rarely spoke them to others. But still, what could she possibly say to a man she never met?

Mabel reached over and quieted Eva's hand, which had been tapping on the paper.

She finally decided to dive in and say *anything.* The man didn't know her, plus no one would read it, so it wouldn't matter how successfully she mastered the activity.

Dear Mr. James, Congratulations on finishing your work. Thank you for your service to our country. I hope you find comfort in the afterlife.

Should she express sympathy for the lack of people in his life at the end? No granddaughter and her fiancé and his uncle in his life? No family willing to give him a home like Eva had been offered? No farm where he could grow lavender and rosemary and vegetables while the grass and woods around the house made applauding sounds every time someone pulled in the driveway? No large barn for refinishing projects?

And that was the home she wanted to escape from.

She finished her note. *Thank you for helping me see more clearly. Godspeed, Eva Gordon.*

She attempted to refold her boat to its original form, but her paper resembled a scrunched and messed-up homework assignment gone awry rather than a boat that might be fit to carry a navy away on troubled, or even calm, waters.

When every pen finally stilled, the mourners got up and marched through the sand like an army invading the beaches of Normandy to place their boats in the basket attached to the balloons. After everyone filed back to their seats, Roberta unloaded a bag of rice that had been weighting down the basket. The niece adjusted something on her phone and an audio recording played "Eternal Father Strong to Save," a hymn for seafaring men, as the bulletin noted. She loosened the basket's moorings, and the balloons drifted heavenward, carried by the easterly wind, leaving this world and all its cares and loneliness behind to bring good tidings to the deceased sailor.

Nine

IN THE DAYS FOLLOWING THE service, Eva took a walk or two, noticing "For Rent" signs, debating with herself about calling the listed real estate agent's phone number, even leaving her packed suitcase in the front hall closet just in case. But then she would remember Hugh James or James Hugh, recall those unexpected moments of gratitude for the companionship in her life, and dismiss the ideas.

Almost as a confirmation of her decision, she got lost one day on one of those walks and had to call for Breezy to come pick her up. Breezy sent Mabel, who apologized profusely for letting Eva get lost. When Breezy encouraged Eva to stop trying to run away and instead start packing up her shop for the move to the farm because their apartment would be rented in the coming months, Eva wondered if she could stay behind in their apartment alone.

"*Absolutely not!*" Breezy had said.

Instead of packing, Eva turned her focus to building a wedding gift for the happy couple as a way to divert her thoughts. Many mornings, the salmon- and blue-colored early morning sun spread across the sky, shining through the garage windows as she worked on her gift— two Federal-style side tables with the neo-classical lines, legs tapering down like a shapely lady, thinner and thinner before reaching the floor. They could sit next to the couch in the living room at Try Again Farm. The Post-its helped her remember the steps, and usually Mabel supervised, passing sandpaper, opening cans of stain, holding wood in a vise.

Tables were the easiest for her to make, although she loved making the decorative boxes like the ones her father taught her to create using two different types of wood and hand-cut dovetail joints.

"Don't waste that wood, Eva! I'm letting you use my good pecan."

For all the harsh words in usual settings, his kindest words came to her in the form of woodworking lessons.

"Wood joints have more structural strength than other joints . . . Use this special saw . . . Measure these sockets . . . use the vise."

Mostly they chiseled out the wood between dovetails, cut the pins out of a piece of wood that would clamp into sockets for a lifetime, all the sides of the box fitting together like fingers held tight with glue.

Each morning, Eva and Mabel Xed out the little boxes on the calendar that trumpeted the end of her time alone with Breezy.

Six weeks. Five weeks. Four weeks.

They bought outfits for the wedding, purged unneeded things by dropping them off at Goodwill, collected boxes to pack her shop and her collection of empty picture frames, stacked in rows against the wall in her shop. For years, Eva had waited for the stomach to fill the frames with pictures of loved ones.

The frames had come from her father's home when he passed away. He had discarded all the photos of her family but kept the frames in case he needed the wood for a project. "Why dwell on the past?" he told Eva when she questioned his reasons for getting rid of the family pictures. "It's over now."

At dinner, in between bites of chicken marsala or grilled shrimp, Breezy verbalized plans for her new life and upcoming wedding: a simple, informal ceremony on the farm—just immediate family, close friends, and students.

Eva listened with subdued enthusiasm.

One night at dinner when Breezy's phone rang, she glanced at the number. Despite their "no phone" rule at meals, she held the device to her chest and spoke to Eva. "Uh oh. I need to get this, Gram. It's my father. I haven't told him yet." She pushed the button to answer. "Hi, Dad. Thanks for calling me back." Breezy took the phone in the other room.

Eva tried to catch the drift of the conversation from her place alone at the kitchen table. From what she could hear, Luke seemed to receive the news of Breezy's engagement with excitement, even though his relationship with his daughter, unfortunately, had sort of fallen off the face of the earth after Sarah's death.

After a while, Breezy returned to the kitchen and stood at the sink, still talking about wedding plans. "I'll be wearing a knee-length vintage dress. Very light purple, so subtle you would think it was beige . . ." She made a pouring motion Luke couldn't see, ". . . like someone took a tablespoon of lilac dye and poured it into the off-white. And the reception will be a simple, catered affair in the yard at the farm. Very low-key, with just sixty or seventy people to watch as I take a new name. We hope you can come."

A new name sounded nice to Eva. She listened to Luke's voice, muffled and bold sounding despite the phone being held close to Breezy's ear. The thought of seeing him again at the wedding stirred up mild dread and resurrected old hurts and memories, the kind she would be fine forgetting permanently.

When Luke first came into Sarah's life, both Wallace and Eva thought he might be good for her. A senior in college, she was excelling in her schoolwork and seemed to be improving in her emotional life—even gaining a little weight. She wanted to take care of herself and began running often down by the seashore. She graduated with honors and accepted a job as an English teacher in a junior high.

At first they thought a love interest might help her eating issues, but within the first couple of years of their relationship, Eva detected mistreatment. Luke pressured Sarah to stay home at night rather than go out with friends, always appearing jealous of other relationships and extremely bossy. He picked at her, pointing out she didn't pronounce "aunt" as "ant" the way he did. He gloated when she lost a political debate between them. And worst of all, he often teased her about putting on a few pounds. "Looking a little flabby in the middle there, Sarah," he said, pinching at her taut skin.

Whether or not he intended to be funny, everyone else in the family considered the topic off-limits. But Sarah took the comments to heart and increased her runs, ate less, and once again obsessed about calorie counts and how her clothes fit. Despite his treatment of her, Sarah insisted on marrying Luke.

Eventually, Sarah ended up in the hospital, forcing her wedding to Luke to be postponed. Thinking that being tough on Sarah for her foolish, dangerous behavior would help her get better, Eva refused to visit her daughter in the hospital.

Wallace went to visit her alone.

Family members hoped the marriage postponement would become permanent, but in a few months, plans were back on track.

After their first year or so of marriage, Sarah rarely called her mother and even more rarely came to visit. Once, Eva called Luke at the university where he worked as a professor to get an honest answer about her daughter's health.

Luke said Sarah was making do. They were both making do. "Oh, and by the way, she's pregnant."

Yet now, on the phone, Breezy spoke to her father as if they were close. Eva knew differently.

When Breezy hung up, Eva asked, "So your father is coming?"

"He wants to. But he mentioned walking me down the aisle." Breezy dropped into the chair at the table and traced her finger over the placemat. "Ugh. I'm not sure how to handle this. I really don't want him officially 'giving me away.' He did that a long time ago. It wouldn't feel genuine, so I changed the subject." Jokingly, she said, "Uncle Rob's been more of a father to me, and he doesn't even live in this country. I could ask him to do it—"

Eva lunged forward. "My son is coming?"

"No. He can't make it from overseas. Not a good time for him." Breezy shook her head. "And I'm just kidding about asking him. I'll walk myself down the aisle."

Eva sat back in her seat.

"But Dad says he'll try to be there. He's never met Ian." She wiped her mouth tidily with her napkin before dropping it on her empty plate. "I'll just tell him the wedding is casual. No need for an escort."

Later in the evening, Eva took Breezy's phone while she was in the bathroom and searched for a long overseas number and jotted it down. Rob's number.

≈

On the weekend after the Fourth of July, Isabella and Mabel gathered in Breezy's kitchen and packed for a get-acquainted cookout at Try Again Farm. Breezy loaded a cooler with water bottles, brie, and Havarti cheese. "It'll be a blast, Gram. Fireworks later on the village green. A ton of people will be there. Who would want to miss all that fun?"

Eva's blood pressure rose at the thought of "a ton of people." She might have to use one of those outside bathrooms to relieve herself when her incontinence struck.

"What's George going to think of me, a total stranger coming and staying with him? Being his chaperone?" Isabella nibbled at her fingernails.

"George is easy to get along with, Isabella. No need to worry about him." Breezy pulled a box of crackers from the cabinet. "Besides, this will be good for him. Allow him to ease into his new life with women." She tucked the crackers into a grocery bag filled with food. "And you can get some preparation for your new eldercare responsibilities. Stop worrying. He's a breeze."

Isabella forced a smile.

Eva nervously paced in the kitchen, watching the activity. "I'd rather stay home."

"No, Gram. This is how you'll get to know your new roommates. No one's backing out of this cookout."

The group collected the packed food and a large, worn patchwork quilt, and headed to the Jeep. While they loaded everything in the car,

Eva stole the opportunity to slip into the hall for a quick peek at her suit-case. Still there, ready to go. But when she recalled Hugh James's lonely funeral, she quickly closed the door.

Outside, Breezy arranged a few of Eva's things in the back. "We'll start fixing up your room. Make it feel like home." The four ladies piled into the vehicle, with Amber sitting between Isabella and Mabel in the back seat. Mabel held a lamp on her lap for the entire ride without complaining.

Supposedly, restorations on Try Again Farm were well underway, but when they pulled onto the property, there was little visible progress. Roof shingles still dangled precariously on the top of the house, some spots bare down to the wood. The driveway remained a cross between a lawn and worn dirt path. Someone had taken the rest of the shutters off the house in preparation for painting and clapboards had been removed, revealing plywood underneath. The poor house looked unclad and vul-nerable, as if ducking behind the shrubs for cover.

"We've been working hard," Breezy said.

"I feel like I've been here before." Mabel looked overdressed, as usual, for the occasion, wearing pantyhose with her pink-and-yellow floral pleated skirt and a sunshine-colored short-sleeved sweater complete with pearls. "What *does it* remind me of?"

"A mess." The words slipped out before Eva had a chance to catch herself.

"Sometimes things look worse before they get better," Breezy said. "You know that from restoring furniture."

"It *feels* like my childhood home, but it doesn't look a thing like it." Mabel climbed from the Jeep and fell under the house's spell while Eva took an inventory of the place from the driveway. The second the others entered the back door, loud laughter, chatter, and cackles spilled through windows, as if the house enjoying a chuckle from deep in its basement and frame, forgetting its nakedness for one second to smile contentedly with the sensation of holding inhabitants inside.

Eva headed to the lonely, empty barn, and heaved open the heavy door. As it grated across the cement floor, the smell of leather, grease, and animals rose to meet her. Ian said nothing had lived in the place for years, but the odor remained behind, embedded deeply in the wall boards. A John Deere tractor sat in the center of the floor, and along the walls hung rakes and hoes, handsaws, spare wire fencing, bags of fertilizer, and seed. Garden tools—a scythe and a push mower—and outdated carpentry tools hung from a pegboard wall. But once upon a time, the cows mooed to the milker who sat on a wobbly stool in that corner in the dark of early morning while the horses whipped flies with their tails and grazed on some hay. New England air blew through the doorway and woke up the sleepy father or child fulfilling their regular morning chore. Over the stall, Eva looked in at them working in dependable silence.

Eyeing a corner, Eva mentally claimed a work spot large enough for her shop. Her workbench there in the middle, toolboxes over on the shelving next to paint cans.

Several pieces of what seemed like trash lay spread out on the floor—empty coffee cans, a couple of old bicycles with baskets filled with plant pots for yards, and many trunks of wood in various stages of being transformed. George seemed to be sanding a child's table and chair set. A vise grip held a painting with a broken frame as if waiting for glue to dry.

Eva's next project, once she finished Breezy and Ian's wedding gift, would be an ancient desk that had belonged to Sarah as a young girl. Over time, the piece had become covered with water rings, dings, and dents, and suffered from a wobble. For the longest time, Eva had tried to hide it, but that desk seemed to have a mind of its own. It haunted her. If she had someone put it in the basement to get it out of sight, Breezy moved it to the foyer. If Eva put it on the street for the trash collector, Mabel had someone lug it up to her apartment and left it on the top of the stairs while she thought of where to give it a home. Thinking it was a fire hazard, Breezy and Ian dragged it back down the stairs and put it in the living room and used it as a television stand.

Recently Eva had given up and decided to just disguise its appearance. That way, she'd walk into a room and say, "Would you look at that adorable little desk!" and never be haunted by memories of the way it once sat buried under teenage diaries, stationery, and schoolbooks, her daughter hunched over homework late into the night, twirling her hair and doodling on the wood top.

Maybe George would appreciate her efforts to clean up his space for him. She moved an old bicycle out of the way, making a spot for her own stuff. Tidiness always made more room.

"What in blazes is going on here?" George bellowed from the doorway. He huffed inside and took the bicycle from Eva with his gnarly hands, worn and dried from work. His unkempt hair made him look as if he'd been startled by an electrical shock. He wore work khakis and a plaid cotton shirt tucked in and secured with a belt high around his waist, clothing in desperate need of a bleach stick and an iron.

Eva held her hand to her chest. "You gave me a start, George. I was trying to help you."

"You're not helping me if you're touching my things." He replaced the items she had just cleared out of the way, once again leaving no space for Eva. He checked the bicycle for damage.

Placating him seemed the right approach. *"Move toward angry people rather than away,"* Breezy liked to counsel, something she learned while teaching difficult students. *"It's the way God treats us, even if it doesn't feel that way."*

"George, I'm just giving the place some order. If we clean up in here, there will be space for both of us. Just trying to help you out. Your litter takes up a ton of room."

"My *litter*?"

"I'll need a spot to do my sanding and refinishing, to store my projects, hang my tools. Wouldn't you say there's plenty of room here to share? You keep that section over there, and I use this section over here." Eva pointed to her soon-to-be-cleared workspace.

"To share? First of all, my stuff ain't litter."

"Breezy told me it wouldn't be a problem for me to set up shop out here." Eva hefted a wooden crate out of the way but sensed silence behind her and turned to look at George.

"Breezy didn't tell you that. She woulda told me first. And second, this is my place of *business*." He paused for a good long while looking at Eva, as if she should find herself trembling at his mean stare. "I fix things out here. It takes a lot of room to do that job."

"I'm just requesting a place to work. Maybe we can decide on a schedule. You come out in the afternoon, and I'll work in the morning." Breezy would be proud of her negotiating skills. "I've been restoring furniture since the start of my marriage, in my own shop. Alone. Now we need to share."

"I have a lot of projects goin' on out here."

"So I see." She glanced around. "Listen, I'm not going to be a boarder, George. I'm going to be a permanent resident. In a heartbeat, I'd rather live alone with my granddaughter—or just *alone*, period—than with you guys, but Breezy wants my company, and I'm trying to make the best of a hard situation. Old folks don't seem to have many choices in matters." She collected the coffee cans from the floor and added them to a box to be stored away.

He came closer. "If you wanna live alone so badly, why don't you?"

She set a coffee can down and faced him, hands defensively on her hips the way she once intimidated her children. "What's your point?"

"Aren't there homes for people like you?"

"What is *that* supposed to mean? 'People like me'? You think I *want* to impose on you guys? Live *here*?"

Stop. Inhale. A still, quiet voice warned her to just shut up or get out of that place.

She ignored the voice and continued. "Well, why do you live with your nephew, George? Is he the only relative who will take you with your *record*?"

Face scrunching like a wadded-up ball of paper, George kicked a bucket of cabinetry hardware across the barn. The contents crashed and spilled over the cement floor.

Eva jumped, shaking.

"Getting acquainted, are you?" Mabel called from the door, sunshine backlighting her form.

Eva broke away from George's glare and bent to put the metal handles back in the bucket, organizing them as she went.

"Sure, sure," George said with the voice of a cheery cruise ship director. "Just gettin' acquainted. Come on in and pull up a seat, Mabel." He dusted off an old, rickety stool for her, but she explored his possessions instead.

"Will you look at all these interesting things." Mabel examined an old milk tin. "This really takes me back. Looks like you're a handyman like my daddy was, George."

The two of them chatted comfortably about handyman work while Eva quietly and slowly lifted a box of old lamps and electrical cords out of her new shop area. One item at a time, she cleared a small but adequate space.

He nodded to the house. "So, what'd you ladies think of Isabella? A real peach of a gal, isn't she?"

"We've known her longer than you have. She seems fine." Eva wiped her hands together, rubbing away the dust. She looked around the barn and offered a muted smile for the efforts made so far on her new shop.

"She's a delight," chirped Mabel. "You'll enjoy her company when Breezy and Ian go away. And this house. It's magical. You're so fortunate to live here, George."

"I am." He moved the box of spilled hardware into a corner. "All the neighbors say I'm such a lucky fella. Spending two weeks in a house after Ian's wedding, just two dames and me."

"Don't get any ideas, George. We're all just sort of helping each other out here." Eva eyed the shelves where she'd stash her stain and milk paint cans.

"Can't a guy have any fun?" He threw a half-hearted smile in Mabel's direction.

Eva picked through paint containers with paint or stain smeared on the outside of the can, many with the same label. "You sure like Sherwin Williams paint."

"Yeah. Sherwin Williams." He tapped the only container of Benjamin Moore. "Holds up real well."

Mabel and Eva shared a glance, then made some light conversation, discussing the differences between staining and painting.

"I've always wanted to learn how to refinish furniture." Isabella had swept into the barn so lightly her arrival went unnoticed. Her wispy presence took up such a small amount of space. It had to do with the way her voice entered the world apologetically, sounding sorry for the intrusion. Wearing a navy- and white-flowered bandana tied around her hair, she looked as if the year was 1965 and Neil Young should be playing on the radio. She sported a pair of hip-hugger jeans with fabric slipped between the side seams, which had been opened to form a skirt, and a T-shirt that read *Here's the Scoop*, advertising a local ice-cream store. She wore the same kind of thick-lensed glasses but with different frames today.

When Eva looked away, then back again quickly, the resemblance to Sarah was uncanny, even the way Isabella drifted along the edge of the room as if hesitant to join everyone. "I guess I could help you learn." Eva softened her tone.

Isabella picked up a paintbrush near the wall and pretended to paint the child's chair. "I once carved my old boyfriend's initials into this old dresser I have. I'd love to get rid of those."

"Do you have to ruin everything?" Eva once hounded Sarah all those decades ago. "My daughter carved her initials in things too."

Everyone turned toward her as if to see if she had more to say.

"Her father was awfully hard on her when she did it."

Isabella handled a metal basket. "I hear you both upcycle things."

"Upcycle?" Eva tilted her head.

George looked equally puzzled by the word.

"You know. Finding old stuff and fixing it up to be better and different. Giving it a sort of new life."

"I just thought of it as a refinishing business." Eva straightened. A new job description sounded so modern and vital. She graced George with a smile. "I guess we do."

"Shopping at secondhand places makes you two pretty cool." Isabella picked up a framed painting and examined it. "I confess. I'm addicted to other people's junk. Thrift stores. Yard sales. Every time I see one of those little signs hammered to a telephone pole, I'm like, 'Whoa. A yard sale,' and the hunt begins. A few weeks ago, I bought this cool, old-fashioned, wooden toolbox, and I'm going to turn it into a gift for Breezy and Ian. Thought I'd put together a 'honeymoon kit' with this thinly shaved floating soap made into the shape of roses and some crystal glasses I got for four dollars apiece at Goodwill. Then I found this book of questions and answers for newlyweds to ask each other on their honeymoon to see how compatible they are. It doesn't look a bit used."

"Isn't it a little late if they find they're not compatible?" Eva asked.

"And I'm going to put them all in the honeymoon toolbox because it's something you quote unquote, 'build your new life around.' Maybe one of you could buy the champagne for me, since I'm not twenty-one."

Oh Sarah, really now. Eva tsked, thinking about the toolbox.

"Who's Sarah?" George asked.

"Who mentioned Sarah?" Eva asked.

"You just said, 'Oh Sarah, really now . . .'"

"No, I didn't," Eva said.

"You don't like the idea, Mrs. Gordon?" Isabella asked Eva, eyes yearning for approval.

"It's your gift to give, not mine, Isabella." Then she pointed outside to the grill. "I'm famished. Let's go see if it's time for the cookout. And I need to talk to Breezy."

George pointed out the child's rocking chair to Mabel and told how he found it in someone's trash one day. Isabella and Eva started off for the house while the other two remained behind.

Inside the farmhouse, the dogs slept in separate corners while jazz music blared through speakers. Piles of paperwork cluttered the pine trestle table.

Eva's blood pressure pumped madly. If she stayed with them permanently, the rest of her life would be spent cleaning and straightening up after those people.

Groceries hadn't made their way into the cupboards and waited on the counter. Pots and pans and plastic cooking utensils—some clean, some not so clean—sat on the stove. To make matters worse, the place was now under construction. Cupboards on one wall had been ripped out, and replacements hadn't been hung yet, leaving exposed plaster beneath. A light coating of plaster dust covered most of the clutter.

Ian came out of the dining room carrying a spackle-covered scraper and wearing a gray shirt with ripped-up, paint-spattered jeans. A baseball cap covered his head. "Pardon our mess, Eva. We're getting spruced up for some ladies coming to live with us." He gave her a quick kiss on the cheek. "Sorry I got caught up working on the drywall. I'll shower and change fast."

"Can you fire up the grill first, hon?" Breezy spooned some kind of orange soup into a pottery tureen. "Then I can work on the food while you get ready. Don't want you to ignore your guests."

"I won't ignore my guests." Ian walked to the sink to clean his scraper.

Eva tugged Breezy by the arm, speaking in a hushed voice. "I need to talk with you. You need to straighten something out right away."

"In a sec, Gram."

Eva followed Breezy to the refrigerator where her granddaughter pulled out hamburger rolls. "George just jumped all over me in the barn about setting up shop out there. You said I could share his space."

Breezy put the rolls on the counter and spun around, holding up a reprimanding finger. "Oh no. You two didn't come to blows already, did you? You're going to have to get along." She pulled out a drawer and moved around the contents. "You misunderstood me, Gram. I never said you could share *his* space. I said Ian has an extra room *off* the barn where you can have your *own* shop."

"You said *in* the barn."

"I said *off* the barn."

At the sink, Ian turned off the water and shook off his scraper. "Problem?"

"Nothing an international diplomat can't repair." Breezy pulled a marinating brush from the drawer. "Gram and George are having territorial disputes over the workspace in the barn."

After stashing his scraper in a bucket on the counter, he picked up a piece of mail on the table. Ian glanced silently at the two. "Eva, there's enough room around here for everyone." He held her gaze for a moment before returning to flip through his mail, waving a brochure from the pile. "Speaking of international diplomats, even with the sign, these jerks still come by and leave brochures?" He revealed a card that read *Barrington and Todd Real Estate Development* and showed a picture-perfect subdivision with houses that matched each other in exact size and shape with large trees in between. "Trees that size take generations to grow." He scoffed before dropping the brochure in the trash, but Isabella confiscated it.

Breezy joined Isabella and the two women leaned together to read the brochure before sharing a concerned glance.

Eva thought about Breezy's words. Maybe a workspace off the barn wouldn't be all that bad. That extension off the side of the barn would be a little more private. She would tell George *off the barn* would be fine. No need to ship her to a home, where she'd eat gray and overcooked meals someone else prepared for her, sitting in a crowded dining room with people who wanted to talk about their checkers game or their favorite television show. If she had to move, she wanted a say in the destination. She glanced at the brochure Isabella held.

The name sounded familiar to Eva. "Isabella, isn't that your last name?"

Ian turned his attention on Isabella as Mabel and George clunked up the back stairs, chattering together.

"What have you two been doing out there? Building a rocket ship?" Eva asked.

"Now Eva, it wasn't that long," Mabel chided.

"That's your father, Isabella?" Ian used a quiet, diplomatic tone.

Isabella dropped her gaze and nodded. Then she tore the brochure into little pieces and tossed them into the trash.

Ian took her hand and sandwiched it between his own as a type of peace offering. "I'm not interested in selling. To anyone."

"This is so embarrassing." Isabella let her hand rest in his. "I wouldn't want to sell this place either if it belonged to me."

He gave her an approving pat and turned to Eva, pointing out a large cut in the ceiling's sheetrock. "Did you see my spot for new lighting? We're putting this giant chandelier up that looks like a dragonfly."

"Oh, please tell me you're not doing that in this old house." Eva counted to ten in her mind.

"Gram, you can mix the old and the new."

"You mean vinyl siding isn't a good idea either?" Ian raised one eyebrow.

"On this lovely old home? Replacing real wood clapboards with that plastic-looking . . ." Her blood pressure increased.

"Gotcha!" Ian slapped George on the back and winked at Eva. "I hate it too. Just wanted to get a rise out of you. And the new chandelier will be tin, as though it was here from the beginning."

"Eva just cares about historical preservation." Mabel accepted some corn from Breezy to be husked. "Pass me that large pot, please, someone."

"Yeah, well, you learn a lot about an old place when you start tearing it apart. Like that sink." Ian pointed. "Never would've known how jury-rigged the plumbing was in this house until we ripped out the old stuff. And the outside? No one bothered to caulk corners or edges around windows. Just applied thick paint to try to keep the weather out, which doesn't work in New England. I have tons of rot out there. But I have news for those developers—no offense, Isabella—when we get started painting, the house will be dressed in a new outfit like that." He snapped his fingers.

"Just don't use vinyl siding." Eva accepted a piece of corn from Mabel and shucked it.

"Gram, there isn't some rule book somewhere that says you can't add new features to an old house. People like conveniences."

"Actually, the restoration police show up." Isabella piped in with her scratchy sandpaper voice. "They come and halt your remodeling job if you're not up to their code."

"Or else you'll get a fine." George laughed at his own comment. "And they'll come at night and take off your vinyl siding and haul it away." His laugh turned into a whistle.

The others began building on the idea, creating a make-believe world where the remodeling police dragged people into court to have their plans approved or to punish violators. Sometimes Ian himself had to go out on calls and arrest people for making a bad color choice on a historical house. The more outrageous the details, the louder the laughter.

And Isabella kept right up with them, the cares on her face smoothing away.

If a story brought a laugh the first time, they seemed to think, why not get a laugh a second, third, or fourth time? "Do you all think I'm not in the room anymore?" Eva snapped. "I get the message." She looked down, fidgeting with her pearl ring.

Abruptly, they stopped, like a symphony responding to the conductor's wave.

"Eva, dear, could you get some water on to boil for this corn? I've shucked enough ears for the whole town of Pemberton," Mabel said.

"Sorry, Eva. No one meant to make you feel bad." Ian dug out a pan and turned on the sink.

An unfamiliar calm swept over her. Eva spent so little time with people who could apologize or ask for forgiveness. And Eva had spent so little time apologizing and asking anyone else for forgiveness. She offered Ian the meekest of acknowledgments.

"Listen, I need to get cleaned up." Ian pointed to his uncle. "Shorty, can you grab Eva's boxes from the Jeep? She'll be in the back bedroom. Just set them in there."

Breezy invited the ladies on a quick tour of the house.

Everyone followed her through the dining room and living room and up the stairs. On the second floor landing, drooping, hideous floral wallpaper with water stains created a serious eyesore.

Mabel reached up and yanked at a piece, tearing it from ceiling to floor. "That will be easy to strip."

"But not today, Mabel." Breezy picked up the wallpaper and folded it up. "There's three bedrooms up here, one bathroom there . . ." She pointed to a closed door. "But Ian's freshening up at the moment." She pointed to the middle door. "Isabella, you'll stay there, in the guest room, while we're away. Ian uses it as an office. And Gram, we're giving you the room at the far end of the hall so you can look out over the back yard." She stepped into the first open doorway overlooking the street. "And here's Ian's room." She allowed everyone to peek through his doorway from the hall.

Eva spotted a large rifle on the dresser. "What in the world is that doing there?"

"Ian found it in the attic while cleaning. It's old and belonged to his grandfather. He's going to hang it above the fireplace."

"Is it safe to have a rifle around?" Eva hadn't grown up with guns.

"It's not loaded, Gram."

She stepped back in the hallway. "Ready to check out your new place, Gram?"

The group trudged to the end of the hall and stopped outside the door.

"Your very first glimpse of your new room!" Breezy motioned for Eva to go inside with a sweeping motion of her hand. "Ta-da! Look at that gorgeous view."

Stepping through the doorway, Eva looked out the back window with approval. She studied pictures of someone else's family hanging on the walls. Black-and-white shots of a couple standing in front of the car that still stood in the farm's driveway and another picture of a family standing in front of Try Again Farm when different shrubbery and younger plants decorated the front. Back then the farm had a lived-in appeal, as if someone was inside making the beds, emptying the trash, and replacing the wallpaper.

"What a generous size, Eva." Mabel followed behind Eva.

The room felt like a museum, furnished with only the necessities. A bed with a white Chenille bedspread, curtains, night table, a slip-covered, striped armchair, scatter rugs on the wide-plank floors, a dresser, and an empty bookshelf. In the empty closet, metal hangers dangled together.

The worn floorboards creaked as Eva explored. On the nightstand sat pictures of a stern-looking elderly couple, arms by their sides. Someone else's memories lived there. Maybe generations of children fell asleep there under a moon-drenched sky, wondering who lived out in space.

People who had left this life, like Matthew Davies. Old and faded and gone.

"I can't live here," Eva said. "It's not home."

"When you get your own things in here, Gram, it'll feel like home. We'll bring down your furniture, your bed, your pictures. Everything to make you comfortable."

George shuffled into the room. "What's in this box, Mrs. Gordon? It weighs a ton."

"Says right there on the side, George. Read it." Her box of memories. He better be careful with it.

He set the box on the floor. "Never mind."

Ian arrived all freshened up and carrying a lamp. "Where do you want this?" He held out the old wine jug filled with sea-washed glass Eva had collected with her children. She took it out of his hands and put it on the nightstand.

The lamp had been next to her bed for so long that the memories from it had diminished—until she saw it in Ian's grip. Rob, Sarah, and Eva would visit the ocean, slip off their shoes, pile them on top of each other in the sand, then skim the shoreline with the day's remaining sun slipping down over the water. They collected shells and examined their ridges, or worn-down glass of all shapes, sizes, and colors—different shades of browns and greens, clears and blues to make a lamp at home. The children struggled to imagine what the glass had been before the ocean washed and pummeled it, making it dull, foggy, and smooth. Was it really just a Coke bottle or a dirty ol' beer bottle, litter, or broken shards of glass with sharp edges? Eva assured them that the power of the storms and waves and sea could take something useless and dangerous, sanding down the sharp edges into something decorative and worth saving.

"I'll be downstairs. Time to get some burgers and kielbasa ready for the grill." Ian left with George following behind. "Don't be too long up here."

The ladies spent a few minutes taking pictures off the walls and nightstand, stacking them on the dresser, before returning downstairs to get the food ready.

In the kitchen, Breezy collected dishes to be set out on the picnic table under an oak tree. Each woman carefully carried a load outside. While Amber and Buck circled the grill, Ian flipped burgers over red-hot charcoals where juices sizzled and kielbasa warmed. The ladies dropped their loads on the red-and-white-checkered tablecloth and arranged the place settings. Luminaries hanging in the tree's branches needed to be lit as the sun set and dusk fell, so Isabella took it upon herself to light them.

On a second run, the ladies brought out bowls of potato salad and green salad. Isabella offered to carry the tureen filled with the carrot soup.

Walking across the yard, Eva commented on the racket of hammers and saws working on a nearby housing development.

"People need a place to live." Isabella tapped Buck with her sneaker to move him back when he came too close to her.

"You think it's a good idea to take down a hundred-year-old farm and put up some cheap, mirror-image homes?"

"You can build a house without tearing down an old one." Suddenly, Isabella tripped on a birdhouse set on the ground waiting to be set on its pole.

The soup tureen broke, sloshing the contents of the soup out onto the lawn.

A bright orange puddle settled on green grass, like an abstract painting.

"Oh, I'm so sorry! I can't believe I spilled all that." She collapsed into a squat and hid her face. With a muffled voice, she said, "You just make me so nervous, Mrs. Gordon!"

"I make you so nervous? This is *my* fault?"

Breezy set down her food and hurried over to help. "What happened?" She helped Isabella pick up the broken soup tureen. "I've been meaning to move that dumb birdhouse off to the side for weeks. It's totally my fault."

George ambled over and stared at the spill. "Would you look at those colors. Beau-tea-ful. Just beautiful."

"That pattern over there . . . the way the swirl looks marbleized and the green grass peeks through? It's a work of art," added Mabel. "Someone should get a camera."

Eva rolled her eyes.

"Totally my fault you tripped." Breezy quickly picked up the largest pieces of the broken tureen. "I should never have given you something that awkward to carry with such an obstacle course for a yard."

Mabel collected a trash bag from Ian at the grill, and they discarded the broken bowl. "Such a shame."

"But that soup took so much time." Isabella looked justifiably devastated.

"No use crying over spilled soup," George said.

As soon as they finished cleaning up the pottery pieces, the dogs licked up the spill.

Everyone sat down at the picnic table, Mabel next to George, Breezy next to Ian, and Eva across from Isabella at the end. One would've thought spilling soup at Try Again Farm was a heroic act, with all the flattery and encouragement poured out on the needy girl.

The table was laden with burgers and salads and other sides. Someone had poured lemonade in the glasses, the sweetness attracting flies that appeared as if on cue.

Each of the older people generously filled their plates, while Isabella only served herself a large helping of salad and potato salad.

"No chicken in the salad." Breezy winked at the girl.

"Don't you want a burger?" Eva asked. Isabella's characteristic gaunt cheek bones reminded her once more of Sarah's aversion to food.

"I'm a vegetarian," Isabella said.

"I'm so sorry." Breezy slumped in her seat.

"Me too." Eva splashed her burger with ketchup and mustard.

"What I meant," Breezy said, throwing Eva a warning look, "was I bought some veggie burgers and forgot to throw them on the grill."

"How in the world do you get your protein? Your body needs protein to survive," Eva chastised.

"I eat dairy products and vegetable proteins: lots of tofu, quinoa, nuts. And sometimes seafood."

"And those are perfectly healthy foods." Breezy was shaking far too much salt on her potato salad.

Ian held a hand in the air. "And let's say grace so we can all eat!"

The group silenced and Ian prayed.

He barely finished his *amen* before Eva charged again into questioning Isabella. "What even is tofu?"

"It's made from soy isoflavones. They're really healthy and the Asian population eats a ton of tofu," Breezy answered for Isabella.

"I grew up on meat and potatoes, and I turned out fine." Eva's burger melted in her mouth as she took a bite.

"It's never too early—or late—to start thinking about taking care of yourself, Gram."

"Besides, if you knew all the steroids and injections they gave those animals before you ate them, you'd lose your appetite. All sorts of studies have shown that eating too much red meat can increase your rate of cancer or heart attack and other stuff." Isabella's voice grew in confidence as if she spoke from her area of expertise.

Eva's fork froze inches from her mouth. "At your age, do you really need to be troubling yourself with heart attacks or cancer? And besides, you look like you don't get anywhere *near* enough food."

"I heard on my radio program that lightning's the number one cause of death in humans," George said. "Not bad diets."

Everyone looked at him in confusion.

"I think that was The Weather Channel, Shorty." Ian spoke calmly. "And they probably were saying lightning is *nature's* number one killer of people."

"Oh, maybe that's it." He shrugged agreeably.

"That's what television does to you." Isabella stirred her salad, toppling the lettuce pieces over each other like waves.

"You probably don't watch television either." Eva studied the girl over her burger.

"Breezy, how do you make your potato salad? It's simply delicious." Mabel cut her potatoes with the side of her fork. "Do you boil your potatoes, then refrigerate them before adding the mayo?"

"Are you kidding?" Isabella responded to Eva, ignoring Mabel. "And get sucked into that Madison Avenue craze for needing to have more and own more?"

"And is this oil vinaigrette on the salad homemade?" Mabel pointed to her plate.

"Isabella has lots of interests, Gram. Acting, college classes, a part-time job, reading. She's even writing a play."

"I've seen someone do *that* before." Eva shook her head, tossing the contents of her salad. "Sarah always had one pipe dream or another going on, but nothing ever came of any of them. I told her, 'Most folks never finish projects like that.'" She looked at Isabella. "Sarah was my daughter."

Breezy made a throat-slicing motion.

"What?" Eva whispered, turning her palms to the sky.

"Oh, it's not a pipe dream," said Isabella. "I plan to finish this."

"I've read what she has so far, Gram, and it's good." Breezy used her sing-song teacher tone. "And please don't characterize my mother that way."

"I'm not doubting *you*, Isabella. I'm just referring to my own daughter. Believe me, she had pipe dreams. I oughta know. I lived with her."

"So did I, Gram." Breezy gulped her lemonade, dribbling some down the side of her mouth.

Suddenly Eva had a flood of memories about her daughter. "First there was the prima ballerina stage, and hundreds and hundreds of dollars spent on ballet training only to have her quit. Then there were art lessons, and she was going to be Georgia O'Keeffe and paint pictures like her desert scenes and her abstract white rose, but suddenly she'd have 'blocks.'" Eva waved her hands in the air.

Breezy put her glass down a little too hard on the picnic table and the bird-shaped salt and pepper shakers flew into the air, then tipped over on landing as if shot down. She stood up the birds. "Please remember it's my mother you're talking about, Gram. Let's not talk ill of the dead.'" Her cheeks looked flushed.

Ian rubbed his eyebrow as if to ward off a migraine. "Ladies, let's change the subject here. What time do the fireworks start?"

"I think I've already started them." Eva stood to go inside. "Anyone else need more ice? I'm getting some."

Everyone was fine.

Walking across the yard, she carefully avoided the birdhouse on the ground, although briefly considered throwing herself down in the grass to get some needed sympathy. Maybe Breezy would regret speaking to her in that harsh tone if she thought Eva had sprained her wrist. But she kept walking. How had a normal conversation turned so tense for her? Maybe a blank memory day would cause less conflict for her.

Inside the kitchen, she collected ice in a bowl and wondered about writing a little note of apology. If she did write out an apology or a little prayer asking for wisdom, she would set the words off in a basket hooked to one of those heaven balloons to sail into the sky for help.

When she returned to the picnic table, she passed Breezy and Ian, who were hosing off what was left of the soup spill and quietly discussing her.

"We never planned for the possibility of Gram and George hating each other." Breezy had her back facing the house.

Eva expected to hear the words "Cedarwood Nursing Home" but didn't. She stopped behind them, knowing she should say something, but what? "Breezy, I . . ."

Breezy spun around, looking as if her grandmother's voice caught her by surprise.

The bowl of ice felt cold in her hands and the words wouldn't come. "Oh, never mind." After returning to the table, Eva slipped cubes into her glass. The ice sounded like the clanking and clinking of keys in a lock.

Ten

AMBER PLAYED AT HER FEET while Eva sat in the shade of Breezy's back yard in an Adirondack chair, a glass of iced tea dripping condensation down her wrist. Next door, the neighbor girls played a make-believe cooking game with a kitchen set on their porch, making roasts and potatoes to offer each other. Sarah loved pretend cooking. She made *hanburgers* and hot dogs on her own kitchen set when she was four years old. While Sarah ran back and forth from the kitchen to her bedroom, giving updates on the assembly, punctuating each announcement with a little leap in the air, Eva wrestled a turkey in the grown-up kitchen sink, pulling its legs apart to insert the homemade stuffing made from crackers, celery, and onions. "Don't ever try to cook a turkey." Eva pressed a large spoonful of stuffing inside the carcass. "Too much of an ordeal."

Eva always sounded so crabby in her memories.

Breezy came outside, keys jangling in her hand. "You ready to go, Gram?" She waited for her grandmother to respond and bent low to examine her grandmother's face. "You okay, Gram? You look sad."

Eva looked into her granddaughter's inviting eyes, opened her mouth to speak, and then closed it again. How could she express her apprehension about the day's appointment—the second doctor's appointment to talk about her memory? After seeing Eva's general practitioner, the doctor recommended seeing someone who worked with the brain. A neurologist.

"You know it's for the best, Gram. We need to know what's going on with you."

"I told you, I'll try harder to remember things. Write more things down." Her voice sounded like a child's pleading. When Breezy didn't budge, Eva stood up from the chair. "Okay. Let's get this over with."

As they drove through the crowded streets to the appointment, Eva tried to remember a few other things, like how Wallace had proposed. Was it at her father's house, on the dock where they used to meet, or in a park? Then she tried to remember Sarah's and Rob's first words, and why she was so stinking angry every day of their lives. Desired memories wouldn't come, yet unwanted memories stormed her thoughts.

In the doctor's examining room, the nurse finished taking Eva's blood pressure and spoke a few words to Breezy while Eva listened to the sound of a car door slamming, like when Wallace had decided to leave.

When he slipped behind the wheel, she'd stood silent and ramrod straight. *Please stay, Wallace. What about the kids?* But she remained mute. How could she make things right when she didn't know how they'd broken?

Sitting in the car, he hesitated for one brief instant, watching his wife with his deep blue eyes expectant and pleading, his hand still on the door as if he'd open it in a flash if she just said the word. Finally, with a shake of his head, Wallace put the car in gear and backed out of the driveway with all his possessions—his favorite record albums, the picture taken with his dad at Fenway Park, his childhood book collection. He stayed with a friend for a while before renting his own place. Eva must've really pushed him over the edge for him to find the gumption to work out a rental agreement and buy a new bed, dresser, and kitchen table. He wasn't a decisive person.

When she took the kids to stay with him for the first time, they were excited to see their father, and excited for a sleepover. As she drove away alone after dropping them off, she wept. Her family was staying in a strange apartment without her. She turned the car around the corner in the direction of her house, away from Wallace's new rental property, adjacent to the Harbor Point Marina, where he had resided until his death.

Breezy drew Eva's attention back to the world by jiggling the plastic skeleton on the counter. "Do . . . da do . . . da do dala do dala . . . do." She sang in rhythm to the clattering, naked bones.

From her cold seat in the corner, Eva hugged her body. "I don't think I ever got over it." Eva looked at Breezy as if she were a priest who could receive her confession.

"Over what?" the skeleton asked with slightly less enthusiasm.

Just then a no-nonsense doctor wearing a white lab coat and a name tag reading *Dr. Howard* entered the room. Her short silver-colored curls made her look as if caring for the ailing bodies of others prohibited time for makeup and style.

Breezy quickly hung the skeleton back on the metal frame.

"The human body's entertaining, isn't it?" She shook hands firmly with Eva, then Breezy. Her warm brown eyes offering concern made up for any lack of primped beauty. "Nice to see you, Mrs. Gordon. What's the reason for the visit today?" She took a seat on a stool in front of a computer, wiggled the mouse, and glanced at her computer screen as if it had the answer.

A flyer hanging on the wall caught Eva's attention: *DO YOU FEEL UNSAFE? LET SOMEONE KNOW IF YOU NEED HELP.* An illustration of an old black dial phone with a long cord decorated the paper.

"My grandmother's having some cognitive problems. She's struggling with her memory."

The skeleton fell off its metal frame, and the three women startled.

Dr. Howard collected it from its splayed position on the floor and sat back down. "One surprise after another around here. So, can you give me some examples of memory problems?"

"Go on, Gram." Breezy coaxed with a nod. "This is your story."

When Eva didn't speak, Breezy tentatively filled in the empty space, beginning with the Post-it notes. When Eva never chimed in, Breezy moved on to the escape attempts, Eva's trip to Phyllis's house . . . where she wanted to live permanently despite the owner having passed away. "And she hasn't driven for a few years . . ."

"Lines or no lines, Mrs. Gordon, three strikes and you're out," the judge said to Eva years ago on Cape Cod before collecting her license. Outside the courthouse, cars filled the street, parking and pulling out, driving away effortlessly to the backdrop of freedom. She'd walked the entire way home.

While Dr. Howard typed notes, her facial expression remained steady.

Eva grew more and more agitated listening to the list. She read the flyer on the wall one more time.

DO YOU FEEL UNSAFE? LET SOMEONE KNOW IF YOU NEED HELP.

"I need help . . ."

Dr. Howard stopped typing and looked over at her patient. "We're going to see what we can do. I'd like to administer some tests . . ." But she paused as she and Breezy suddenly followed the path of Eva's gaze to the flyer and back to Eva.

"Oh no you don't, Gram. Don't do this."

"Are you saying, Mrs. Gordon, you feel unsafe?" Dr. Howard removed her hands from the keyboard and turned to face Eva. She pointed to the flyer.

Eva pulled on her shirtsleeves and nodded.

"I see." The doctor nodded, scrunching her lips together. "Maybe we should talk alone for a minute, Mrs. Gordon? Would you like that?"

"Breezy can stay."

The doctor seemed as confused as Eva. "Mrs. Gordon, do you understand what that flyer means?"

Breezy leaned in, as if waiting for her grandmother's answer.

Doors closed out in the hallway, and a mother tried to comfort a crying child. A nurse dropped a heavy clipboard into a box outside an exam room.

"That I need help. Sometimes my brain feels dull and I make bad, bad decisions . . . Sometimes I make myself unsafe." She paused a moment. "But I can still refinish furniture . . ."

Breezy looked as if she'd fall soon on the floor with relief and land where the skeleton had earlier.

"I thought you were saying something different. Just to be clear, you feel safe with the people you live with?"

Eva looked up. What was the difference between being unsafe with herself and unsafe with the people she lived with? She wasn't staying safe living with them, because she made decisions she didn't always understand. "What do you mean?"

"Being 'safe' means no one is going to harm you in your home." Dr. Howard pressed her hands between her knees.

"Oh, Breezy would never harm me. Is that what you mean?"

"Yes, that's what I'm asking. Why don't I administer some tests, ask a lot of silly questions about days of the week and the time. We'll test your word recall." She asked Eva to write numbers on a clock, draw specific times, name the date, their location, the season. Then she named three objects and wanted Eva to repeat the names: *street, apple, hammer.* She pointed to objects on the counter and asked Eva to name them. They drew pictures like children, Dr. Howard drawing a shape, and then Eva copying it. She wrote a sentence. Eva copied it. "What were those three objects I mentioned several minutes ago? Repeat after me . . . What do we call that? Count backward from one hundred . . ."

"If we're just going to lose all our memories, why make any at all?" Eva gave her hefty thigh a good swat. What if Eva lost the memory of her family and replaced it with nonsense memories? What if she remembered Mabel but didn't remember Sarah and Rob? She was fond of Mabel and didn't particularly care to forget her, but not in place of her children, whom she spent so much time forgetting during life.

If she could pick and choose memories to keep, she'd hold on to Breezy with her hair down and loose, dancing to jazz music while cooking dinner. She'd keep Sarah's holding Breezy on her lap, the baby staring up at her mother, brushing Sarah's cheek with the very tips of her pudgy fingers. They loved each other so.

Dr. Howard focused on Eva and spoke with quiet compassion. "When it functions well, memory is quite a gift, able to keep our past with us long after the moments are gone. Losing our memory is a great loss."

The doctor's kindness beckoned to Eva's hurt. "I lost a daughter, and I think I'm starting to forget her."

"Oh, Gram . . ." Breezy moved closer to her grandmother, kneeling beside her.

The doctor turned in her chair. "I'm so sorry about your daughter. I lost a son to cancer a few years back. My memory keeps him here." She tapped her head.

"Will my memories still be inside of me someplace . . . even if I can't communicate?" Eva quavered.

"I haven't given you a diagnosis yet. But elderly people with dementia or Alzheimer's often respond to stimulus—the cry of a baby, a photo, a song—which suggests their memories still live deep inside." Her words wrapped around Eva. "For now, we'll do some more testing. In the meantime, you can hide yourself away—or you can make the most of your life. Take care of any unfinished business. Enjoy your family. Spread kindness. Watch the sunset. Mend anything that needs repairing."

Eva's mind scrambled at the prospects. "I don't want a diagnosis for this." She stood up and left Dr. Howard's office.

Breezy hurried behind her, down the hall, past the reception desk, calling her name. "Gram, do not leave without me!"

When Eva pushed through the door of the waiting room, other patients looked up. Lips formed smiles. Some people looked away, as if offering respect. A little girl stopped drawing with her crayon.

Breezy caught her grandmother's arm and spoke close to her grandmother's ear. "You need to come back. Right now. You left your coat and purse . . . and me."

Eva passed her eyes over the other patients getting a glimpse into her private family struggles and turned toward the exam room, head lifted high like a regal queen walking through Buckingham Palace.

Back in the room, the doctor held Eva's coat and purse. "Let's schedule a few tests and a follow-up appointment, Mrs. Gordon."

Eleven

SUDDENLY, AS IF SNEAKING UP on her like a cat burglar, the day of the rehearsal dinner arrived. Eva and Breezy drove out to the farm on one of those New England nights where the light air danced in the treetops underneath passing wispy clouds. Only good could happen on a night when the air feels like a Cape Cod breeze blowing in. When they arrived, the farm looked unrecognizable, wearing a whole new outfit and standing mighty, tall and proud. Painters had finished their work, and the outside of the house sported a new color scheme of pale-yellow paint with crisp white trim, and a black door and shutters to match. Shutters hung in their proper place, while holes in the clapboards had been patched. The driveway had a new batch of gravel spread on top and new bricks lined the sides. The hedges had been trimmed, the gangly shrubs removed, and the gardens weeded. Eva stared up at all the changes as she got out of the car.

Even the UPS delivery man whistled long and slow as he took in Try Again Farm in its brand-spanking-new attire, as if he was eyeing a curvy, beautiful woman. "Haven't been on this route for a while, but it's looking good."

Breezy collected Eva's suitcase while Ian waited for them on the porch, her ship's bell mounted right beside him outside the kitchen door. Just as Eva breathlessly made it to the top step, he reached up and pulled the gong, ringing the bell three times.

Unable to stop herself, she clasped Ian's cheeks in both her hands and kissed his face.

Inside the kitchen, it was as if someone had shoveled out all the clutter—the place looked like new, the dust of years past sent packing. More painting and wallpapering needed to be done, but the wood floors boasted a shiny face-lift. Breezy pointed out the beautiful tin chandelier over the pine table.

"Goodbye dark, stuffy feel." Ian swept his arms in a display of introduction as they entered the kitchen.

"It's quite an improvement." Eva nodded her approval before rolling her suitcase into the dining room on her way to check out her new room. Half a dozen friends and students worked diligently in the dining room to prepare decorations for the wedding celebration the next day. They had spread wispy, white tulle over tables and banisters, tucked with enough wildflowers to stock a store. Breezy's theater students had decided to aid in throwing the wedding for Breezy and Ian by putting their set design and decorating skills to work. And their efforts created quite a commotion.

"Pass me that glass cylinder." Isabella pointed, holding sweet pea blossoms in her hand. "Mrs. Gordon, hello. Everyone, this is Breezy's grandmother, Mrs. Gordon." Despite making the introduction, her voice still held a reticence, a sort of shy apprehension attempting to push itself into the world.

The group briefly looked up from their tasks and offered greetings and waves.

Dressed in a long, sage-colored skirt, with her hair pulled back in a ponytail, Isabella's soft honey-brown eyes behind her thick glasses looked expectantly at Eva, as if she were an acquaintance who had appeared to rescue her from loneliness. "I can move over and you can squish in by me and help us, Mrs. Gordon."

A lumbering girl with terrible posture held up some pillar candles. "When will we place all of these?"

Isabella told her they would go out tomorrow. "Not too early, so they don't melt in the sun."

The only male in the group wore a military-style haircut and a neatly trimmed dark beard. He requested someone put on more music.

A tall young woman, who looked vaguely familiar, addressed Eva. "We really could use more help, Mrs. Gordon."

Eva brushed her off and waved to the others. "Everything looks wonderful, but I need to check out my room. Get settled." Looking at Isabella, though, she felt Sarah's thin presence appear as she continued toward the stairs.

"Would you like help carrying your luggage upstairs, Mrs. Gordon?" Isabella asked.

Eva glanced up the stairway. "Actually, I'd appreciate that." She released the handle and moved over to study the framed caterer's menu and wedding invitation, propped on a welcome table by the front door. Eva would've gladly shared empty frames from her collection. Family pictures sat clustered on hallway tables for viewing—Ian's and Breezy's parents, grandparents, and shots of the couple's growing-up years, Eva's stern father, then Wallace, Sarah and Rob, and Eva with Breezy. Group shots seemed an improvement over solos.

"See, Mother," Sarah might say. "Look at what a nice family we have after all."

Earlier in the week, Breezy and a few friends had moved the rest of Eva's worldly possessions out to the farm, and tonight would mark her first official stay at her new residence with her new zip code—for the time being.

Upstairs, the girl left the suitcase in the hallway. "You can manage from here?"

"Yes. Thank you." She rolled her bag down to her new bedroom, where she slipped it under the bed. Maybe someday she could find a home on the street with a carriage house out back where she could live alone, cook in her own kitchen, sit by herself and watch the television show of her own choosing in the evening rather than something from Netflix Eva never would've chosen. Or maybe Breezy and Ian could build her a carriage house on the far end of the property.

She spent a long time alone in her room that day, unpacking, organizing her boxes in the closet, listening to the creaks of the house and the way the wind rattled the old windows like someone knocking to come inside, the same way the windows rattled on a safe day in her grandmother's house. From the dining room, voices rose, carrying an unfamiliar kind of joy to accompany Eva's inexplicable loneliness.

She opened her door to eavesdrop on the conversations below, where young people planned their own weddings, deciding to forgo tradition for something simple like Breezy and Ian's wedding. Someone declared she didn't want to be walked down the aisle by her father but to enter the church with her husband-to-be, side by side as equals. Others planned beach weddings, hoping the weather would hold out, and condemned "destination weddings," expecting guests to travel thousands of miles for an event. The topic of eloping introduced a long silence followed by a collective "no way," probably with all their heads shaking in unison when the group decided they didn't want their weddings to be a private affair without a true celebration.

Eventually Eva lay down on her bed with a light blanket to keep her warm, listening to their rising voices, offering her own whispered opinions about the silliness of their ideas and how they hadn't thought this or that issue through all the way. And oh, did she ever want to tell them to stop imagining marriage to be some trip to Paradise Island.

Mabel's cheery voice interrupted the flow of young people's voices from time to time to offer her aged perspective, especially on keeping marriage vows. "They're meant to be for a lifetime." Her mature voice sounded a warning. "So many hurts and problems in this world would be avoided if people kept those important vows. When my husband and I married in the last century, we always knew we were making important promises to God. And those promises were like life jackets in the stormy days."

Later in the afternoon, Mabel came up and said they should be getting ready for the rehearsal. Weeks earlier, she had helped Eva buy a yellow linen suit, with long sleeves to hide her sagging arm skin, and loose enough around the tummy to tuck in the extra weight. They had purchased a necklace with clay beads painted with accenting shades of green. While Mabel dressed in the bathroom, Eva slipped on the suit.

Outside near the barn, the two older women sat side by side in the front row during the wedding rehearsal, which seemed interminably long. Goodness, she'd fall onto the grass if they didn't stop soon.

Finally, they loaded into cars to head off to the rehearsal dinner. Breezy sent a couple of large flower arrangements in the car with one of her students to spruce up the restaurant. Their party formed a caravan of cars not unlike those of funeral processions from recent memory.

When they pulled into George's and Ian's favorite restaurant— Mortie's—the restaurant looked far from the upscale place described by Ian and George when they had passed around the invitations to everyone. Apparently, the restaurant had decayed considerably since the years when the Ward family would frequent the establishment, celebrating special occasions dressed to the hilt. Eva felt quite special in her new outfit, but foolishly overdressed at the rundown restaurant. Ian and George seemed oblivious to Mortie's decomposition filling the background, instead recalling the establishment as it stood in past decades before the years beat it to smithereens. On the sidewalk, Ian adjusted his uncle's slightly askew red tie, his massive hands guiding his uncle's wrinkled arthritic ones. The drab restaurant behind them needed trim paint, landscaping, and a fresh sign to replace the one out front filled with changeable plastic letters that seemed to have run out of *R*s. Mortie's was sandwiched between a bar and a gas station with an attached convenience store, and surrounded by a chain-link fence plastered with windblown litter.

"We're the MacPherson-Ward party, and we have twenty hungry folks." Ian made his announcement to a stone-faced hostess. She waited at the front door, perusing everyone's dressy attire, offering a smirky smile. No "hospitable greeter" here. The hostess led everyone over the worn and stained carpet to the far corner of the restaurant, passing a buffet table and diners dressed in an assortment of jeans and band T-shirts, and one patron whose shirt proudly labeled her a "Spoiled Brat." Plates piled high with food sat on their tables, as if a sudden rush would prevent a second trip to the food line.

George leaned into Eva and spoke on the way to their seats. "They have the best biscuits here."

The guests encircled the long rectangular table, their voices growing louder as they adjusted to their surroundings and found their seats.

Isabella exclaimed about the restaurant décor, apparently seeing something Eva missed. "Awesome restaurant. Feels so retro."

Military haircut guy introduced himself as Kelton and pulled out a chair in a gentlemanly way, offering the seat to Eva. She accepted, but couldn't she sit alone over there, at a separate table away from the confusion? She'd love to quietly do a crossword puzzle or just listen in on other people's conversations.

Breezy and Ian took seats across from her, speaking to everyone, including the folks at the far end, which unfortunately required raised voices.

She mentally slipped away from all the hubbub and confusion, as the noise drained her cognitive abilities almost immediately. To battle the strain, she made a mental restoration of the restaurant, returning it to its former glory: The red carpet brightened, the worn spots vanished. The waitresses transformed into people who enjoyed their patrons, jokingly taking orders, offering winks and delivering drinks to customers along with a compliment, using first names, flirting with some of the men. Smoke rose from many of the patrons who flicked ashes in glass ashtrays on the table. The image appeared in black and white.

Then the ashtrays disappeared, and it was Breezy sitting across from Eva, whispering to Ian, wrapping her fingers with his. Ian stood, clanging his spoon on his glass to gather everyone's attention before he dove into a long thank-you speech to each person for sharing in his long-awaited journey toward marriage to Breezy. To Eva's dismay, he recounted *everything*. How they dated when they were younger, broke up after a rough patch, and ran into each other at a restaurant one day.

The group gave Ian their rapt attention, sipping drinks after the waitresses delivered sodas and iced tea to the table. Holding their empty trays against their hips, even the waitresses stopped for a minute to listen. Ian's talk brought Eva's own relationship with Wallace to mind, and how they never divorced but never got their second chance by reconciling either.

While Ian told all his humorous stories about trying to win back Breezy, such as enrolling in one of her aerobics classes at the YMCA, falling off exercise balls, and memorizing poetry to impress her, Eva thought of Wallace. Once, or maybe twice, she considered trying to get him to return home and forget all the silliness between them, but she couldn't decide on a plan of attack. Make him a delicious lasagna and drop in under the guise of discussing Sarah's issues?

He had still helped her with her taxes year after year. She could never figure out all those exemptions and deductions. Once, while he sat there hunched over the tax forms underneath the dim desk lamp light, Eva, speechless, stepped closer, words all tangled on her tongue, unable to form an invitation for him to come home to try again, mouth unable to form the shape of an apology.

And then Sarah took ill. Very ill. She and Luke loved being parents to young Breezy, but Sarah continued to grow sicker. "Being a parent never scares away someone's demons," Wallace said to Eva during Sarah's very last hospital stay.

"The damage to her body is irreparable," the doctors explained to them. Wallace, Eva, and Luke sat by her bedside on her last night, watching as her breathing slowed and her consciousness faded. How could Eva express all her parenting regrets in just a few short moments when she'd never practiced asking for forgiveness in the past?

"She's gone." The doctor turned off the machine before Eva had a chance to speak.

Luke and Wallace wept and wept.

Eva found an empty hospital room and slipped inside the darkness, where she sat on a chair and pummeled her own legs with wounding punches no one else would see, wailing on her thighs with a powerful grief. The next day, great bruises appeared on her body, as if she'd been in the worst fight of her life.

Ian had moved on to reciting poetry to Breezy, lifting her by the hand from her seat and standing intimately close. "This is called 'Destiny' by Edwin Arnold." He recited a poem about how *somewhere there waiteth in this world of ours for one lone soul another lonely soul—*. The couple seemed unaware when trays of appetizers arrived—stuffed mushrooms and bruschetta and bread and butter. The guests loaded their appetizer plates and passed baskets of bread around as Ian and Breezy pulled themselves from their reverie to return their attention to their surroundings and hungry guests.

Eva tried to focus on cutting the stuffed mushroom on her plate while keeping the insides intact.

A baby-faced girl, Jasmine, sitting next to Eva, seemed to have the task of building community among the guests, asking questions about everyone's plans for the rest of the summer. The girl sat erect at the edge of her seat, shoulders and back so straight it was as if she were propped up by a metal bar.

Eva only gave her the briefest nuggets of information. "Weeding a few gardens at Try Again Farm, I suppose." She stabbed another mushroom on her plate with her fork.

The girl remained undeterred, adding her irritatingly sweet voice to so much other chatter up and down the table.

Eva's brain could not decipher the girl's voice from other voices or the competing music coming from speakers in the ceiling. "Could you repeat that question?"

Jasmine looked over at Breezy and Ian, who were engaged with people standing behind them. She held up her hand, as if shielding her words from Breezy and Ian. "Don't you love Isabella's idea for the honeymoon kit? So fun."

Eva applied pressure to her arms and legs, expecting to feel bruised from the powerful memory of Sarah's passing. "Seems a little immature for a wedding gift. To me." As soon as she said the words, a pained expression overtook Jasmine's face.

Eva turned and there was Isabella, standing at their side.

Jasmine grabbed Isabella's arm, as if preventing the girl from making a hurried escape. "Your idea's so clever, Isabella. It's *so* creative!"

Isabella fiddled with a card. "I was hoping everyone could sign this, write some practical tip for Breezy and Ian for their marriage. I was going to put it in the basket." Her eyes looked wounded, as if Eva introduced an insult to her fragile psyche. "Maybe it's too immature." She looked to Eva for feedback. Maybe an apology?

"I'm just repeating what I already told you in the barn," Eva explained. "Isn't it a little late to 'get to know' someone . . . ?" But Eva's voice trailed off.

Jasmine stood and turned Isabella away from the table.

Eva followed.

"It's Breezy." Jasmine slid her hands in a referee's "safe" gesture. "That's all I can say. It's Breezy. She'll love all the creative hodgepodge gifts."

"It doesn't make any difference." Isabella's disappointed face said the opposite.

Eva wanted to say something to help Isabella. If only she knew what would help. Her mind blackened, words vanishing. Jumbled conversations and confusion overwhelmed her. As if moving on without her, Eva imagined her body standing and heading for the door, desperately in need of outdoor air and a moment to compose her thoughts.

"Hey, where are the flower arrangements we made? Didn't anyone bring them in?" Breezy looked up and down the table.

Eva pointed to the door. "I'll go get them. Can I have the keys?"

Breezy pulled the keys from her purse. "You'll need some help, Gram."

Kelton stood. "I can help." He followed Eva to the door.

She led him outside in the dark to the Jeep and unlocked the door. She pointed to the arrangements in the back seat, and he lugged one out.

"If you pass me that other one, I can carry them both." He shifted the one arrangement in his arms to make room for a second.

Just as she handed him the second arrangement, music started playing next door. A band was warming up. "You go on in, Kelson. I need a minute of quiet out here."

"Kelton. And are you sure?" He wore a hesitant expression.

"Absolutely. Run along. I'll be fine."

Slowly, he walked to the front door, looking back at Eva once or twice. She waved him inside with her hand.

The music calmed her, slowed her breathing. Suddenly she was eighteen again standing outside The Fisherman's Tavern on a summer night, excited to go inside and hear Wallace's band play. She could hear his jazzy trumpet from right there in the parking lot. Her legs trembled with excitement at the thought of seeing him onstage with his band. As she opened the door, the brassy sound grew louder, but she couldn't see him anywhere. Her girlfriend, Carol, dated the drummer, so Eva scoured the place for her friend who showed up for most of the shows. Eva made her way through the club to get closer to the stage as they warmed up and tuned their instruments.

As he played some notes, the trumpeter caught Eva's eye and smiled. She smiled back.

But he wasn't Wallace.

The band nodded to each other and started a new tune, filling her ears with strange and unfamiliar music.

Where had Wallace gone?

She turned to the young girl standing next to her. "Carol, why isn't Wallace playing tonight?"

The girl turned and spoke to Eva through lips pierced with multiple metal objects. "Which one's Wallace? I don't know the band members' names."

Eva turned and hurried out of the dance hall and rushed across the parking lot to find Mortie's, reaching for the pleats on her skirt as she walked, only to realize she was wearing a yellow linen suit—the scratchy one Mabel bought with her—instead of her favorite skirt from long ago. The darkness of the parking lot left her feeling blind.

Wait, there were flower arrangements in the Jeep, but where was the Jeep?

As she walked, the night club music grew more distant sounding, but the Mortie's sign never appeared. She needed to ask someone for help.

The shadows ahead of her shifted as two men approached her.

She backed up to get away from them. What might men do to a woman alone in a dark parking lot?

A low voice spoke and something metallic jingled. They moved in close.

They could grab her and stuff her into the back seat of their car. Or worse, their trunk. She would kick out the taillights if they took her, like the news report had once said to do. *Kick out the taillights and wave your hands to people in other cars.* Was she strong enough to kick out a taillight?

Suddenly they were next to her, metal objects clanging in their hands.

"You look lost. Need some help, ma'am?" The taller of the two men spoke.

"Lines or no lines, Mrs. Gordon, you can't drive. You can't live alone anymore, Gram. You can't live near Mabel. You can't see your son. You can't talk to your daughter. You can't."

"Get away from me or I'll scream!"

"Eva?" The call came from behind her.

She turned.

At just that moment, Ian jogged around the corner and through the parking lot yelling her name.

"I think she's over here," the shorter of the two men called. "Are you Eva?"

She nodded.

When Ian arrived, Eva threw herself into his arms.

"We just came out to get some percussion equipment." The taller man held up a drum stand.

"Yeah. And found her wandering around. Just wanted to help." He looked as if Eva had frightened him as much as they'd frightened her. "Sorry to scare you, ma'am."

"She threatened to scream." The taller one again spoke to Ian. "Glad she didn't."

Ian thanked them for their concern, and the men wandered back inside. He gently released Eva's arms from his body, then turned her around to escort her back to the restaurant. "You okay, Eva?"

She just nodded. Her knees felt as though they might buckle beneath her. She grabbed Ian's arm for support.

"All right. All right. You're safe now. Got yourself a little turned around? You're out behind the building." He towered over her like he had earlier with his helpless, old uncle.

"I just went next door. To hear the music."

When they arrived back at Mortie's, Breezy was pacing the sidewalk outside the restaurant. "Where have you *been*, Gram?" She shored her up on the opposite side of Ian. "Kelton said you wanted to hear the live music, and we went next door to find you, but you weren't there. He's very apologetic about leaving you."

"She's had a bit of a scare. But she's going to be okay. We'll get her some prime rib, and she'll forget all about it." Ian led her back inside and pointed Eva toward her seat.

Before she walked away, her good ear picked up part of Breezy and Ian's discussion.

Shorten the honeymoon. Able to leave her with Isabella? Getting worse?

〰

Back at Try Again Farm, Eva hated to be left alone with strangers while her granddaughter went off to spend her final night as a single person with her bridesmaids—Tara and the other girls. But Eva stoically kept her thoughts to herself to allow Breezy her wish of staying with her friends at a bed and breakfast, and getting the royal treatment of a special breakfast and massages in the morning.

"You're sure you'll be fine staying here, Gram? We can squeeze you in at the B and B . . ."

"And stay up all hours of the night listening to you all chatter? No thank you, ma'am. I'll be climbing into bed and getting my beauty sleep." Eva waved her hand toward the car. "You go now. Scat." Then, warding off second thoughts, she gave Breezy a brusque kiss on her cheek and a little pat on the back.

Twelve

EARLY THE NEXT MORNING, SOME sort of early bird sang a forlorn call outside Eva's window. Her mind scrolled through her listings of bird songs, failing to decipher the species. She looked at the door. Why was it to her right rather than her left? Studying the placement of the windows didn't orient her either. To add misery to her troubles, a pervasive feeling accompanied the typical morning fog—a grief over someone's departure, or a grasping and longing for some desire just out of reach—either something lost or something never experienced, but something to do with family. Either way, the experience felt beyond her ability to recapture.

The dim light of dawn cast only the slightest illumination on her room, leaving her unable to focus on the human form across the room. Young Sarah bringing her breakfast in bed again? A tray laden with eggs, pancakes, and a napkin folded with a child's precision?

With eyes still shut, never really looking at her daughter, she yelled. "Get out and stop waking me up the one morning I can sleep in!"

Footsteps hurried from the room. The door shut quietly, fearfully behind.

Underneath the blankets, Eva's foot moved this way and that, completing her morning stretch routine. With the morning light, the figure at the end of the bed came into focus. Not little Sarah but Breezy's 1940s-style satin wedding dress, "with a hint of lilac," hung from the closet door.

Ah, the big day lay ahead, including the parade of strangers invading her life.

She slowly swung her feet out of bed, then struggled for balance as she stood and walked to the dress. She smoothed its glimmering fabric, picked a little at the rosette on the hip. Why did Breezy choose a dress from Eva's teenage era, a V-neck bodice with ruching and thin straps? Rather than going downstairs to join all those people whose names she could never straighten out—especially when her granddaughter greeted the morning somewhere else—she slipped on casual cargo pants and a saggy shirt appropriate for hiding in the barn for the day. She would change later when Breezy arrived.

The back door in the kitchen slammed often, and footsteps bustled about the house.

Eva stepped out of her room.

"Good morning, Mrs. Gordon."

Eva flew back inside her room, trying to calm the rushing heart rate caused by the unexpected greeting.

She shut her eyes. When her heart returned to normal, she stepped out of the room and looked down at the girl who sat on the floor by Eva's door.

Isabella calmly held a cup of coffee in hand and a book on her lap. On the floor next to her sat her phone and journal.

Eva asked with slow precision, "What in the world are you doing sitting outside an old woman's door, young lady? Knowing I might have a heart attack from being startled? Why not sit outside your own room?" Eva aimed a pointed finger at the room next door.

The girl didn't immediately answer in cohesive sentences, instead stumbling around for an excuse she should've planned well in advance.

"Well, Isabella, let's go on downstairs and see what everyone's doing to get ready for the big day."

Isabella collected her belongings and quickly caught up to Eva, following her down the hall.

The spirit of the wedding began at the top of the stairs, descending down the banister with lush garlands of hydrangeas sprinkled with white roses and sheer ribbon. The aroma of flowers and coffee filled the air. And the delicious smell of something baking in the oven.

"Do you know what she made for you?" Wallace rebuked. *"She's been working for an hour to surprise you! And you threw her out of your room?"*

Eva descended the stairs as if being pulled into a fiery inferno for all her crimes, trying to steady herself by gripping the slippery, prickly banister wrapped in flowers.

Isabella's ghostlike presence followed her.

"She scraped every bit of the food in the dog's dish." Wallace pointed an accusing finger at Eva, no longer looking like the freckle-faced boy she grew up with. *"Do you know how hard she worked? She threw the daisy out the back door, then washed the dishes and put them away."*

In the living room and dining room, daisies and willow sprigs soaked in glass jars, waiting to be taken outside later in the afternoon. Throughout the first floor, a heavily caffeinated group of about a dozen young people worked with energetic smiles and chatter, moving around vases of greenery and flowers. Some stood back from the group, chatting in groups of two or three while sipping from their mugs. A few raised a hand in a morning greeting as Eva passed.

Ian stood in the kitchen, talking on the phone, wearing jeans and a short-sleeved shirt. His five o'clock shadow said he hadn't shaved yet. "Gram's doin' good. She just came down for breakfast, and we'll put her to work as soon as we feed her." He tried to hand Eva the phone, but she waved him off on her direct path for the coffeepot.

"Just tell her I'll see her later today." Eva selected a mug from the cabinets and poured herself some coffee.

Ian hung up his phone. "How you feelin' this morning? You had quite a scare last night."

The tender press of his hand on her back made her suddenly sad with remorse, wanting to inhale her harsh and bossy words to Isabella for guarding her door. She ignored his comment and poured some cream into her coffee. "I hope you know what you're getting yourself into, letting me live with you."

"My eyes are wide open." He widened his eyes as if demonstrating.

"I'm not the easiest person to get along with." She took a sip of the warm beverage.

"Nothing I can't handle, Eva."

"If you're sure." She looked out the window at the yard. "I think I'll go check out the preparations." She raised her coffee mug as if in a toast.

From the back porch, she studied the yard. A young woman with arms covered in tattoos was draping small bundles of white lights in the tree's branches to glow brightly at dusk. Jasmine helped drape tables with rented linens while an easy breeze rippled the cloth beneath the simple, lovely settings. Arrangements of candles—some under glass hurricane lamps of different sizes, some clustered in jars, and some strewn about in pierced tin votive holders—graced each table.

Isabella approached Eva. "Looks beautiful, doesn't it? Would you like to help Mabel light all those candles when the time's near, Mrs. Gordon—at dusk, just before the ceremony?"

"Sure. I can handle lighting candles."

Ian called out the back door. "Cinnamon rolls for breakfast! Come and get 'em while they're hot!"

"Lines or no lines, Mrs. Gordon, three strikes and you're out," said the judge in his last words.

"Lines, Mrs. Gordon?" Isabella fidgeted with her ponytail's elastic.

"Lines?" Eva looked at the girl with confusion.

Isabella held a book. "I'm putting this on a table up near the front by the street, so guests can write a poem for the bride and groom in the guest book. Or, try their hand at being Shakespeare, writing a brief synopsis of Breezy and Ian's future. It's going to be a creative crowd."

"Great idea. Speaking of the front, I'm going to check it out." She left Isabella to her tasks and ambled off, having to dodge Amber and Buck, who wrestled with each other on the lawn.

Standing at the end of the driveway, she could feel them all standing beside her—Ian's parents and grandparents, the Wards who had poured themselves into life on that farm for generations, dressed in their casual clothes, leaning on rakes and shovels. They would be admiring Ian's work, remarking on their pleasure with their descendant's choice to stay at the farm and marry Breezy. In their deepest hopes, they probably all wished for the farm to stay in the family for generations to come.

The whole lot of them nodded with approval seeing the farm dressed in its wedding attire when their own had been so simple, a ceremony in the living room and some cake and punch in the dining room. They smiled and pointed at the *No Developers* sign and the white tulle and arrangement of lilies and hydrangeas draped over the mailbox. Eva stood comfortably silent in their presence, encouraging them to step back as a pickup truck pulled into the driveway. A couple of men unloaded speakers and a fold-up dance floor in the yard.

The original plan had been to hold the ceremony under a large canvas tent in case of inclement weather, but Breezy, the penny-pincher, decided if worst came to worst, they'd clean out the barn and get married in there.

Fortunately, the weather cooperated. In fact, the early morning news forecasted perfect dry air with no moisture in New England and clear skies all the way to Chicago.

Isabella followed behind as the rental guys dropped the chairs into a pile in the barn's shadow. She snapped each one into place next to the barn where the ceremony would be held, all the while talking with Jasmine. They tied tulle at the end of each row, then adding a daisy on the end seats.

As Eva made her way inside to get one of those cinnamon rolls for breakfast, a white van pulled up with the words *A Catered Affair* painted on the side of the vehicle. Four people, two men and two women, hurried out of the van and started unloading food steamer trays and coolers.

Eva greeted them in the kitchen, where she buttered her roll. "Feel free to use the fridge. I made some space for you."

A heavyset woman with gray hair squeezed into a tight bun set up trays of food on the counters. "Thanks. Hopefully our coolers will do." She turned to the others and passed out instructions. "The hosts want the food served outside, but we'll make a staging station here on the kitchen table to replenish the outside trays."

Her crew nodded and set down crates filled with dishes.

"I'd be glad to help you set up." Eva started unpacking their paper plates and coffee cups, but the woman's hand stilled her own.

"We're fine. We'll take care of everything." Her no-nonsense manner included no smile.

Her employees hurried up and down the back stairs, arms loaded with bags and boxes to go out on the buffet table in the back field.

"I can take something outside." Eva's arms felt empty.

"We've got it. Thanks for the offer. If we could get you to step out of the way . . ." With a brief smile, the supervisor continued setting up.

"The cake is going—"

"The dining room. Yeah, we know. Thanks." She gently took Eva's arm and guided her to the back door.

Eva grabbed another roll from a plate on her way outside. Standing beside the screen door, she munched and watched as people arranged the coolers by the back field.

Unsure of how to occupy herself and be useful, she headed to her secluded new shop, where she rummaged through boxes, lining up her supplies to order her work area, finding a place for brushes, paints, and sandpaper in the drawers of the sturdy workbench. But there was a steep reduction in her tool collection. Missing were her electric tools, anything that plugged in and offered power or heat. A number of chemical substances seemed missing as well. However, sandpaper must've been deemed safe for the aging woman.

The sound of a swishing skirt strolling back and forth by the entrance of the shop drew her attention. "If you're going to keep an eye on me, might as well join me in here." Eva turned and saw Jasmine.

The girl came inside. "Watcha doing?"

Eva pointed out Sarah's old desk, explaining her restoration plan.

Jasmine raised her eyebrows. "Sounds so cool. I've always had this funny idea when I see old, abandoned furniture on the side of the road." She smoothed her hand over the desktop. "What would the owners do if I took one of those finds, fixed up all its wounds, gave it some fresh paint, and just for giggles, revamped it with a new feature—like a built-in chess board on a coffee table, new cane on a rocker, a slab of marble for a tabletop? Then late at night, I'd sneak the piece back to the street where I found it."

Those people would be so shocked when they found their throwaway junk all fixed up and worth some money. Maybe they would wonder why they failed to see potential in the piece. Or maybe some people would still hate the piece, thinking its flaw existed in the core of its being. It was *just* a pine dresser after all. But the idea appealed to Eva in all its weirdness. Maybe she could make something new with Sarah's desk?

"But I wouldn't even know where to begin." Jasmine picked up a pack of sandpaper and read the label. Her cell phone rang and she answered it, then gave the caller directions to the farm.

"It's easy." Eva glanced at Post-its. "Just remove the old finish with a rough grain sandpaper, then move to a finer grit until you have a smooth finish. Run a tacky cloth over the top, add paint or stain and some hardware, and you're done. But it's too messy to do on a wedding day. Can you help me with this tarp?" The two women covered the desk for protection before they left the barn.

Jasmine's cell phone rang again. "Sure. We'll get Michael to come pick you up. See you later!" She hung up.

As they crossed the yard, a car pulled into the driveway and parked.

A woman got out and opened her hatch. She spotted Ian attaching a nylon rope between trees to tie up the dogs during the festivities. She called to him. "Yoo-hoo, Ian! I've got a cake for you!"

He finished connecting the dog run and met her at her vehicle. Together they unloaded a collection of separate boxes, probably each holding a layer. "Let's go in through the front door to stay out of the caterer's way." He noticed Eva and Jasmine. "Ladies, can you give us a hand?"

"I'd be glad to carry something." Eva held out willing arms.

The baker passed a box to Jasmine. "Looks like we're good, but thanks. If you could just grab the door."

Inside, they set the boxes on the table in the dining room, away from tree droppings, bugs, and active dogs. The cake was a replica of a Scrabble board, complete with squares of alphabet letters, as a tribute to Ian's proposal to Breezy. Over a game of Scrabble, he had spelled out the words *Marry me Breeze* in small, block letters, to which she spelled out *Yes.*

The caterer stuck her head into the dining room to talk to Ian. "We have box lunches, like you requested. They're stacked in your refrigerator."

Ian turned to Eva and Jasmine. "Want to be sure everyone knows there's some lunch in here? Just carry the boxes out later and set them up on the porch so people can eat outside."

The ladies agreed to the task.

Yet again, Jasmine's cell phone rang and she answered it. "Uh, no." She shook her head as if the caller could see her annoyed expression. "No dogs as guests." After hanging up, Jasmine hurried off to help Isabella with decorations.

Not knowing what to do with herself, Eva slipped upstairs to her room and sat on the edge of her bed, looking down over the fields below. The sense of loneliness and uselessness compounded by being in a crowd of strangers made her pensive. If only she had her own family members here. If only she had Sarah. And Rob.

A thought occurred to her.

She collected her phone from inside her purse, then opened her address book. As she flipped slowly through the pages, she ran her finger down the listings of names. After finding Rob's contact information in Breezy's phone, she had been certain to save it in her address book.

And here it was. Would he speak to her? Would he hang up? She sat down in the armchair.

Carefully, she punched in the international number on her phone, double and even triple checking the numbers as she dialed.

After several rings, a man's voice answered. "Hello?"

She sat upright in her seat, posture forming a prominent exclamation point. "Rob?"

The man didn't respond.

She lowered her voice. "Rob. It's your mother."

Static crackled on the line before he responded. "Mother? *What the* . . . ? Isn't there a wedding going on there today?"

"Yes, a wedding going on here today. But it's been a while, Rob. I just thought this was a good time to call. I'm living on the farm now. With Breezy. You'd love this place. And you still live in London?" If she kept talking, blathering words, she hoped she could tether him to herself so he couldn't hang up. *He* was what she was longing for. *He* was what she was missing. She wanted to iron his shirts, creating a defined crease in his sleeves and flattening down his collar. She would steam the pleat in his pants and offer the clothes to him one item at a time while he waited, telling her about his travels, the other people on his overseas flight, what he planned to do in the States.

"This is out of the blue, Mother."

"Son, are you . . . are you receiving my letters? You never write back." She fiddled with a place on the chair's upholstery where the threads were straining and coming apart at a seam.

"Mother, this isn't a good idea today." He paused and sighed into the phone as if battling a migraine. "Look, I've been thinking. I heard about your trip to Phyllis's house. Breezy filled me in. It sounds tough. But not today."

Eva couldn't form a response. She didn't want him to hang up. She wanted him to keep talking, to let his voice wash over her with all its associated memories.

"And it's an international charge. Just tell Breezy 'Congrats.'"

"I wish you could've come for the ceremony."

"Well, you know me and family get-togethers."

"Rob . . . wait." Eva leaned her hefty frame forward, arms on her knees and head bowed, in her own way offering up a confession. "Did you know Sarah once made me breakfast in bed?"

He didn't answer.

"I hurt her so badly. I screeched at her like an owl. For making me breakfast in bed. And now I can't . . . I can't even apologize to her."

His voice softened. "I'm not sure what to say to you. You've caught me off guard here." Something brushed, as if he was rubbing his face the way he did when he was young and his mother exasperated him but he wanted to hold his tongue, maybe counting to ten.

"I'm sure I did similar things to you. I'm just missing you all." She sat wordless, the sounds of wedding preparations coming in through the window, voices and music and car doors slamming. Finally he said, "I need to go. For now. Please give Breezy my very best wishes." And he hung up.

For the longest time, Eva sat there holding her phone in her hand, long after the wireless company had stopped calculating the cost of the transatlantic conversation. "I've always loved you, Rob," Eva whispered.

When she finally went downstairs for one of those boxed lunches, Ian rushed past her looking for a volunteer to go pick up Breezy's father at the Logan Express. "He needs a ride to the farm."

Ugh. Luke. He wasn't here yet?

Kelton volunteered, snatched keys from Ian's hand, and headed out to the car. Wearily Eva sat down in a sagging living room chair decorated with laced doilies on the arms. For a long while, her mind turned blank, simply tracing the lines of the braided rug round and round in a widening circle, round and round over the fabric. Mrs. Ward had likely cut up old sheets and curtains that had served their purpose as coverings for her family. Now they would serve her loved ones in a fresh way. She would've formed long strips of fabric, braided them, then sewed the pieces together to make a rug that would keep the bare feet of family members warm in the long, hard winters. Round and round Eva moved her eyes while her brain slipped into quiet mode.

She let her head fall back and her mind grow distant, dipping into a listening posture. Joyous voices. The back door opening and slamming. Mabel arriving, exclaiming about how grand the place looked, how tired Eva looked, could they help in any way in the kitchen?

Eva shook her head, offering only a weary, dull look to Mabel when she bent down close with a hand on Eva's shoulder, silently watching her for a minute before moving her mouth to ask questions and glance toward the kitchen.

Then, Mabel inviting herself into the kitchen commotion, introducing herself, passing around compliments about the aroma of their quiches and meatballs. Mabel bringing in two boxed lunches and water bottles, sitting down on the ottoman in front of Eva's chair, exclaiming about the very good cleanliness practices of the caterers. Eating quietly together. Mabel giving Eva a gentle lift by the elbow to encourage her to stand and walk around, go outside, get her blood flowing to wake up. Poking at flower arrangements in the yard, petting dogs as they chased each other through the chairs. George kneeling by Buck's side where he was now tied up out back, rubbing his fur, whispering into his ear. George and Mabel preparing a spot in the shade for Eva, where they lowered her into a chair to wait for Breezy. Falling asleep to the unfamiliar yet comforting sounds of people caring for her, sitting near her in silence, just the squeak of a chair when they changed positions, the sound of breathy whispers when someone else came to check on her, giving her something she missed or longed for.

When she heard Breezy's voice, Eva opened her eyes and sat up straight in the chair. Jasmine shooed Ian into George's room off the kitchen so the bride wouldn't be seen slipping upstairs to get ready.

Mabel spoke. "Here we go, Eva. Are you ready to get dressed?" Mabel helped her friend from the chair, and they walked inside the house together.

"I think I might need some coffee."

Mabel retrieved coffee and then ushered Eva upstairs.

Eva stopped at Breezy's door and stuck her head inside. "Hi, dear. I'll be right back. Going to get my outfit on."

"Hi, Gram. You ready for my big day?" She was laying out makeup on the dresser, still wearing jeans and a cotton shirt.

Her bridesmaids were pulling their dresses out of garment bags and waved to Eva.

"I'm ready." She looked down at her messy outfit. "Well, not *fully* ready. But I'm getting dressed now."

In Eva's room, Mabel had pulled Eva's clothes out of the closet and laid them on the bed. "I'll just turn away while you dress." She focused on the view out the window.

Eva donned her formal blue skirt and matching lace jacket over a sleeveless top. "How do I look?" she asked Mabel.

"You look gorgeous, Eva."

"Not gorgeous like the bride, but this will do." And they walked down the hall.

Mabel went downstairs to wait.

When Eva knocked, Tara opened the door and stepped back to let Eva slip inside. There, standing by the bed stood Breezy wearing her vintage wedding dress, looking like a vision from Eva's past. And looking so much like Sarah. Her breath caught in her throat.

"Why don't we give you a minute, Mrs. Gordon." Tara and the others left the room.

Eva hated to admit she couldn't remember their names. And now they all looked exactly alike, wearing the same dresses.

Eva paused.

"All this anxiety over a wedding? Sure you're making the right decision?" Eva hounded.

Eva badgered her daughter while the young woman ironed her own dress, since Eva refused to help. How could Sarah be getting married when Eva's marriage had fallen apart?

Eva silently took Breezy into her arms for a long hug. "I don't ever want to forget how beautiful you look at this moment."

Breezy smiled warmly in return. "Thank you, Gram. And I haven't even done my hair yet." She patted the mass.

"You look so much like—"

"I wish . . . she was here." Breezy's eyed filled to overflowing. She pulled away from Eva and waved her hands. "Oh, I can't cry! I've already done my makeup!"

Eva took a tissue from the dresser and gently dabbed at her granddaughter's eyes. Her own eyes threatened to fill. "I shouldn't be the one here with you now. She should be here." She noticed Breezy's dress wasn't zipped on the side and carefully tugged the zipper on the soft satin fabric.

"In a perfect world, you'd both be here." Breezy finished with the tissue, then looked out the window.

"You'll be a much better wife than I ever was. That's for sure. I'm happy for you." Eva sat down on the bed.

"It won't be hard with Ian for a husband." Breezy turned to the mirror and swept her long locks up into a loose chignon on the back of her head. "Okay. Time to get my emotions under control and do my hair. Can you call in the girls again? Tara's going to help me."

Eva let them back in and watched as Tara secured the chignon with bobby pins and hair spray, allowing a couple of wisps to hang free on the sides.

Outside, a car door slammed.

Breezy moved to the window. "It's my dad." She blew him a kiss. "Hey, Dad! See you in a minute." And she returned her attention to the room. "He looks shorter. Much shorter than Ian. Tara, could you bring my dad up so I can say hi to him?"

Eva moved to look out the window at Luke.

Isabella knocked on the door and asked if Eva was still going to help light the candles and luminaries with Mabel. Breezy looked finished, so Eva went outside with Isabella, who handed her and Mabel wands to light the candles.

By the time they finished, a crowd had gathered. Students dressed in a hodgepodge of outfits—camouflage skirts, heavy eyeliner on some of the girls, a pretty cotton flowing skirt with cowboy boots on another—while a violinist wandered through the yard, bowing a peaceful melody.

Amber and Buck were restrained by the dog run, and someone had attached lily-of-the-valley corsages to their collars. But Buck spun in circles trying to pull the flowers from his collar, unraveling the edges of the ribbon holding it in place. Amber endured hers patiently like a lady, sitting and watching the gathering crowd.

Luke stood up from one of the chairs where he had been sitting and called out a greeting to Eva. "Hello, grandmother of the bride. It's been a long time, Eva." He walked over to join her and offered a slight reserved bow.

She held out her hand but he instead leaned in to give her a perfunctory kiss on her cheek. His splotchy, red face suggested he still enjoyed a few too many drinks.

He glanced around. "I'm just taking my seat, since I'm not walking the bride down the aisle." Luke shifted nervously, looking out toward the pasture.

"Of course." Eva pointed to the front row. "We're supposed to be up there." He followed behind Eva and Mabel, who would also be sitting in the front row, just as the eerie sound of a lone bagpiper drifted through the dusk. Bagpipes always sounded like pleading wails to Eva.

At least the bagpiper stood at a distance.

The tune summoned everyone to their seats, and the crowd hushed. Ian, George, Ian's brother, and the pastor strode to the front and lined up with the barn behind them. The photographer positioned himself outside the back door waiting for Breezy. A hush passed over Try Again Farm.

Eva looked down the row at Luke. *Let's get this show on the road so we don't have to be in each other's company much longer.* He nodded to her as if reading her mind.

The men all wore khaki pants, navy jackets, and red ties, which gently rippled with the breeze. George's wild hair looked slicked down with gel, and he had shaved his whiskers. While the groom looked at the house expectantly for his bride-to-be, Eva's mind displayed a black-and-white version of the participants and guests waiting for Breezy, envisioning the scene as a memory etched on yellowed paper, stuffed in a book.

The bagpipe's melancholy invited tears from a hidden, lonely spot in Eva, who saw herself standing before her grandmother, ashamed of who she'd become and unable to explain all her bitter, persnickety behavior. She wanted to say she was trying to be different, but Grandmother had a stern look on her face, a look that pained Eva. The tears bubbled up, but she didn't have a tissue and hated to cry in public.

The click of the photographer's camera drew everyone's attention to the back door. The bridesmaids walked down the steps carrying bouquets of lily of the valley tied with a wide strip of white satin ribbon. As they strolled down the aisle between the chairs, the fabric of their pale-pink dresses rustled like field grass.

Thankfully, the bagpiper ended, replaced by the violinist. And it was at just that perfect moment, when the wind lifted the leaves in the trees and the birds lowered their tunes to a faint song, that Breezy appeared barefoot at the back door. She descended the back steps, crossing the driveway to the soft grass, where she slowly walked through the crowd, greeting guests with nods and smiles before latching her gaze onto Ian. Eva had suggested shoes but Breezy had just smiled and patted her grandmother, as if the suggestion humored her.

When she reached her groom, Breezy passed her flowers to Tara and joined hands with Ian as the violinist finished playing. A man's voice rose up from behind the guests.

Eva turned to see who was speaking and why they were speaking, taking a few moments to orient herself to the fact that one of Breezy's students, possibly Kelton, was reciting something from the Bible with a deep stage voice: "Love is patient; love is kind. Love is not envious or boastful or arrogant or rude . . ."

When he finished, Jasmine approached the bride and groom from Breezy's side and recited a poem from memory. "How do I love thee?"

The poem resided in Eva's memory in its entirety.

Once, Wallace had recited those very words to Eva as they stood on a Cape Cod beach. *"I memorized them for you, Eva."*

Eva's eyes stung as she recalled his loving gesture.

As soon as the girl finished reciting the poem, a young man's voice rose from a different place in the yard, reciting the poem they heard last night at dinner about someone *waiting for a lone soul, another lonely soul.*

After the poetry, the pastor thanked the crowd for joining them for this holy moment. He read from the book of Genesis Breezy's favorite story, about the young man Joseph, sold into slavery by his jealous brothers and carried off to Egypt. The pastor wove that strange story about Egypt and slavery into something fit for a wedding couple, telling how Joseph's past one day intersected with his present when his brothers reappeared in his life after a long absence, needing help to survive a famine in their land. He confessed his choice of a story seemed an odd pick for a wedding, but he rarely married a couple who were given a second chance like Breezy and Ian, whose pasts joined with their presents like Joseph and his brothers. "Joseph's family spent years apart, dead to each other, not knowing that there was a heavenly plan for their relationship to be restored in time. The story shows us God can go even into our pasts and 'restore the years the locust has eaten.'"

After the sermon, the couple recited their vows from memory, eyes fixed on each other, tears forming a silent line down their cheeks. A guitar player led the group in singing a hymn. Rings were exchanged. The minister offered a blessing on their future life together and told Ian he could kiss his bride.

Applause rang out as the two embraced. After the kiss, Ian held his wife's arm in the air like an act of victory. The crowd cheered even more.

On cue, caterers brought out trays of meatballs, finger sandwiches, quiches, cut-up vegetables and dip, several tureens of clam chowder with oyster crackers and loads of breads, fruit trays, cheeses, and crackers. Large carafes of decaf iced coffee were set up on the tables near the orchard. The happy couple led guests through the food line.

The boisterous crowd swirled about Eva, leaving her disoriented as Mabel led her from one place to another, her thin hand guiding Eva's arm. Isabella skittered around the edges of the group with the same uncertainty until she caught up with Mabel and Eva and encouraged them to sign the guest book. "And can I get you a plate?"

Mabel declined, but Eva was starving.

On their way to the guest book, Luke stepped directly in their path. "Wonderful ceremony." He balanced some appetizers and a glass of punch, giving Eva a cautious smile. His rumpled suit jacket looked as if he slept in it the night before and hadn't had it dry-cleaned in years.

Eva expected disdain, but he seemed a little more reserved than in the past.

"Pardon me, you two." Mabel placed a hand on both Eva and Luke. "I'm going to go help George with the guest book." And she hurried off to collect George.

"I'm surprised you could get the time off." Luke taught college out west somewhere.

"It's my daughter's wedding. Did you think I'd skip it?"

"I never could guess what you'd do, Luke."

He closed his eyes and briefly dropped his head. "I always thought you and I were cut from the same cloth." He sipped his punch. "But anyway, it was easy to get here. I'm on sabbatical this year from teaching."

The conversation stumbled along with a decade's worth of painful memories falling in between them.

Eva accepted a plate of food from Isabella.

Luke nibbled at a piece of quiche as people pulled the chairs from the ceremony off to the side to unfold the dance floor. Someone announced Mr. and Mrs. Ward, and the newlyweds stepped onto the floor for a dance.

A bluegrass song? Not very traditional.

"She looks like her mother, doesn't she?"

"I see it in her, definitely." Eva shifted her weight, eating a meatball off a toothpick. "I'm surprised an important professor like you was able to come. How did you get the time off?"

His eyes narrowed ever so slightly as he pondered Eva, sizing her up with a silent stare, nodding to himself as if grasping some hidden truth. "Ah, yes. Yes." After a few moments, his manner changed, turning to his professor persona. "I'm on sabbatical. That means I have a lot of time to pursue my own studies or interests." He jutted his chin at the dancing couple. "Do you like this guy?"

"I do. He treats her exactly the way you'd want her to be treated."

Luke had lost some, but not all, of his smugness over the years and seemed a little weathered, like an old New England farmhouse. Lines and age softened his dark, coiffed looks into something less conscious and intentional, as though he'd had a shift in priorities. They stared at each other briefly without any words passing between them.

Eva imagined them both taking responsibility for Sarah's loss, but they just turned to watch the dancers.

"You never got along with Sarah, but somehow you're *living* with Breezy. Quite a turn of events." Luke took a hard swig of his drink and stared off beyond the barn into the forest. Either his thoughts or the drink seemed distasteful. "Breezy still keeps me at arm's length— like you'd treat a neighbor. Cordial and nice enough, but guarded." He tossed the rest of his drink out on the ground and stared at the empty glass as if the solution to all his life's problems should be written there on the bottom.

Later in the evening, Eva saw him several times, standing off at a distance with his head cocked, watching his daughter, or walking out to the road to carefully read the signs posted there, engaging with George, who probably came out to explain the problems of developers in the area. A few times he made attempts at joining conversations, but whenever Eva passed by, they were stumbling over awkward words.

Ha. Maybe they *were* cut from the same cloth.

Eva wandered toward the kitchen to see if she could help replenish trays, but the caterers shooed her away, telling her everything was under control. When she went to find Mabel, she and George were dancing together, holding hands and doing some version of a swinging jitterbug to modern music, spinning and whirling about like youngsters.

Eva took a seat in the yard near the guest book table stocked with paper and pens for writing poetry or a synopsis. Eva took a piece of paper.

Could she concentrate enough to write something? She was so tired after the full day. But if she could find the right words to express it, she'd write about their life living in a house that seemed prone to belly laughs when filled with occupants, moving with rolls of gaiety despite the rough times that inevitably visit every married couple from time to time. Maybe unemployment, deaths, or illness. Or she'd write about the way she imagined Breezy with her own children, and how'd she'd be a gentle mother, more like Sarah than Eva. She picked up a pen but found herself scratching out more than she wrote on the paper. When she finished her note, she saw the toolbox sitting on the table holding the guests' letters to the couple—the toolbox from the "honeymoon kit."

"There you are." Mabel walked across the lawn. "Why are you sitting over here? Guests can figure out the guest book themselves." She wore a flowered wreath on her head comprised of daisies and lily of the valley, either made by someone else or it was a centerpiece she'd stolen. She took the chair next to Eva and sat down close, holding a wedding gift in her hands. Mabel gazed suspiciously at Eva's glimmering eyelashes. "Are you all right, my friend?"

Eva brushed away the tears. How could she tell her all that pained her? The call with Rob. Her daughter's absence from the wedding.

"Wasn't it a lovely ceremony, Eva? Breezy looked radiant. And all that poetry!"

Eva looked up at Mabel, whose kind face and personality could break down every border erected to keep her out. She always appeared at Eva's side at the loneliest moments, offering companionship neglected by Eva for so long. Eva reached up and gently stroked her friend's soft skin, causing Mabel to blink quickly. How does one survive so many years without loving people like Mabel in their lives?

Mabel continued her exclamations about the day. "And Breezy's father came all this way. I hope they heal their relationship."

The brides blended together, the same dress worn by both Breezy and Sarah.

Mabel noticed the toolbox on that table. "Interesting choice of a wedding decoration. It certainly goes with the farm theme."

Eva offered her second confession of the day. "It was supposed to be part of Isabella's 'Honeymoon Kit' to Breezy and Ian. But I questioned her choice of a gift. The fragile girl was hurt and had second thoughts about giving it to them."

"Oh, Eva, go apologize. Ask her to forgive you. You'll feel much better when you do." Mabel tugged at her friend to stand her up. "I don't ever let time pass if I need to settle something with someone. Never let your sins pile up. Just go do this one simple task."

For some people, like Mabel, getting along with others seemed as easy as making an apple crisp from fresh-picked fruit from a backyard orchard. Eva could make an apple crisp any old day. But she couldn't get her son to visit her. She slouched, heavy with self-pity and frustration, but Mabel's simple words ran through her mind—*Just go do this one simple task.*

Toward the end of the evening, young people passed out sparklers from boxes, giving instructions to line up in the yard with a passageway between for Breezy and Ian to escape through on their way to their car.

As the waving swirls of light spit out sparks, Breezy appeared beside her grandmother, extending her arms for a hug. "Gram, we're leaving. I'll see you in a week. We're cutting our honeymoon short . . ."

"No . . ."

Breezy put her finger to her grandmother's lips and shushed her. "I'm not discussing it."

"Don't make me responsible for ruining your honeymoon, Breezy."

"One week instead of two isn't ruining our honeymoon." She kissed her grandmother's cheek. "Thanks for all your help with the wedding. And no trips. Okay?"

Tattoo girl handed Eva a sparkler. With the lines formed, Breezy and Ian ran through the shocks of light, and just like that, everything was over. Before climbing in the car, though, Breezy stopped Ian and turned and walked over to her father, who was standing back from the crowd, empty-handed, elbow resting on his knee with his foot perched on an old stump.

He had watched their getaway like an unrelated spectator. But as she approached him, surprise transformed his face, and he straightened.

She offered him her arms, and gently wrapped them around his waist with her face tucked against his chest—like once upon a time. Then she was off.

Luke stood, trying to compose himself, straightening his tie, stretching his neck in a couple of different directions, rubbing his hands together nervously.

After the bride and groom drove away, Isabella and Jasmine passed out favors to the guests from an old milk crate. Breezy had made homemade blueberry jam and orange-flavored honey from the farm's crop earlier in the summer with the Try Again Farm label on the front—a new image of the farm decked out in pale-yellow and white trim for its new day.

Eva selected one of the jars and studied it as a couple of people walked around with trash bags, picking up sparklers and napkins from the ground. Later, she took the jar to her room and left it by her bedside. She would mail it to Rob.

Thirteen

EVA SLEPT DEEPLY THE NIGHT after the wedding—until the nightmares came on. She sat in the living room of her old house on Cape Cod in a lifeguard's stand, watching a cooking show, when her husband sailed into the driveway on a boat. As he approached her door, she noticed the clutter in the living room and bustled around, straightening up and putting things away—yesterday's news, dirty dishes from her snack of crackers and cheese, envelopes and mail, embarrassed for him to catch her in an untidy state. She checked herself in the mirror and saw she was young again, wrinkles gone, dressed in her pink 1940s dress.

Wallace hurried up the steps, while Sarah waited outside on the boat in the driveway. He always left that girl in a running car while he ran into the drugstore for some Wintergreen mints. Now a boat! Suddenly, waves of rough water appeared like a rushing river from down the street, steering around the corner, spreading out into driveways. Sarah saw the impending trouble and screamed for help, but Wallace kept his back to their daughter, looking at Eva as if he had some account to settle with her. The waves made the boat unsteady, rocking Sarah back and forth. Eva pointed and yelled. Sarah was only a young girl, for heaven's sake. Her little hands gripped the sides of the boat, but still she struggled to stay onboard.

Wallace ignored both his wife and daughter. Eva grabbed a flotation device tied to the side of the lifeguard stand and unlatched it, throwing it to Sarah from the front door. Sarah struggled to keep her footing on the boat as rushing water hauled her down the road, her young voice growing smaller and smaller, fading into the distance.

Wallace finally turned and waded into the water to chase her, making little progress with the rapids slowing him down. Suddenly both Sarah and Wallace disappeared, leaving only a compass with the needle spinning wildly on Eva's front door mat.

She woke in a sweat.

The outside morning air arrived through her bedroom window with misty humidity, as if a river of water had traveled down her street and into the driveway, allowing steam to rise to her room. The air suffocated Eva, adding to her claustrophobic feeling of being trapped and left to fraternize with near strangers for a week. Even from her window on the second floor, she could see the flowers hanging their heads and the way the field grasses rolled to the east and to the west. She could hear the caterers in the kitchen. They likely had returned for their tables and equipment.

She thumped down in her chair, haunted by the dream and the mental sound of Sarah's voice crying for help. If only Eva knew how to pray. She would pray for their safety, for the waters to recede, for the life preserver to reach her daughter. But even if she knew how to form words into a prayer fitting enough to rise to God, even if she asked Mabel to pray, it was too late for the well-being of her family members who had passed.

"Lord have mercy," Mabel would say.

After a long while, the emotions of the dream dissipated, but Eva continued sitting in her room. What were the things she wanted to get done that week? She should've written them down.

Rob came to mind, and their talk the day before. She wanted to talk to him again.

Rob playing in the snow for hours, building snow forts and having snowball fights, cheeks rosy from the cold, overheated from running with his friends, Timothy and Glenn. Rob alone at the kitchen table, only twelve years old, with a National Geographic *magazine spread out before him as he studied the maps and planned the places he would live when he was older: Malaysia, Uzbekistan, Prague, Cape Town, New Zealand. Rob counting the dimes and nickels after collecting money from delivering newspapers. Rob defending his sister when neighbors claimed she was a mean babysitter by going over and speaking to the mother. His voice, still high like a girl's, but his words, angry like a man's. Rob studying for hours and hours for exams with his short dark crew cut and Scottish-looking freckles across his entire face like his father once had, writing himself notes on index cards to review on the walk to school. Rob shoveling the driveway, and shoveling the neighbor's driveway, and learning Spanish then Latin. Amo, amas, amat, over and over again. Then Swahili. Habari. Jina lako ni nani? Jina langu ni Rob.*

Rob working summer jobs, caddying at the golf course, saving to take a trip, distancing himself from his mother, who had tantrums he deplored. Rob driving by the house one day at the wheel of his father's new Chevy Impala he bought with who-knows-what-money as Wallace taught him to drive, never looking at his mother who worked in the garden. Rob weeping over the crumpled-up body of his dog, hit by a car and bleeding out. Rob typing a letter to the editor of the newspaper to commend a local hero who rescued a potential drowning victim. Rob applying for college after moving in with his father. Rob, at his sister's funeral, refusing to look at his mother, allowing his father to hold him tightly while they wept together. Rob cutting off most contact with his mother after his parents separated. Rob playing army with his toy soldiers. Rob playing army with his friends in the yard. Rob at war with his mother.

Suddenly, as if her blood sugar dipped, she grew dizzy. She needed to eat. Opening her door slowly, she peeked around the corner, looking on the floor for a posted guard.

No one sat there.

A good beginning to her day.

Downstairs, the first floor looked a little like Eva felt that morning. The quiet of the house made it seem as if nothing much had happened the day before. The stillness allowed for the beating of the living room clock to mimic the pumping of a heart. In the living room and dining room, she picked up forgotten plastic forks and cups. All the wrapped wedding gifts towered grandly on the living room table, waiting for the newly-weds to return, along with the toolbox now filled with poems and scripts penned by the guests. In the bathroom, Eva found the shaved soap from Isabella sitting in a soap dish after earlier finding the sparkling cider in the pantry, and the two champagne glasses up in the cabinet. Breezy's chairs sat side by side with Ward family bookshelves and tables, giving the place a shabby, thrift-store feel of two families mixing together.

Isabella sat at the kitchen table with an open book and a cup of tea, wearing flannel pajama bottoms, a loose jean shirt, and flip-flops, her hair draped to the side in a long and tousled ponytail. Her ever-present phone sat upside down on the table in front of her while she wrote in her journal.

Rob, casting his fishing rod and standing patiently for an entire sunny afternoon only to catch one measly little fish that he later threw back. Rob, kneeling beside his bed to say nighttime prayers with no one telling him to do so. Rob, trying to build a model car, the instruction booklet open on the table, studying the diagrams with an earnest expression.

Eva poured herself coffee and sat across from the girl in silence.

Outside a truck or van door slammed and the engine started before they drove away.

"Sleep well?"

"Like I was in a coma." Isabella looked up while shutting her journal. She watched Eva with her magnified eyes, as if she might see more than Eva wanted to display.

"What do you write in there?" Eva nodded to the journal.

"It's part diary, part snippets of my life and observations I make. I use the notes I collect in my writing. Lots of writers do the same thing." She picked up the book and flipped through the pages, creating a mild, refreshing breeze that reached Eva like sea air, taking her back to her days with cousins and a husband and children.

Isabella stopped flipping pages and set the journal back down on the table. "I've made some notes about your personality and George's personality. You guys are *interesting*." She smiled a mischievous smile at Eva.

What could possibly be interesting about two old, cantankerous people? "Well, we might start taking notes about you, my dear. You're quite interesting too."

"And I make lists of things I want to change about myself." The mischievous smile turned grave. Her appraising expression seemed to measure the level of empathy in the room. "Things I hate about myself. Number one . . ."

"That you don't stand up for yourself."

Isabella's gaze scanned the room as if she'd misplaced the truth somewhere among the pots and pans. "Actually, I was going to say I talk too much out of nervousness when conversations get quiet, saying idiotic things—way too much personal stuff." Isabella sat back in her chair, then reached for the journal, opened to a blank page, and picked up her pen. "So, you think I don't stand up for myself?"

"And you take things so *personally*. You might want to write that down." Eva pointed to the open page.

Isabella scribbled for a few minutes, furrowing her brow as she wrote. "I also like to write things in here that I admire in other people, trying to create this idealized person in my mind of who I hope to be. I really want to think less often about myself."

"You want to think 'less' of yourself?" Eva asked.

"Less *often*," Isabella reiterated. "The perfect me would be totally oblivious to the impression I make on other people and just free to be and laugh and talk. A little like Mabel."

Eva's idealized woman had no regrets and greeted each day with exuberance and song. Everyone loved her. Then Eva's brain scrambled with confusion at the thought of regrets. "Oh, I know what I wanted to say." Eva grasped tight to the memory before it could slip away again. "About the honeymoon kit . . ."

"Don't worry about it." Isabella closed the journal and traced the writing on the cover with her pointer finger. "I thought about what you said, and you were right. Onward and upward, my grandmother liked to say." The girl offered the brave phrase with a determined point to the sky but then dropped her limb heavily. "I just added that to my list—I want to stop being so sensitive when people don't like my ideas. Like right now, you might think it's stupid I keep a list at all. I don't care what you think about it . . . well, I do actually care, but I'm going to start stepping into my new persona, and maybe my feelings will catch up."

George's footsteps sounded out in the hallway outside his room. He entered the kitchen with his hair slicked back like the day before, as if trying to put his best foot forward for all the *dames* in the house.

"Good morning, George. I have some cereal here for you and Eva. That's what you like, right?"

"Yup. Special K." He collected one of the bowls Isabella had set out and poured his cereal. After scooping some strawberries from a bowl, he added milk.

Eva sipped her coffee for a while before collecting her own bowl and pouring some cereal.

While the two older people ate, Isabella offered some activity suggestions for things they could do during the week to keep occupied until Breezy and Ian returned. "Play cards, do a project or two in the shop. Go to the old drive-in movie theater that reopened across town and see some classics like *Rear Window* and *Casablanca*. And we could cook together, making ratatouille from all the garden's ripe tomatoes." She pointed to a basketful she must've picked earlier. "I thought we could have it tonight."

"Rat-tat-what?" George asked cheerfully. "I'll do whatever you want." He got up and poured his coffee, then held up the pot. "You ladies want some more?"

Eva and Isabella shook their heads. While chewing her breakfast— masticating, the girl would probably note in her word book—Isabella got up and grabbed a recipe card from the counter, holding it close for George to read.

He pushed the card away. "I'd need my glasses to read that."

"I think we have all the ingredients for the ratatouille. It's mostly vegetables from the garden. But I thought we could make this bread too." She held up the recipe card.

"I have an idea for something that might be fun to do." Eva kept her eyes focused on her coffee. "Have you ever made those birds with folded-up paper? Probably we can get some paper at the store . . . at the end of the street."

Isabella picked up her phone and typed with her thumbs. "Origami. I googled it." She turned her phone for George and Eva to see pictures of folded paper birds in many colors.

As they looked at the photos, Isabella's phone rang. The caller's name popped up as *Tyrant*.

"Hey, Dad. You got my message?"

A loud male voice boomed through the phone.

She stood up from the table and walked over to the door, growing quiet, listening. "I'm not trying to be *an inconvenience*." Her voice had turned a bit sour. "I just need a ride to get my car from the mechanic. It's fixed and ready to be picked up." She paused while he spoke. "Remember? I'm at my friend Breezy's farm while she's on her honeymoon, helping with her family. You dropped me off here a couple of days ago. I can't just walk up to the garage on my own."

The phone might as well have been on speaker, his voice coming through loudly enough for Eva and George to plainly hear his tirade while not making out specific words.

To give Isabella some privacy, Eva went to the counter and collected the recipe card, flipping it over a couple of times, trying to decipher the instructions for bread.

The letters were perfectly legible, but putting them together to form instructions was a different story.

C-O-M-B-I-N-E-W-A-R-M-W-A-T-E-R-Y-E-A-S-T-A-N-D-O-N-E-T-B-S-P-O-F-S-U-G-A-R

A blankness swam in her brain and she slammed the recipe onto the counter. "Making bread used to be a cinch to me."

George approached the counter, eyes locked on Isabella as he walked. Once next to Eva, he stared at the recipe before sharing a look with Eva.

With silent understanding that the words and letters on the card meant nothing to either of their brains, Eva suddenly realized their disabilities didn't seem so very different.

"I can't ask anyone else. I don't *have* anyone else available this week."
Isabella stepped outside onto the porch.

They busied themselves hunting for ingredients in the cabinets, not
even sure what they needed, pulling out arbitrary items: flour, garlic
salt, baking powder, turmeric, and sugar. George rummaged through
the fridge for eggs and milk.

Eva walked to the door to peek out at Isabella, who remained amaz-
ingly poised under the pressure of the call, but her neck jerked as if someone slapped her, and her hand went on her hip in defiance. Eva had seen
that gesture before from Sarah. Isabella's father clearly liked to interrupt. The girl slipped around the corner and spoke in a muffled voice,
"If you can't be respectful, I'm going to hang up the phone, Dad." A few
moments passed before Isabella returned to the kitchen, unzipped her
purse, and stuffed her cell phone inside with a jittery hand.

A look of mutual concern passed between George and Eva.

"Everything all right?" Eva asked.

"Fine. Everything's fine." She picked up a zucchini from the pile and
slammed the knife through the poor vegetable on the counter with a
vengeance. "I guess I'll have to get it when Breezy and Ian get back. He
won't help me. *Too busy.*" She spoke with a vibrating shake to her body,
as if mocking her father's excuse. "I have the keys to Ian's truck, and they
said I can drive that."

"Maybe Mabel can help you," Eva offered. "Is this the bread recipe
you wanted to make for tonight?" She held up the index card.

Isabella dropped the knife, staring at the recipe card for several
moments before saying, "Hmm? Oh, yeah. I thought we could have it
with the ratatouille."

"I used to make something similar. How much flour does it call for
again?" Eva asked. "I can't make out the quantity."

Isabella came over and retrieved the recipe from Eva's hand, but
didn't seem to connect the words on the card any more than Eva or
George.

Eva chuckled. No one in the house seemed able to read a recipe. The
words looked like placeholder text Wallace learned as a typesetter to

save certain spots for graphics: *Lorem ipsum dolor sit amet, consectetur adipisicing elit, sed do eiusmod tempor incididunt ut labore et dolore magna aliqua.* They always laughed and tried to make up meanings for those words, with Wallace pretending they were words to woo a woman, and Eva saying they were words to woe a man.

Isabella handed Eva the card. "Would you go ahead and start that for me, Mrs. Gordon? I'm going to run upstairs for a little while."

"Tell me what to do and I'll do it," Eva said.

Isabella lined up the dry ingredients on one side of the table and the wet ingredients on the other side before walking Eva through the instructions of mixing and kneading and letting the dough rest.

Breadmaking returned to Eva's mind just as Isabella vanished around the corner. Eva looked at George. "I guess we'll give it a whirl, huh?"

He finished drying a bowl from the sink, then dropped a white dish towel on the counter between them as a white flag of sorts. Nodding toward the second floor, he said, "Poor kid."

They added ingredients to the bowl, water to the yeast, and mixed everything together before kneading, pounding, and pushing. The dough seemed hard and stiff at first, so Eva added a dollop of water, which made it mushy.

George added more flour.

The couple talked little as they worked. At least he didn't try to make small talk while they concentrated on the work.

When Isabella rejoined them, her face looked freshly washed and a bit splotchy with red marks from crying. She dampened a towel to cover the bread bowl. "I guess I totally failed the 'new me' test today," she said. "He got under my skin. Again."

"We made that bread pretty well for *amaturs*," said George.

"Well, hopefully it'll rise enough before Mabel gets here. George and I are going yard saling today. Right, George?" She looked to the man for confirmation. "Mabel's going to keep you company, Mrs. Gordon. Maybe we can pick up that origami paper too. I'll throw dinner together now, so it's ready and all the flavors have a chance to mingle." Isabella started sautéing vegetables in a pan for the ratatouille. While she threw together the dinner, George collected all the trash bags from the day before to load into Ian's truck.

Eva went upstairs and donned her work slacks and overshirt, and headed to the barn to work on the old desk. Alone.

At roughly lunchtime, Mabel's Buick pulled into the drive and she yoo-hooed. Usually Mabel yoo-hooed for just Eva, so she focused on the work at hand, waiting for Mabel to appear in the doorway of the barn and exclaim over Eva's long face, but Mabel never came. Voices rose in a chorus of greetings and well-wishes in the yard, engaging even George in the hullabaloo.

Everyone except Eva. In fact, no one came to see her in the shop, even as the car doors slammed, the engine started, and the car left.

Finally, as if Eva was only an afterthought, Mabel called out from the kitchen door, "Where *is* that Eva? Eva?" Within a few moments she stuck her head in the doorway. "There you are."

"Don't mind me. I'm just working out here all by myself."

Mabel approached Eva until she got good and close to Eva's face. "Why, Eva Gordon . . . are you jealous?"

"Not jealous. But it sure took you long enough to come find me." She smoothed the wood filler and gave the surface a rigorous swipe with a rag to dispose of dust. What was dust other than the past in powder form?

"You're *jealous.*" Mabel clamped her hands together in victory. "Well, I'll be. I never thought I'd see the day when Eva Gordon felt jealous that people were accommodating her wishes by leaving her alone." Her voice turned more conciliatory. "Eva, I just arrived. Barely had a chance to set my purse on the kitchen chair and give the dogs a pat before I came to find you, and here you are mad that I took too long. Let's just remember that most of the time you act as if you're irritated that I'm even—"

A car pulled onto the driveway gravel at a high speed.

Mabel crooked her neck. "Back already? And why are they driving like a passel of skunks is chasing them?"

Eva followed Mabel outside.

An unfamiliar car sat in the driveway outside the barn.

Before they could even call out a greeting, a man jumped onto the porch and pounded hard on the screen door. "Isabella! You in there?" The man spoke with a husky-sounding voice, the male version of Isabella's voice.

"Can I help you with something, sir?" Eva called out as she wiped off her hands on a rag.

"You know where my daughter Isabella is? She said she needed a ride, and now she's not even ready."

"She seemed to believe you were previously engaged, so she went on an outing with a friend," Eva explained in her most diplomatic voice.

"Can't be too desperate to pick up her car at the garage if she went off on an outing with a friend. You sure she's not inside, avoiding me?" With arms crossed against his chest, he looked inside the screen door, as if Isabella sat inside ignoring him.

"Is there a reason she'd want to avoid you, sir?"

He smirked. "When'll she be back?" He swaggered down the back steps toward Eva while Mabel waited near the barn, uncharacteristically quiet. Even though he was dressed the part of a businessman in a suit and tie, something about him looked like a thug.

Eva wished to lock herself inside the barn away from the burly man, but she stood her ground.

Buck and Amber came around the corner and sniffed him good. The man stomped in their direction, and the dogs growled. When he approached Eva, Buck blocked his way.

She smiled. "He's not comfortable with certain people. But I'll tell Isabella you came by looking for her." Eva turned back toward the barn.

"No, you tell her I'll be back. I'll be checking out the work on one of my construction sites nearby." He nodded toward the woods before letting the words sit there like a threat and a jab. Then he got back in his car, started the engine, and pulled out toward the street, shooting gravel all over the yard, hitting Amber with a few stray, speeding pebbles.

In her mind, the Ward family members joined her, arms crossed against their own chests, shaking their heads as he drove away.

≈

The ratatouille simmered on the back burner, the end-of-summer deep red tomatoes blending with squash to give the dish a bright hue. Mabel whirled around, trying to read a Langston Hughes poem painted along the ceiling's edge, tilting back her head as if to admire the black scrolled letters painted over the green color of the room. *"Bring me all of your dreams, you dreamer—"*

George and Isabella had returned from their excursion with some origami paper and one find from a yard sale: a new soup tureen to replace the one broken in the yard in July. At the sink, Isabella scrubbed out the years of dust and filth from the bowl's insides, while George turned on the evening news in the living room and immediately talked back to the anchor as if having a two-way conversation.

"Well, listen everyone, I need to get on the road before it gets too dark." Mabel collected her keys, nuzzling the dogs in farewell. "I'm known to lose my way in strange towns." She gave Isabella's hand a good pat before doing the same with Eva's hand.

Isabella resorted to lifting the top of the pan of simmering ratatouille, waving the aromatic steam in Mabel's direction. "You sure you won't stay for dinner?"

"It's not going to work tonight, dears. I'm plenty tired from these past busy days." She called out her goodbye to George in the living room, then collected her pocketbook and vanished out the screen door with promises to *be back soon!*

Isabella and Eva set three place settings on the table, and Isabella was about to scoop the ratatouille into the soup tureen when Mabel suddenly rushed a bit breathlessly into the kitchen.

"When you say *soon,* you mean *soon.*" Isabella handed Eva a contraption to scoop out the soup.

Soup scooper? Super scooper?

"What's wrong?"

With one hand over her mouth, Mabel wordlessly pointed outside.

A familiar male voice roared from the yard—Isabella's father.

"That man appears to be intoxicated," she said.

Isabella and Eva both rushed to peek through the kitchen window. "My father's here? I talked to him on the phone after you told me he stopped by earlier. He never said he was coming. What's he want? It's not as if we're picking up my car *now*." Her voice filled with panic.

The lines on Mabel's forehead etched with deep concern. "He was quite rude." They all turned as the man's yells erupted again outside. "And now he seems under the influence of alcohol."

"Isabella, we need to . . . ttt . . . talk in private!" he called.

Buck and Amber appeared from the other room. Buck growled low and threateningly, while Amber barked.

"Father or no father, he sounds downright unreasonable." Mabel quickly locked the screen door. "You stay here and we'll handle this." She spoke with a calm voice through the screen. "Isabella is busy making a lovely dinner. Can we help you with something, sir?"

"Oh, she's making 'a lovyey dinner,' huh?'" His words sounded as wobbly as his steps on the back porch, one foot thudding down long before the other one landed on the wood.

George appeared at Mabel's side in response to the man's cynical laugh, suddenly looking taller. "What's the problem?"

"I want my daughter out here. Now."

"She's busy." George reached to unlock the door, but Mabel brushed back his hand.

"Then I'll come in there . . . while she cooks the lovyey dinner."

Eva had created many similar scenes in the past with her own family, but without alcohol fueling the fights. Here and now, though, something felt different, unfamiliar.

The man's outburst attacked like an unwanted enemy reintroducing war when everyone was sick of battle. Isabella needed to be protected, and her father needed to leave, but what to do? Call the police? Call a neighbor? Or just let the dogs out?

While the man pounded to get in the screen door, Eva hurried to the second floor.

Mabel continued talking to the man calmly. "Can we call you a taxi, sir? You don't seem like you should be driving right now."

Upstairs, Eva collected just what she needed from Ian's room.

The rifle felt awkward in her hands.

Breathless, she slipped the weapon behind her back.

When Eva returned to the kitchen, Mabel and George had closed the back door and were conferring with Isabella, trying to prevent her from going outside.

"He's harmless. Really." She nudged them out of the way and unlocked the door. "Keep the dogs here." She stepped onto the porch and led him down into the yard, where he grabbed her by the arm and dragged the girl toward his car. Isabella rolled her shoulders and dropped her head to focus on her flip-flops, as if he might strike her.

Most of his words were indecipherable, but Eva heard the words "schtaying at this dump that should be torn down." He tottered back and forth in front of his daughter like an ocean buoy in a summer storm, spewing some sort of abuse close to her face.

"Why that dirty, blasted, son of a gun . . ." George's clawlike hands folded in anger.

Mr. Barrington tried to steady his wobbly balance by leaning on his daughter's shoulders and nearly toppled to the ground.

"Enough is enough." Mabel opened the door and the dogs crashed onto the porch. Mabel hurried down the steps to get to Mr. Barrington.

George followed.

Both tried to insert themselves between father and daughter as the dogs circled the group, agitated and growling. Mabel spoke in a consoling tone, while George tried to assert his role as man of the house, and Isabella pleaded with her father to leave. Their voices blended into a discordant choir, moving no closer to resolution.

Eva stepped out onto the porch and shouted, "Let her go! I have a gun!" The instrument felt strange and heavy but gave her a sense of command.

Everyone whirled around to look at her holding the rifle.

She aimed toward the roof of the barn over their heads.

Isabella's father looked stunned, his reflexes slowing enough to loosen his grip on Isabella's arm, allowing her to wriggle away from him.

"Mr. Barrington, let go of your daughter and behave like a gentleman." Eva raised her eyebrows. "We'll call the police unless you leave. Now."

"No." Isabella shook her head emphatically. "No police." She moved farther away from her father.

For several moments, no one moved.

A lone car drove past the house. Would they notice all the commotion in the yard?

The dogs continued growling at Mr. Barrington, low, like rabid animals. The Wards looked frantic, encircling the entire group.

Isabella ran up the worn stairs to the house.

Her father shouted threats, but with less bravado, as he backed toward his car. He bellowed one more command as he slipped behind the wheel. "I'll see *you* at the house, young lady."

"That man shouldn't be driving," Mabel said.

Too late. He reversed his way out of the driveway, up onto the grass, just missing Ian's go-away-developers sign.

After he was out of sight, Isabella coaxed Eva to give her the gun. "Keep it pointed down toward the ground as you hand it to me, Mrs. Gordon." Isabella reached for the weapon. When she had it in her own hand, the girl seemed to droop with relief.

"Eva, do you know how dangerous it is to bring a gun outside during an argument?" Mabel asked.

"Is that Ian's? You shouldn't have it." George seemed like an adult scolding a child.

Eva dismissed their chidings. "Isabella, that man shouldn't be allowed to treat you that way. It's downright—"

"Abusive. Yeah, I know." The girl still hung her head.

"Does he do this often?" Mabel asked.

"Often enough—if I don't do what he wants. So there you have it, folks." She threw waving hands in the air. "Now you know the truth. I have a father with some 'issues.'"

Mabel hugged Isabella tight around the waist, leading her up the back steps to the kitchen while the girl gingerly held the rifle way out to her side.

In the house, Isabella set the gun, pointing it toward the back wall, on the table and picked up her phone. "I need to call Breezy and Ian. They're going to want to hear about this." She hit Breezy's number. "Breezy, please don't panic, and I *really* hate disturbing you on your honeymoon, but um, something kinda big happened here just now." Isabella recounted the situation. "No! You are not coming back early. Everything's under control. I just thought you should know. We'll be fine."

Eva could just envision Breezy trying to speak calmly into the phone then covering the mouthpiece to whisper hysterical words to Ian.

Later, after Ian came on the line and gave Isabella specific instructions to secure the weapon and she took it to a secret place without anyone looking over her shoulder, the foursome stood in the kitchen, recounting the event over and over, building the story with each retelling. After pulling out bowls for dinner and slicing bread, Isabella suddenly needed to sit down. "I hate thinking what could've happened out there." She shuddered.

"Can I serve your nice dinner, Isabella? Why don't you rest? George, you sit too." Mabel pulled one more bowl and plate out of the cabinet for herself, then ladled ratatouille for everyone while Eva put the bread on a wooden cutting board and cut it into slices. Then she placed a butter dish on the table before sitting down next to George.

Isabella still shook her head every few moments, as if trying to shake the images of the event.

Mabel folded her hands on the table. "Let's just have a quiet moment of thankfulness before we eat. George, how about you ask the blessing."

"Me?" He shook his head furiously.

"It's just a matter of saying 'thank you.' I believe you can say thank you, George."

They all waited while he drummed up the courage.

"Well, I guess it's just talking." He looked around the table and folded his hands. "Okay, I can do it."

They all bowed their heads. Eva even closed her eyes.

"We've had a pretty big day around here, God. But no one got shot. No one got in a bad fight. And now we're sittin' around the table about to eat this good smellin' food. Phew. We just wanna say thank you. Amen."

Afterward, Mabel scooped a large spoonful into her mouth. "This has to be the best ratatouille I've ever had." She generously buttered a slice of bread Eva had served her.

After getting some food into her system, Isabella seemed to relax. In between bites, she suggested they all do something to calm themselves down, get their minds off the event. "Anyone up for the drive-in tonight? Mabel, can you stay?"

Mabel did seem like her nerves were all in a "jittery jumble" and agreed to stay "for a sleepover."

"We can put you in Breezy and Ian's room. Or you could take the guest room where I'm staying. Your choice." Isabella scrolled and tapped on her phone.

"Oh, I don't want to steal your guest quarters, Isabella. I'll stay in Breezy and Ian's room."

"Okay. The movie doesn't start for a couple of hours." Isabella thought a moment, then suggested they play the *Getting to Know You* game from the honeymoon kit. "To lighten us all up. We can even put on our pajamas for the drive-in, like we used to do when I was a kid."

"A sleepover pajama party." Mabel's face turned younger before Eva's eyes, as if banishing the years that separated her from her last sleepover as a young girl.

George seemed to think out loud. "The guys at the thrift store aren't gonna believe this."

After they finished eating and cleaned up the meal, the three ladies went upstairs and found some pajamas. Eva loaned one of her cotton nighties to Mabel. On the petite woman, Eva's nightgown dragged and dusted the floor, making her look like a princess with a train. George chose to stay in his work clothes. Isabella brought out the game, made some popcorn, and sifted through game cards looking for a place to start.

Eva stared at the mixture of hands sorting and straightening cards and adjusting water glasses on napkins—bluish black, veined hands with age spots; arthritic and bent hands; and Isabella's dainty smooth hands, decorated with mismatched silver jewelry, even on her thumb.

So many of Eva's evenings had been spent with one lone pair of hands. The youngest hands shuffled and sifted through the cards while the older hands sat folded or fidgety, drumming and tidying up.

Perched crossed legged on the ladder-back chair, Isabella explained the object of the game. Each player would read a personal question from a card, and other players decide if the answer is *true* or *false*. "I'll start." Isabella read from a card. "If someone else was telling your story, which moment in your life would they describe as your hardest?" She daintily wiped butter off her hands from the popcorn. "You first, Mrs. Gordon."

Couldn't the girl have started with a slightly easier question? "Begin with someone else."

"Say anything. It doesn't even have to be true." Isabella searched on her phone for something, settling on music by Frank Sinatra. "The Way You Look Tonight" played through her speaker. "But it sort of makes it fun if you tell something a little risky and personal." The usual sad wariness of her eyes vanished for the moment. "That's how we get to know each other better."

"I'm not sure I want anyone to know me better." Eva picked up four or five kernels of popcorn from the bowl to eat.

"OK . . . let me show you how it's done." Isabella grabbed a handful of popcorn, stuffed it into her mouth, and kept on talking. "I think people would say the worst time for me was in high school, when I stole a stop sign from an intersection and this guy in my social studies class got in a terrible accident afterward and had to go to the hospital. He died." Her face turned somber and serious, tears filling her eyes. "Now, do you think that's true or false?"

"True." Eva tapped her finger on the table accusingly.

George looked at Eva like she had gone batty. "False. You wouldn't do that."

"Half false." Isabella's tears vanished as quickly as they appeared, replaced by a slight smile.

Eva tried to imagine someone half dying.

"I was with the people who took down the sign, and the accident was only minor. But we got in big trouble."

The theater girl had tricked everyone.

"Oh, Isabella . . . that's serious." Mabel scolded, shaking her head. "'You may choose to look the other way, but you can never again say you did not know.'"

The room hushed, anticipating her explanation.

"William Wilberforce."

"It's pretty miraculous teenagers survive until adulthood, all the dumb things they do."

"We're in the company of one of those young people right now." Mabel looked disapprovingly at Eva.

"Your turn, George," Isabella said. "How would others describe your worst moment?"

"I don't want to play . . ."

Eva sifted through hard memories like Isabella had just sifted through the game cards. Feeling emboldened by Isabella's turn, Eva unexpectedly blurted out her answer. "The day my husband walked out the door and I never fought for him to stay." Her voice dropped to a hush when she realized the depth of her verbal confession.

The mood in the room turned somber as they went around the circle and each said, "True."

Eva confirmed her regretted behavior with a reluctant head nod.

"Eva, that's a serious moment. Did you still love him?" Mabel asked.

Their three faces looked at her with such trust and softness. With the concern they were showing on their faces, Eva could confess all her bad behaviors in exchange for the power of their mercy. "Until the day he died." Her table-tapping sped up, faster and faster. "Not something that can be fixed now." She wiped up a wet ring under her glass and dropped the napkin on the floor by accident. She leaned to pick it up. "If I went, you can go, George."

They waited while he batted around a piece of popcorn on a napkin with his fingers. "People would say it was me failin' in school for never learning to read." The words blew past as quickly as a car out on the street moving on to its destination.

"False. You can *read*," Isabella argued. "You get around too well not to be able to *read*."

"True," Eva said. "But isn't going to prison even harder?"

Isabella's upper body did a slight bob, and Mabel gasped, eyes wide with shock.

"If I was going to describe your hardest moment, I'd certainly say it was going to prison."

Mabel set down her tea and spoke in a scolding tone. "This isn't your story to tell, Eva."

"False. You never went to *prison*." Isabella unfolded her legs to scoot forward and plant her feet on the floor in an attentive posture.

"They're both true," said George. "I did go to jail. Thanks, Eva, for letting everyone know." He scowled at her. "I hurt someone bad in a fight once. I used to have an anger problem." George directed his comments to Eva. "And that's all I'm saying."

"Maybe we should quit now." Isabella's voice quivered nervously as she collected the cards, nodding to the window. "Looks as though it might be getting dark enough for the drive-in."

"Dunce. That's what they called me all my life for not being able to read." He turned to Eva. "You ever get called that, Eva? You think that's a nice way to talk to a kid?"

His outburst stunned Eva. She saw him as she recalled Rob, a little boy vulnerable to the meanness of the world. "No. It's a terrible way to talk to a child."

"And teachers? They were the worst—hitting me with a switch or a ruler for not doing schoolwork I couldn't understand."

Mabel's face burned and she trembled with anger at his experience, uncharacteristically slamming her hand down on the table. "No teacher should treat a student that way, George. They should've found a different profession to work in. If it would help, it's not too late to learn to read. Probably you have a little disability. Did you ever think of that?"

"I have friends with dyslexia, and after they got tutored, they could read. I could find some names of tutors for you, George." Isabella sounded so compassionate.

"Maybe." But he was on a memory roll. "I got fired from one job when I couldn't follow instructions. Another time, a guy made a fake flyer with the picture of a brain inside a big crossed out circle, like a 'No guns allowed' sign, and taped it to my locker. I went berserk. I'm small, but I'm strong." He paused. "He ended up in the emergency room with a broken jaw, and I went to jail for assault."

"Phew." Isabella fell back against her chair seat. "I didn't expect a group of older people to have so much baggage. Wow. Heavy stuff."

"Confession is always good for the soul, George. Like lancing an infected wound. Do you feel better?" Mabel patted his arm.

"I hope it was cathartic for us all?" Isabella solicited an answer from the group.

Was *cathartic* written in Isabella's word journal?

When no one responded, Isabella glanced outside the window at the darkening New England sky. "Let's pack up the game. Time for a drive-in movie!"

Eva looked down at her outfit. "But we're in our pajamas. Shouldn't we change?"

"Remember? We put them on for the slumber party. Just throw a light jacket on top." Isabella collected the popcorn bowl and asked them to grab a coat. "Let's live dangerously." She mischievously rubbed her hands together.

After donning summer jackets and slippers, they all piled into Mabel's car to see *Rear Window*, a movie Eva hadn't seen in years. Wearing a coat over her nightgown reminded Eva of packing her pajama-clad kids in the old Fairlane for the drive-in. After the movie, she and Wallace would carry the exhausted, heavy children into the house and up to their rooms, where they would slip them into the soft warmth of their beds, as if safe from all the world's dangers.

Fourteen

At the ticket window, Eva pulled out her wallet to pay, but Isabella argued with her. "Mrs. Gordon, you don't have the money to spend on something like this. Besides, Breezy gave me some cash to do things with you."

"I insist." Eva passed the money to Isabella, who bought the ticket and stuck it on the dashboard.

She drove through rows and rows of parked families who had left their comfortable homes with wide-screened televisions and access to any movie they wanted to watch while curled up on the comfort of a private, overstuffed couch to come to the drive-in theater and sit in their car.

"This is so retro." Isabella pulled in and out of a parking space until she could reach the speaker just right before attaching it to the side of the car.

"We went all the time when I was younger." Mabel sounded wistful.

"We did too." Eva recalled the sound of the speakers echoing from car after car down the row, each family being fed the same story privately.

Isabella turned up the volume switch on the beat-up speaker and an announcer narrated the images of floating popcorn and cokes on the big screen. "Last chance before the feature starts. Take advantage of our special tonight. Buy one bucket and get as many refills as you can eat." Advertisements for local businesses filled the screen: Avery and Hawt

Law Firm, Mortie's Restaurant, Miss Sally's Academy of Dance. As their four bodies heated up the Buick, they slipped off their coats, using them as pillows and back supports.

Finally, Grace Kelly and James Stewart replaced the popcorn and soft drinks on the screen, and the plot came back to her—a man lives in a Manhattan high-rise apartment, where he's recuperating from an accident that left him in a cast. To pass the time, he watches his neighbors out his rear window through binoculars, guessing the stories of their lives, loves, marriages, and relationships, spying on both their fortunes and misfortunes.

Moments into the film, Eva got a tickle in her throat. "I'm going to get a drink. Anyone else want one?"

With eyes glued to the screen, they mumbled *no*.

Eva slipped out the back door and made her way to the concession stand, weaving between the cars to purchase a bottle of water. While there, she noticed gift cards to the drive-in. She bought one for Breezy and Ian, certain her granddaughter would love the "retro" experience.

She headed back to the car, near the screen. Or were they parked farther away? Recalling the panicked feeling of being alone in the Park and Ride on Cape Cod, she felt helpless without anyone to turn to. Finally, she saw the Buick and pulled open the rear passenger door.

"Can we help you?" An unfamiliar man spoke to her from the front seat.

She looked from person to person. She knew no one in this car. Eva's thoughts swirled with questions. Who did she come with and where were they?

She scrambled backward and slammed the door. Rushing toward the middle of the parking lot, she tried to find Mabel's car. Maybe someone could make an announcement to the whole audience? Would her friends leave without her, thinking she'd walked home? She stopped to let her heart settle a bit before returning to her search. A few deep breaths steadied her trembling hands.

"If you're going to stay out after curfew, girl, you must really have somethin'

to be outside for," her father growled from the upstairs window. "Stay out all night, then. That'll teach ya."

Eva tried the front door.

Locked.

Wallace dropped her off late and had not stuck around. Frightened and cold, she thought of walking to Wallace's house, but the idea of going across town at night seemed alarming. Instead, she went to the back yard and curled up in a lawn chair on the patio.

Eva looked around for a lawn chair where she could settle for the night.

Eva listened to her mother's fading breaths with her head resting on Mother's hand on the bed. When she breathed her last, Eva lifted her head and left the house, walking and walking until she found herself down at the shore, where she spent the entire night outside alone in the dark, the waves keeping her company with her fear and sorrow.

But she didn't want to sleep outside again. She wanted help finding her companions at the drive-in, but her thinking felt so cloudy. Maybe someone could make an announcement for her.

A man shouted at her, "You make a better door than a window, lady!" A few cars later, a driver tooted their horn in a short warning sound. A teenage voice heckled her. "Maybe she's looking for her bathrobe."

She looked down. Why was she lost outside in her nightgown?

An older gentleman stuck his head out of the window and kindly asked if she needed assistance.

Her mouth opened to respond, but her inner panic twisted all the words up and held them.

Through glasses, the distinguished man looked at her with caring eyes. He got out of the car and steered her over to the side to restore the view of the other patrons. "What kind of car did you come in, ma'am?" He spoke with a soothing voice, as if he was a pediatrician tending to a sick child afraid of needles.

"Well, I think it was a Ford Fairlane station wagon."

"Hmm." He scanned the parking lot. "Haven't seen one of those in years."

"Oh, silly me. That's not what we came in. We came in my friend's car—a brown Buick, I believe."

"Well, we're going to have a hard time seeing colors tonight in the dark, but maybe you remember your view of the screen?"

"That's what I was doing when people became nasty. I was trying to remember my view." Heat filled her face as she thought of this handsome older gentleman holding her elbow out in public while she wore only her nightie. Eva pulled the buttons tighter at the neck, aware of her thick ankles protruding beneath the gown. "It wasn't my idea to wear pajamas, by the way. It was—" Isabella! She'd come with Isabella and George.

"No need to explain, ma'am. My grandkids always wear their jammies to the drive-in, and sometimes I'm jealous. You just did your own thing."

Footsteps shuffled up behind her. George called her name.

A few people shushed him out their windows.

"Oh, shush yourselves!" he answered back before turning to Eva. "I saw you from over there. You looked lost." He spoke gruffly but took off his jacket and placed it over her shoulders. He thanked the kind man for helping her, as if he was recovering his elderly mother who needed special assistance.

Two men, rushing to her aid in one night.

Without saying another word, George walked Eva back to the car, which turned out to be only two rows away.

She didn't need to thank him for coming to find her because he surely knew she was grateful. Isabella never took her eyes from the screen, and Mabel simply offered her some candy as she settled in the back seat.

George never let on. He just turned and offered Eva a kindly wink.

Eva sipped her water, contemplating Jimmy Stewart's character. If he were real, he'd probably attend the funerals of strangers and watch people's hard-luck stories play out from the upstairs farmhouse window— and he wouldn't be much better at solving the mysteries of life than she.

Fifteen

SEVERAL DAYS LATER, HEAVY MORNING rain greeted the crew at Try Again Farm, soaking the farm, and bringing with it the kind of dampness that seeps into bones and causes a chill. Before going downstairs for breakfast, Eva stood at the edge of her meticulously made bed listening to the *pat-pat-patter* of the drops falling on the roof and the metal gutter, staring down over her packed suitcase for a long time. She tried to remember distant plans and desires to go somewhere but couldn't recollect where she should go. Some niggling idea told her she was missing something *out there*. The young people often called the feeling FOMO: Fear of Missing Out. At other moments she felt she'd be missed by the others if she left the farm. And lastly, she might miss out on life at the farm if she left—like missing the way the birds outside her window woke her each morning with their merriment. After grabbing the suitcase by the handle, Eva dropped it down on the floor and pushed it back underneath her bed, willing to stay around a little while longer in case she was needed to help out with the place.

When she entered the kitchen for breakfast, Isabella picked up a plastic-wrapped package from the table and waved it at Eva. "Origami paper. You up for a lesson?"

Mabel walked through the porch door at just that moment, as if Eva had never left the former apartment and her friend still lived upstairs. "I ran home to change and pick up a few things." Canvas bag filled with who-knows-what flung over her shoulder, she wore pressed white linen pants with a baby-blue jersey-knit shirt. Her favorite kitty pin sat on the upper left shoulder. A pair of rubber overshoes protected her pumps against the downpour. She dropped the full bag on an empty chair with a thud and a sigh of gratitude, as if to be free of her burden.

"It's our inimitable friend, Mabel Maguire."

Mabel gave Eva a quick kiss on the cheek, leaving a whiff of her familiar sweet perfume lingering on Eva's skin. "George and I made some plans this morning." Mabel pointed to her bulging bag. "We're going to do some reading."

"Saint Mabel," Eva said.

"Someone called your cell phone, Mrs. Gordon." Isabella pointed to it on the table where Eva left it the night before.

Eva picked up the phone and played the message in case it was Breezy. But it was the doctor's office calling to say they had a cancellation and could get her in today for the follow-up.

Eva laid the phone back down. She had forgotten about the first appointment at the neurologist's, the silly plastic skeleton, and her own confused behavior in front of the doctor, offering many clues to her diagnosis before official testing began. Breezy would want to accompany her grandmother to listen intently to the doctor with deep concentration and notebook in hand.

But Eva wasn't ready to go.

She deleted the voicemail, then retreated into her private thoughts of nursing homes where people were pushed around in wheelchairs and never took bus trips or worked in barns on woodworking. Her heart felt heavy with loss, imagining her likely future.

"George and I have plans to attend a funeral later today. We'd like you to join us." Mabel pulled a newspaper out of her canvas bag and set it down on the table.

George came through the door from his room with a wag of his wrinkled, aged finger. "Not sure I said I'd go to the funeral. A reading lesson is enough for one day."

He took a seat at the table and Isabella served him some coffee and toast. They sipped their coffee and slathered toast with homemade Try Again Farm jam produced from the farm's crushed and sweetened berries. Similar to the chickadee's chatter outside her bedroom, Eva's friends serenaded her with sounds of community while she grieved the potential imminent threat.

Everyone finished eating and making plans for the day. Mabel helped Isabella clear dirty dishes from the table and rinsed hot water over the plates with the hand sprayer. Once they had finished loading the dishwasher and wiping down the table, Isabella used sharp scissors to open the packages of multicolored paper. She slipped the contents from the packaging, spreading the sheets evenly over the table's surface within easy reach of everyone. "Time for an origami lesson. I'm no expert, but YouTube teaches you just about anything these days."

"George and I can give it a shot for just a few minutes," interjected Mabel. "But we really do have plans this morning." She selected a few pieces of fluorescent orange paper, handing one piece to George, who flipped it over and over in his claw as if trying to decode a secret message.

Isabella held her phone so everyone could see the YouTube lesson, which began with flapping birds. First they folded the paper in half, then folded the corners on the right and the left toward the crease in the middle of the paper to make the paper look like a kite. Eva heard the instructions as: *to the right and in half and over again and in half and over and over and over making "squash folds" and "valley folds" and folds and folds and folds.* Slowly, methodically, she formed the paper into sickly, deformed creatures, while everyone else's paper transformed into healthier-looking birds, possibly ready for flight. From the living room, Eva collected her wooden bowl, which Breezy had set out on the coffee table. As each bird came into being, she dropped the origami pieces inside.

After everyone made several birds, stars, and whatnots, Mabel grabbed the newspaper from the buffet where Isabella had set it when she cleared the table. She searched for a moment. "Here we go." As usual, she settled on the obituaries. "This is the funeral I'd like to attend this afternoon. He was a special friend."

"Not up to it today, Mabel." Eva turned on the kettle for tea.

"The funeral will give you a better perspective on life. And George will have the opportunity to escort two ladies for the afternoon."

George flashed a grin from the sink, where he washed his hands, softening to Mabel's strange invitation.

Mabel read aloud from the obituary for Mr. Bruce Themlan, who died last Monday at his home after a brief illness. Mr. Themlan was born in Quincy, Massachusetts, and had been married for forty years. He was survived by five children and five grandchildren, many nieces, nephews, and friends. The funeral service would be held that afternoon at 3 p.m. at the Redeemer Lutheran Church in Quincy, with a burial to follow at Greenbrier Cemetery. In lieu of flowers, donations could be made to the town youth hockey league that Mr. Themlan had coached for years.

"Are you up for it?" she asked Eva.

"You're the driver. I assent to you." Eva sipped her cup of tea.

Isabella took out her notebook and made a note.

"George, let's go do our lesson, and when we're done, you can put on that outfit you wore for Breezy and Ian's wedding."

"But *I* don't know that person." He jabbed a finger at the paper.

"That doesn't matter. Would you be upset if *extra* people showed up for your funeral to honor you and say goodbye?" She didn't wait for his answer. "Of course not. And, as I've taught Eva here, a funeral does a person good."

He flung Eva a look, as if discovering for the first time his newfound friend might be just as dimwitted as Eva. "Funerals break my heart most of the time," he said quickly. "You sure nobody's gonna get mad or get us in trouble for doin' this?"

"Doesn't say a thing in the paper about this being a private event." Mabel folded up the paper and returned it to her canvas bag.

George didn't really need to know that sometimes the folks weren't lonelies. Bruce Themlan, for example. The obituary sounded like plenty of people would send him off, especially his family made up of a cast of thousands.

When plans had been decided, George and Mabel slipped into the dining room for his reading lesson, Eva spent time alone in her room, picking out something to wear, listening to the birds, watching a rabbit scurry through the field.

After lunch, George appeared in the kitchen freshly showered and dressed in his disheveled suit, wearing a slipped-on tie that hung crooked around his neck.

After straightening his tie, Mabel scraped off some of the wedding cake on his lapel with her finger. "Our chariot awaits!" She hustled Eva along with a light hold on her elbow.

George straggled behind obediently.

Eva sat in the back seat, and George sat up front with Mabel. To a passerby, the vehicle probably looked self-propelled without a driver or passenger tall enough to be seen over the headrests. George chatted the whole way about life on Try Again Farm back when there was a steady stream of traffic up and down the street and in and out of the driveway as people came to visit and buy herbs and plants and pick apples. "Breezy has a mind to fix up that farm stand one day, since she's off in the summers," said George. "We're gonna sell vegetables and herbs again."

The drive into Quincy felt like hours and hours to Eva but only took twenty minutes according to Mabel when Eva voiced her complaint. They drove down familiar Hancock Street, past the Memorial Stadium, Central Middle School, and a carwash. "Does anyone have a Tylenol?" Mabel asked. "I seem to have hurt my arm carrying that big bag filled with reading material."

With concern, Eva rummaged in her purse and handed her friend a pill, watching Mabel carefully. The woman never admitted to battling pain.

Without any water, Mabel just gulped it down and continued her drive to the funeral.

Pulling into the full parking lot of a beautiful, classic brick structure, the threesome found the lot to be full. They circled the block two times before finding a space for the Buick.

Once Mabel parked the car, she and George walked across the parking lot. She patted his back and he patted hers in return.

A greeter held the front door open for mourners, ushering them into the lobby area.

Inside, the church gleamed with polished wooden pews and red velvet cushions. A cordial greeter handed them a program at the entry to the sanctuary.

"Seems he had lots of folks willin' to send him off and didn't need us." George didn't bother lowering his voice.

Mabel held her finger to her mouth to shush him. "But just think, we'll have some great answers for Isabella's icebreaker game."

Nearly two hundred fifty people must have packed into the place, sitting shoulder to shoulder with strangers on either side of them. Before the service even began, a line of people stood along the back wall as ushers scurried around. They brought in extra folding chairs, lining them up and down the side aisles nearly to the front of the sanctuary. The room quickly overheated since they were packed in like flowers in a sympathy arrangement.

The pastor appeared with another man and called the congregation to order. The organ music quieted, and the pastor led everyone in a prayer. They sang hymns chosen by the family: "Great Is Thy Faithfulness" and "O Love that Will Not Let Me Go."

The pastor announced that Bruce Themlan's son and daughter would speak in remembrance of their father. A very composed young man stood and walked to the podium, dry-eyed and confident. He talked of his father being his best man at his wedding. "For the life of me, I can't think of anyone who's been a better friend." He told story after story about his father, who sounded a little too good to be true. "He even left his golf clubs at home when the family went on vacation so he wouldn't neglect his kids or grandchildren. He didn't bring them along until we were old enough to play with him."

The daughter, dressed in a dignified, fitted gray suit, replaced the son at the front of the church and immediately apologized for her teariness, saying that she was going to speak anyway to honor her father. She told stories of her father getting up in the middle of the night with her kids when he came for a visit, having a bottle ready in the fridge so he could feed the baby while his daughter slept. He used to play Barbie with his little granddaughter, giving Barbie and Ken a wedding, then afterward he'd let his granddaughter paint his fingernails red. And he shared his deep faith with the entire family, both by his words and through his actions.

Eva must've let out a deep, exasperated sigh because Mabel shushed her with a finger to her lips, like she'd shushed George earlier. Eva sat rigidly straight, rolling her eyes.

Apparently, Mr. Themlan had all the answers, and they involved a willingness to be inconvenienced, to dress like someone one didn't want to dress like, and to engage in one's least favorite activities without complaint.

George's shoulder shook ever so slightly, pressed against Eva's. The lady next to Eva leaned over her to hand him a tissue. Eva impatiently patted George's knee, bestowing more of a near-spanking than a comforting stroke.

The air became stifling and humid and seemed to bother Mabel. She spoke to Eva, waving her hand in front of her face. "I'll be right back. I think I need some air." Mabel stood and stepped over the stranger at the end of the row to get out.

The attendees continued to sing hymns and recite prayers, but throughout the remaining service, Eva felt Mabel's absence strongly, looking down at the empty seat several times and back toward the rear of the church.

In the lobby, a few people made a bit of a ruckus off to one side. If Mabel were here, she would have sent a sharp glance strong enough to cease the commotion. Finally, after another hymn and a pastor's blessing, they were dismissed.

"Mabel never came back." George's brow wrinkled with concern as he studied the entry to the church.

"I know. Let's go find her." Eva collected her purse and their bulletins, then waited in the slow procession down the aisle to leave.

Out in the lobby, voices rose as people fondly recalled the service, but George and Eva searched the church for Mabel.

A small crowd was gathered in the corner near the stairs leading up to the balcony. And the bottom of Mabel's pumps peeked through their legs.

Oh, please not Mabel. She clutched George's sleeve and pulled him in that direction.

Folks circling her prone body held cell phones, conferring with each other about calling ambulances or doctors and finding whoever she came with.

"She's with us!" George roughly pushed folks out of his way and knelt by Mabel's side.

"I'm fine, George. Just got a little dizzy suddenly in the heat. There's nothing the matter," Mabel said.

Eva knelt beside Mabel, suddenly feeling the urge to pray.

A gentleman with graying sideburns, outdated eyeglasses, and piercing blue eyes held Mabel's head in his hand to keep her off the floor. "She felt weak suddenly and collapsed. I think she needs to get to the hospital."

"Really, this is quite silly, me down here, making a scene. Eva, could you give me a hand? And we'll be on our way. I'm feeling much better now." She reached her liver-spotted hand to Eva.

The kind man shook his head, his facial jowls giving a slight wiggle.

A woman in a dark A-line dress watched Mabel, a cell phone propped in position, as if ready to dial 911.

"You don't need to have that look of panic, Eva. There's nothing going on here we can't handle."

"You really should let us call an ambulance," the kind-faced man said.

"We'll just take ourselves right on over to the hospital," Mabel told him. "As soon as someone helps me up. No need to spend the entire budget of the state of Massachusetts on an ambulance ride."

"Fine. As long as you're not the driver, ma'am," said the kind man.

"Maybe an ambulance would be a good idea," George coaxed, as Eva smoothed back the hair from Mabel's forehead. "I saw this once on my program. The person fell on the floor, and he was in a coma . . ."

LINDA MACKILLOP

"I am *not* in a coma, George. I'm talking to you, aren't I? I didn't even *fall*. I just sat down to rest."

The kindly gentleman shook his head again. "That's not quite how it happened."

Eva looked wearily at Mabel's graying face as George fanned her furiously with the funeral program, mussing her hair with the draft. Eva stilled his hand.

He started again, talking a million miles an hour: "It could be heart problems. On my program once, there was this guy with a heart arrhythmia . . ."

Another gentleman brought Mabel water and sat her up to take some sips before helping her stand. George directed the men outside to the car, where they slipped Mabel into the back seat to stretch out.

Eva and George both waited outside the car, stealing a couple of glances at each other. *Now what do we do?*

"Sorry, didn't bring my wallet, Eva." George patted his back pocket. "You'll have to drive."

Turning away from the waiting gentlemen, Eva speared him with her eyes.

Mabel certainly wasn't going to be allowed to drive, and George had "forgotten" his wallet. That left one person to get them to the hospital.

Eva turned back to the men who were waiting and watching. "Well then. Let's get this show on the road." She opened the driver's side door and slid into the seat. Passing her hands over the steering wheel felt so good and familiar. She adjusted the rearview mirror and slid the seat back.

George buckled his seat belt, giving a slight wave to the gentlemen outside.

From the back seat, Mabel handed Eva the keys from her purse. On a good day, Mabel would never allow her friend who hadn't possessed a driver's license in many years to drive.

The kind gentleman leaned into the window. "Are you sure I can't call for help?"

Eva turned on the engine and slowly put the car in reverse. "We'll be fine. Thank you all for your help and concern." And she backed out of the parking space without hitting any other cars.

"Glad you still remember how to drive, Eva. Never driven in my life."

Slowly and cautiously, Eva pulled out onto the street, put her foot on the gas, and accelerated down the road, noticing how the familiarity of driving returned as if she'd only been without a car for a few weeks.

In the back seat, Mabel sat up. "Oh, I'm really feeling much better." She rolled down the window and scooted over next to the door. "Please don't take me to the hospital, Eva. It just seems so silly. I'll call the doctor tomorrow. I promise. Why, I could make you all a nice dinner tonight!"

Were they all just overreacting about Mabel's symptoms? Eva hesitated but then headed for the farm. A road sign up ahead read Raynham. "Is Raynham anywhere near the farm?"

Mabel read from a map and mumbled, "No, I think we're too far west. You need to turn around, Eva."

Once they finally turned into the farm entrance, Isabella burst through the back door waving arms above her head. "Where have you been? I expected you back an hour ago! I was starting to imagine losing all three of you and having to explain *that* problem to Breezy and Ian." Her words screeched to a halt. "And why are you in the driver's seat, Mrs. Gordon?"

Sixteen

ONCE ISABELLA HEARD THE TALE, she refused to let Mabel leave. "Let's get her upstairs and into bed. She can stay in Breezy and Ian's room."

"Might I borrow that nightie again to sleep in, Eva?"

Eva collected the gown from her bedroom hamper and dropped it on Breezy and Ian's bed, leaving to give Mabel some privacy.

A few minutes later, she returned and found Mabel propped up slightly with pillows.

"Another pajama party! Why, I hope you folks have—" Mabel stopped talking mid-sentence when Eva leaned over and hugged her.

How many times had Mabel put aside her own loneliness to tend to Eva? With sudden deep gratitude to God for their friendship, Eva stroked her friend's hand. "Why are you friends with me, Mabel Maguire?"

Mabel's eyes grew large. "What a silly question. Why ever would you ask such a thing?"

"Answer me, please," Eva said in the softest voice to ever exit her mouth. "What have I ever done to make you want to be friends with me?"

Mabel closed her eyes for just a moment, maybe to rest, maybe to gather her thoughts. When she finally opened them, she averted her gaze and fiddled with the bedspread stitching, speaking with halting words. "Eva, I've known you before." She glanced up and waved a hand up and down in front of Eva's frame. "Not *this* you, but people just like you from my past. People who couldn't find their way to the very place where they needed to go to heal—living smack-dab in the middle of people who cared about them." She closed her eyes again, gathering some fortitude. "And you may not believe this, but I've always seen a bit of myself in you."

Eva scrunched up her face at the thought.

Mabel shook her head and added quickly, "No, no. Maybe not in your gruff exterior—but we're not so different in our wants. We both want a familiar place to live, some trusted folks around us, and a purpose when we face each new day. I try to offer you what I know would heal you— and what I wished I had given others from my past. Love, patience, and a picture of God's unwavering grace, no matter what you did."

"I haven't always been very nice to you."

"No, but you give me good practice turning the other cheek." She offered Eva a wink and a squeeze of her hand before shutting her eyes again.

Eva tucked Mabel into her bed, leaving the bedroom door open with instructions to call them if she needed anything. Isabella made a little campsite outside Mabel's door, where she would sleep wrapped in a pile of blankets, keeping an ear out in case Mabel called.

When Eva finally fell asleep, she dreamt again.

Sarah made herself a "suicide tool kit." In a red toolbox identical to the marriage kit, Sarah collected coupons to the funeral home where she'd save money on her coffin and cemetery plot, along with dusty silk flowers, snacks for the family at the reception, and a note to her mother.

Way before dawn, Eva woke with such deep regret and longing she couldn't fix, wanting just one more conversation with her daughter, where she would fill the silences with words that mattered. She would move toward her rather than pushing away. After the disturbing dream, Eva had no chance of falling back to sleep. For a while, she lay in the blackened silence, listening to the clock tick downstairs.

If Sarah really had written a note like the one in the dream, what would she have written?

Finally, Eva threw off her covers, got out of bed, and donned her robe. She tiptoed down the creaky hall, careful not to step on sleeping Isabella as she peeked in on her friend.

Mabel waved a hand weakly in the semidarkness.

Eva stepped closer to the bed.

Propped up against pillows, Mabel clasped a hand against her chest, breathing with labored gasps. "Eva, dear. I think you might want to call that ambulance now."

A half hour later, as the paramedics drove away with Mabel in tow, Isabella, George, and Eva stood in the yard, wrapped in bathrobes, on a sunless early morning with none of Mabel's relatives to call—no immediate family left in her circle. She had *less* people left in her family than Eva.

After getting dressed and stuffing down some nourishment, the threesome drove in Mabel's car to the hospital, where they sat most of the day in a waiting room, Eva and George sitting side by side, flipping through magazines, looking at recipes. Isabella sat beside Eva, pointed to food that looked good and chatted with whomever dropped into the seat on her other side.

"I heard recently rosemary's really good for memory problems, Mrs. Gordon." Isabella pointed to one particular recipe for grilled chicken with rosemary. "Can't remember where I heard it though. Isn't that ironic?" She pulled out her phone from her purse. "We should search for rosemary recipes for you." She snapped a picture of the rosemary-covered chicken. Then she googled "rosemary recipes." Together they began a list of rosemary-infused dishes: lamb with rosemary; focaccia with rosemary; herbed breads with rosemary; rosemary sprinkled over potatoes.

"Rosemary grows on the farm," George said, but soon dropped his head back against the wall and fell asleep, mouth wide open like a cave entrance. No one in the waiting room seemed to notice or care when he started to snore.

"I hope this isn't my fault." Isabella rubbed her neck as if experiencing severe muscle tension. "We should've taken her to the hospital sooner. I'm a failure. A rotten elder-sitter. A gun episode? Someone ends up in the ER? I'd be fired for sure if this was a real job."

"Don't be hard on yourself, Isabella. We all listened to Mabel." Eva squeezed the girl's fidgeting hand. Then she retreated into memories. *The soft feel of a baby's skin, seagulls on a summer day at the beach, the kindest words ever spoken to her, the last time she saw her daughter's face before she died. The tenderness in Wallace's eyes just before he kissed Eva for the first time.*

She looked at Isabella and George, adding their faces to her list.

A nurse appeared in the doorway with a chart. "Eva Gordon?" Her eyes passed over the crowd, settling on Eva when she rose and collected her purse.

"Your friend is requesting your company. But just a few moments. She needs to rest and we'll be doing tests."

Eva, Isabella, and George followed the nurse to Mabel's private room. Once there, they gathered on the side of the room while the doctor spoke to Mabel.

When she finished, the doctor turned toward the friends. "Are these your family members?"

"In a way. They are very dear friends." Mabel wore the expression of someone setting their eyes on their loved ones. She seemed to be comfortable, no outward signs of pain. "You can share medical details with them."

"A small army. You're very fortunate." Turning to the group, she explained the diagnosis. "Your friend has had a very mild heart attack but should recover." She explained a few test results and then patted the side of the bed before heading for the door. "I'll leave you alone for a visit. A quick visit."

Eva walked to her friend's side and fluffed Mabel's covers, rubbed her hands, and said they would pray for her. Mabel settled comfortably back onto her pillows, smiling.

≈

When Isabella pulled into the driveway at the farm, the sun was dropping low in the evening sky and Breezy and Ian were home, unloading luggage, shopping bags, and a cooler from of the back of their car.

Looking tan and relaxed, they sported mauve-colored Bar Harbor baseball caps and sweatshirts over their shorts. Amber circled Breezy with wiggles and yelps, tail slapping the ground with unspeakable glee.

Breezy dropped her load, turned toward the car, and held empty palms toward the sky as if begging for an explanation of their whereabouts. "At least the dogs were here to welcome us back. Where have you all been?"

"You're home early. We thought you were comin' tomorrow." George whisked away a load of bags from the ground. "Welcome home, lovebirds." He gave Breezy's browned cheek a sweet kiss and then one-arm hugged his nephew.

"Have you been at the hospital?" Ian asked.

Isabella had texted them the update about Mabel from the hospital waiting room. Unfortunately, they decided to cut short their honeymoon. She trailed behind, shaking her head. "You're probably not going to want to pay me for my caregiving."

George explained. "The doctor at the hospital told us 'doting friends should go home for the evening to allow Mabel recovery time.'"

Looking like scarecrows standing in a field, Breezy and Ian stood stiffly, listening. Finally, Breezy said, "I can't believe she had a heart attack." She turned to Isabella. "You didn't sign up for this, did you?"

Isabella's face spoke regret. "Yeah, things got a little crazy. All mayhem seemed to break out, but I'm just grateful I was here to help. Wouldn't have wanted to be anywhere else."

"I knew this had the potential to be a challenging job, but not *this* challenging." Breezy hugged the girl. "Honestly, we can't thank you enough for letting us get away." She picked up a cardboard lobster cooler marked Down East Seafood on the sides in red font. "So we brought lobster to show our appreciation!"

Scratching sounds came from within.

"Whoa. Lobsters make everything worth it. Almost. I may not eat meat, but I eat seafood!" Isabella relieved Breezy of the cooler.

Settling her eyes on her grandmother, Breezy held out her arms for a hug. "You okay, Gram? A lot of action this week."

Eva stepped into the welcoming hug. "Doing fine. Can we visit Mabel tomorrow?"

"Of course."

They all turned toward the house, divvying up the luggage between the group. But at the kitchen door, Ian stopped the crowd like a traffic director, his commanding hand firmly held in the air. "I need to carry my bride over the threshold, folks." He dropped an armload of luggage on the porch and scooped up his wife, keeping the screen door open with his behind. With the group of humans and animals following, he entered his partially restored home, set her down, and planted a gentle kiss on her lips. "Welcome home, Mrs. Ward," he whispered, brushing her hair behind her ears.

Eva smiled when she saw the rest of the Wards watching from the garden, applauding the arrival of a new Mrs. Ward. Memories of Wallace invaded Eva's thoughts, the night he carried her over the threshold of their first small apartment with his strong, protecting arms, giggles and kisses abounding. She was much lighter back then. For a moment, she recaptured the feeling of young love, that hopefulness that accompanies newlyweds into their first abode. For Eva, her new life with Wallace meant being free from her father's unreasonable tirades for the first time and living with her one protector in life.

Inside the farm's kitchen, everyone bustled about, putting water on for the lobsters, pulling out dishes to set the table, moving luggage over to the stairs. Amber and Buck constantly got in the way as they sniffed the cooler. George interrupted at every moment possible. "You shoulda seen my program, kid. This guy was caught stealing a priceless diamond, and the FBI came after him and they had this car chase and they drove side by side right next to this train track . . ."

"That's what you wanna talk about after all that's happened here, Shorty?" Ian briefly scanned the mail on the counter. "Anybody try to tear down the place while I was gone? Put up a new development?"

"Not exactly." Isabella eyed Eva and George with a mutinous glance.

"Are you talking about the gun incident?" Ian shook his head and pierced Eva with his gaze. He lifted his baseball cap up and down, adjusting it several times on his head as he smoothed his dark hair. After a quick glance through the dining room into the living room, he focused on the pile of wedding gifts waiting to be opened. "Man, people were generous."

"Let's open gifts after dinner, hon."

The late-day sun poured a lovely, warm light into the kitchen, giving a glow to everyone's face as if they'd all been to Maine together and picked up a tan.

Isabella pulled out the homemade bread they made the other day.

After a while, Breezy announced the water was ready for the lobsters. "If someone wants to throw them in the pot. I hate that part."

Eva took a seat at the table. *Wallace's normally serene face looked so weary and agitated. Once again, she greeted him at the door with a list of complaints about the kids and their lack of help. "Am I the only one who does anything around here?"*

"Not again, Eva. Just one night I'd love to come home to a wife who was happy. When we were first married, I thought I could make you happy. Kiss all your bad experiences away. But I don't even know you anymore." He said the words once, then twice, then they became his mantra. "You're not the person I married. Even I can't crack your tough shell."

Isabella opened the cooler and rubbed the backs of one of the lobsters. "There's a compassionate way to cook them."

"Oh for heaven's sake. They're lobsters," Eva mumbled. "Even I don't have a shell that tough."

The group gathered around the cooler, staring at the six lobsters until George picked one up and let it scamper free on the kitchen floor.

Amber and Buck ran in circles around it, yapping.

"You can try relaxation techniques on them, so they calm down, like this. Rubbing their backs . . ." Isabella cradled one of the lobsters, rubbing the outer shell as if holding a beloved pet.

George clapped his hands together. "And then—Wham! You stick 'em in a pot of boiling water."

Isabella lifted her eyes to the ceiling. "People have done actual experiments in killing lobsters humanely. This is for real. Or you can put them in the freezer for a few minutes—to numb them a little. They slow down and start to mellow. Then you take them out and slip them gently into the water." Isabella performed a faux slide, as if demonstrating a gentle introduction to the lobsters' death.

If only Mabel, and Eva, and George could slide through their own transition to the other side in peace and find someone waiting there to meet them. Maybe even God.

While Isabella continued touting the idea of compassionate killing, Ian grabbed the lobster from the floor with its tail and claws slapping wildly in an effort to escape. "Or you can do it like this." He stuck it headfirst into the pot, splashing and splattering boiling water all over the stovetop. "That way they don't know what hit 'em." He wiped his hands on his Levi's before he grabbed the next one.

"Okay, then." Isabella threw up her hands. She and Breezy covered the kitchen table with newspapers, located nutcrackers, and melted some butter.

Everyone chatted while the lobsters cooked and the kitchen filled with a steamy, fishy smell mixed with melted butter. When they finally sat down to their feast, Ian asked Isabella if she'd miss the farm, now that her house-sitting gig had come to an end.

Her face dropped before she looked at Ian with the saddest smile. "Definitely. I wish I could live here."

"Careful. Someone might start moving you in." Ian wiped bread in the butter drippings on his plate.

Throughout dinner, Breezy's eyes remained on her grandmother. She attempted to engage Eva in conversation to no avail.

When the last morsel of lobster was devoured and all the remains collected in a bag and secured in a trash can outside, Eva excused herself, encouraging them to go open their wedding gifts. She needed to be alone.

"We can wait and open them later, Gram. When you're up to it."

"Don't let me spoil the excitement. I'll see them all in the morning." She pointed to a small wooden box where she had moved the poems and scripts from the wedding day, a box she once made with her father.

"You'll find lots of poetry and words in that box. Don't forget to show that to the newlyweds." She started toward the stairs but returned to Isabella, placing a hand on the back of the girl's dreadlocked hair, pressing a kiss on the top of her head.

As Eva climbed the stairs, Breezy said, "Whoa. *What* has happened around here?"

Isabella's voice rose to the second floor, bold and confident, telling how Breezy and Ian had a crowd of Shakespeares at their wedding, which she discovered after she came up with this idea to give people an assignment . . .

Upstairs in her room, still fully dressed, Eva climbed under the bedspread, leaving the door open in the hopes that the camaraderie of happy family voices below would silence Wallace's chiding words. But she could still make one thing right. From the nightstand, Eva collected the slip of paper with Rob's phone number, just as downstairs Ian gleefully celebrated a new toolbox for a wedding gift.

"Now *that's* a wedding gift I can appreciate."

Isabella's voice protested. "It was a gift meant for the honeymoon."

Breezy read the words. "A marriage kit to build your life around. With love, from Isabella."

Eva smiled.

"A gift card to the drive-in! And luxurious bath lotion, carved soap, sparkling apple cider with champagne glasses, and a book called, *How to Love Your Spouse for a Lifetime*." Their voices read the cards from the *Getting to Know You* game too.

With a shaking hand, she picked up the phone and squinted to turn it on, carefully looking at her address book with the scratched lines indicating numbers, pushing each corresponding button to dial him.

An automated voicemail responded with Rob's instruction to leave a message and he'd return the call.

As if talking to a silent priest through a confessional and unable to hold it all in any longer, Eva proceeded to leave a message. "Rob, it's me, your mother. Could you call me . . . so we could talk? I have some things I need to say to you."

Rob's hand shook her awake roughly.

Eva turning to see if he had disturbed his father.

Wallace's side of the bed, unwrinkled and unslept in for two years.

"I don't want to live with you anymore, Mother. Neither does Sarah."

The girl's silhouetted frame in the doorway, nodding.

"You're not like a real mother."

"I . . . I made so many mistakes with you and Sarah. I ranted and raved and blamed you both for things you shouldn't have been blamed for. You were just children. Is there . . . is there any way to make it right?"

The children recounting so many of her episodes of mistreatment: accusing them of being careless with pets, household chores, and turning off the stove, folding the laundry poorly, turning in sloppy school papers. The way their teachers offered less condemnation on their schoolwork than Eva.

The voicemail cut out and Eva called back, slipping down onto her knees beside her bed.

"I feel like it's getting late—but it's not *too* late. Please call me?" She closed her eyes and sat in silence on her knees, picturing Rob's young face when he protected Sarah. Without any more words to purge, Eva clicked off the phone and wearily rested her head against the bed.

Outside, evening sounds filled her room: tree leaves rustling, an owl hooting in the distance, crickets chirping above the wind, an occasional car drifting past the house. Throat dry, she put on a sweater before plodding downstairs for a drink, passing the group who were still examining the wedding gifts, sitting in the center of a pile of gifts. Tablecloths, a wedding album, and silver frames for their pictures, referring to someone who had "regifted them," whatever that meant.

"Gram, don't you want to watch us open gifts now?"

But Eva silently waved to them and kept walking.

In the kitchen, Eva poured a glass of water, taking long, deep drinks as if thirst had pursued her for years.

Amber trotted into the kitchen, nudged Eva, then walked to the door, looking imploringly at Eva.

They would go for a walk and breathe in some night air. She collected Amber's leash, which the dog rarely wore, then opened the back door,

letting the animal lead the way. As she followed behind, the wind serenaded her with whispers sounding like taunting voices.

*Rob and his unreasonable devotion to his father and sister, the way he
never stood with his mother.*

Amber headed through the back field to a dirt road that skirted
the edge of Ian's property. A last glimpse of the evening light peeked
through parted clouds. Just a few steps down the road, the slithering
shadow of a snake slipped by.

Eva hiked up her denim skirt and hustled backward to let him pass.

*Other rants, slaps for accidental spills in the kitchen, talking back disre-
spectfully to her, or for taking a drink of orange juice late at night. Mocking
them for having only a few friends, predicting their catastrophic futures of
failure after a bad grade, finally pushing her children to the brink.*

If only she could walk and walk and walk and find herself firmly situated in a past decade. Eva longed to return to a day when her beloved
husband slipped into bed beside her each night after the children had
been safely sequestered in their own rooms. She would be different.

*"When we make mistakes, you could've lightened up, stopped your scream-
ing, helped us learn, been a shoulder to cry on." His voice sounded like a chas-
tising parent, his sister's protector yet again. "Dad's picking us up soon."*

Amber took a dip in a small stream, clear and clean, with polished
rocks as stepping-stones. Eva's kids had done the same during their
escapades in the woods.

At a beach funeral, a helium balloon sends well-wishes for the
deceased toward the sky.

If only Eva's sins had traveled along as stowaways.

The setting sun over the treetops gave a splotched look to the woods.
A neighboring house sat at the edge of the tree line, smaller than the
surrounding farmhouses but rural in its appearance. It was a one-story
English cottage, nestled in a partly manicured but partly relaxed state,
penned in by a weathered picket fence in need of a few replacement
boards, while bordering neatly trimmed and edged grass and gardens.

Eva came through the woods and walked up to the cottage's gate. The
steeply pitched and varying roofline, along with an arched doorway,

described Rob's house, though she'd always imagined a thatched roof instead of asphalt shingle.

As a child, Rob kept his room neater than Eva would've asked of him—probably to ward off the same scolding she often delivered to Sarah. Unless he just liked order. His house would be orderly as well.

Eva opened the gate and walked up the stone path to the front door and tried the knob, which opened.

Rob really should lock his doors.

Eva stepped inside to the sight of his well-worn leather furniture, so many books filling the bookshelves. He had an eye for design, filling the space with framed world maps, photography of the Greek Isles, and a large brass compass.

His kitchen looked practical and functional. She decided to make him a pot of tea—the British love tea. The gas stove startled her when the flame burst to life, red and yellow waves. As she rummaged for his tea bags, she heard a man's voice behind her.

"Who are *you*? What are you doing in here?"

The anger in his voice frightened Eva. She turned quickly, arms extended to implore him for understanding. Didn't he know she wanted to make things right? "Rob! She was just a little girl who made a mistake, wasn't she?" She hoped to hear him say his mother just made a mistake too, absolving her of all her sins, but the words came out before she carefully studied the person before her.

"Where did you come from?" The man sounded wary. He watched her with a puzzled sideways expression. He was an older version of Rob, eyes more worn than her son's—but a different color, blue rather than brown—and much longer hair.

"We don't know each other, do we?" She backed away, setting the tea down on the counter behind her. "I thought you were Rob." She slipped over to the door to put the table between them.

He nodded slowly as if understanding the situation. "Okay. I think I see now. You thought Rob lived here?" His eyes lost their wariness and waved his hand toward the kitchen chair. "Why don't you have a seat and rest. We'll figure this out."

A beam from a flashlight illuminated the wall through the open screen door, allowing his figure to create an eerie shadow hovering over Eva. The beam of light appeared as a spotlight announcing an important event.

A voice called and called, getting louder and louder, becoming clearer.

Wearing a light jacket as if he had just come inside from an errand, the man looked toward the light source and back at Eva. He slowly moved toward the door, keeping his eyes latched onto Eva.

Breezy's voice calling, "Graaaam? Eva Gordon? Are you out here?"

"Are you Eva Gordon?" he asked.

Eva nodded, feeling like a silly child.

The man walked over to the door. "I think someone is trying to find you."

The familiar sound of the water rumbling in the kettle on the stove settled her, and she felt herself returning. "Oh, I'm so sorry. I'm not sure what I've done."

"Everything will be fine. You wait here—I'll be right back." The screen door slammed behind him as he walked out into the night.

Steam escaped from his kettle.

Eva walked to the steaming kettle, and shut off the burner.

Moments later, the sounds of footsteps and chatter preceded the man through the door as he made way for a panicked-looking Breezy to come inside.

Detective Breezy had questions. "What are you doing over here, Gram? Amber came back wearing her leash, and I thought something had happened to you. You should always tell me if you want to go for a walk. I thought you might've fallen . . . or worse." She nodded toward the man leaning against the counter. "You met Ned?"

He appraised Eva with a painfully tender smile.

"We . . . well—"

"Sure, we met," Ned said. "I think your grandmother just got a little confused. We were straightening some things out when I heard you outside."

"I see." Breezy kept her eyes trained on Eva. "I'm sorry, Ned." She emitted words between ragged breaths. "Thanks for watching her."

Ned swatted the air in dismissal. "No harm done. I'm just glad everyone is safe."

"I'll be getting her home," said Breezy. She escorted Eva to the door. But where was Rob? They were going to have some tea.

Breezy shepherded her grandmother home through the woods while the flashlight's beam danced over the leaf-covered path. Their feet crunched along, first on leaves, then on gravel.

"Isabella said to say 'goodbye.' She had nice things to say about her time on the farm this week." Their two stark shadows led them home, walking side by side, formed by the moonlight.

Eva looked out at the darkness of the woods. As the truth rose to the surface in her mind, her body trembled in fear. In a mere whisper, she said, "I don't know if I can trust myself anymore. For the life of me, Breann Macpherson . . ."

"Ward."

"Breann Ward, I'm all turned around in my head—" They stopped in the path, and Breezy pointed the flashlight toward the sky. "I don't know how to explain what's wrong with my mind."

Breezy kept quiet and held her grandmother's hand, listening to Eva's jumbled thoughts.

"I've been feeling myself slip away for years, as though I'm a stranger to myself. I live in a world set up like one large safety mechanism—reminder notes hanging from every wall, no mobility, and frustrating, elderly sitting arrangements with strangers. You can't experience all those things without knowing something is changing permanently."

Breezy waited and nodded. "I'm listening, Gram."

"It's not normal to walk uninvited into a stranger's house. Or go to a doctor's appointment and make a fool of yourself. I'm moving further and further down a strange road, away from any normal, everyday existence."

"We're here for you, Gram. You're not alone."

"I'm giving up, Breezy."

"Please don't. Let us help you."

She wanted to send balloons and other things to the sky. She wanted to make life easier for her granddaughter and Ian. She wanted help saying goodbye.

Eva silently begged her granddaughter for understanding and some sort of reassurance.

Breezy squeezed her grandmother's hand, promising to do the best she could. With a thin ray of light shining the straight way down the gravel road, the two women walked slowly toward home.

Seventeen

FOR MUCH OF THE NIGHT, Eva sat in the dark of her room, staring out over the yard as if keeping guard over the farm and its occupants, ready to scare away stray coyotes or potential burglars with her strong, commanding voice. A family of skunks, six in all, skittered along the wall of the barn on their way out to the field, the parents leading the way as protective guardians, their white stripes both ominous and luminous. For the sake of their offspring, they took on enemies, not with a spray of toxic words, but with a simple foul odor.

Watching their formation, the parents in the lead, Eva knew what she needed to do. As an assurance against morning forgetfulness, Eva found paper and scratched three words that would change her life—and protect Breezy and Ian's future. As the colors of dawn inched above the horizon, the determined decision ushered in sleepiness. Eva shut the drapes, climbed into bed, and fell into the heavy, dreamless slumber of an exhausted child.

Bright and early the next morning, Eva shuffled into the kitchen for breakfast. Breezy sat at the table wearing a Patriots sweatshirt, forehead pinched, looking both exhausted and sad. She was writing some sort of note while scratching Amber with her foot. She stopped and motioned for Eva to have a seat. Breezy scraped back her chair, stood up, and collected a mug from the cabinet. She buttered a bagel, steeped some tea, and fried an egg. Then she served her grandmother a breakfast sandwich.

While they ate their food, Breezy made conversation about the weather. "Oh, and I had a call from Rob this morning, Gram. He said he received a long 20-minute series of voicemails from his mother. He wanted to know if you were all right."

A faint memory formed of the comforting expulsion of her words into Rob's voicemail. "I'm not . . . well, I guess . . ."

Breezy's voice gentled. "I told him about your struggles, Gram. He has a right to know."

"I had some things I needed to say to him."

Breezy mentioned Mabel had a rough night, according to the hospital. "We could put together a bouquet for her with some fresh flowers from the yard and pay her a visit."

The women cleaned up the kitchen, then strolled through the yard and field finding flowers, enjoying the end-of-summer brisk air while picking black-eyed Susans, asters, and daisies, forming them into a bouquet. While they collected, Breezy pointed out the work that needed to be done outside. Pruning some of the larger branches on those neglected apple trees. Replacing some trees filled with deadwood. A new retaining wall along the house, and a healthier lawn. "But with no chemicals."

The sun warmed them, and the birds sang for them as they collected enough flowers for arrangements for Mabel and for the tables in the living room and dining room at the farm. Just before climbing the back stairs to the kitchen, Eva spotted dandelions speckling the grass. She picked a few for Mabel's arrangement.

Inside, they wrapped the flowers in wet newspaper while Breezy rummaged for an old vase she could leave at the hospital.

Later in the hospital gift shop, after Breezy read nearly every get well card on the rack to Eva, they picked out a whimsical card appropriate for Mabel. Breezy signed the card while Eva dictated words: "Get better so you can support all the Matthew Davieses in the world who need you." And they purchased some helium balloons that read *Get Well!*

The nurse directed them down the sterile hall lined with vacant hospital beds and medical equipment on wheels. In Mabel's room, they found their friend dozing and difficult to wake, probably from medication.

A shadowed look of darkness passed over Breezy's face at Mabel's sallow appearance, her itsy-bitsy body dwarfed beneath the tubes and baggy hospital gown.

After tying the balloons to the end of the bed, Eva set the flowers on the nightstand, causing Mabel to stir.

"Look what you brought me! Flowers from God's good creation." Mabel spoke in a weak, scratchy voice. She rubbed her eyes and nodded to the balloons at the end of her bed. "Can those wonderful balloons carry me to the heavens?" She smoothed down the silver locks of her hair that lay flattened against her scalp and in need of a shampoo. "I look awful. They won't let me wear any jewelry, and I haven't even run a comb through my hair all day."

"I can brush your hair, Mabel." Breezy picked up a brush from the bedside table.

"Oh, what a luxury. I'd love that, dear."

"I can dab on some makeup, too, if that would help you feel more presentable." Breezy looked around for Mabel's purse.

"Oh, yes. Over there on the chair." She nodded to her purse. "I would be so grateful, Breezy."

While tenderly brushing the locks long so every strand was in place and dabbing some rouge and color on Mabel's lips, Breezy made light conversation about the honeymoon, sounding as nonchalant as possible, even offering Mabel a place at the farm when she was discharged. "You don't want to live alone anymore, Mabel. Do you?"

"No no, dear," said Mabel. "You have so much on your hands as it is. You're a full-time teacher and a newlywed. You don't need to be running a nursing facility as well. I'll just come for visits if I get better—"

"*If* you get better? Of course you'll get better, Mabel," Breezy said.

"I will *not* be a burden to anyone." Then she shut her eyes. "Any new replacements for the downstairs apartment yet?"

"Been too busy to work on that task yet. Now that I'm home, I'll advertise."

Eva tried offering Mabel a sip of water through a straw and some applesauce from a plastic container.

Mabel refused both, instead giving them a whispered rundown on the nurses, like the sweetest night nurse who really should lose a few pounds. "But she's going through a painful divorce." Another nurse with tattoos might have been better choosing a different profession. "She seems a tad annoyed with the patients. She was a little gruff with me when I asked for some medication . . . until I offered to pray for her. Then she was nicer." Mabel turned her head in Eva's direction. "And how is my dear friend Eva doing?"

"I'm starting to make some plans. I don't want to be a burden to Breezy either."

"Stop, Gram. We'll talk about this later. Right now we want to cheer up Mabel."

"Eva, you're a strong, strong woman when you put your mind to something," said Mabel.

"My mind is the problem."

"I think I'm ready for a sip of that water now. Could you pass it to me, Breezy?" Mabel took a brief sip from the offered straw. "Eva, getting old is the most natural thing on earth, no matter how hard we fight it. Look at those flowers right there in the vase. They bloom and bring beauty for just the briefest of moments, like us. The only thing we can control is whether we go out singing or not."

The list of fears preventing her from singing paraded through Eva's mind. Fear of losing her faculties, of wandering off and never being found, of being forgotten. Fear of suffering with stomach pain but being unable to communicate the problem to anyone. Fear of a tightening in her heart, a locking in a joint, a choking sensation on her food and never being able to ask for help.

Mabel turned to Breezy. "Dear, could I have just a few minutes alone with your grandmother?"

Breezy sat straight at the request. "Oh. Of course. I'll just wait outside." She set down the brush and stepped outside of the room.

When Breezy shut the door, Mabel fidgeted with her fingers on the blanket. "I don't know if this would help you, Eva, but some days, when I'm feeling alone, I like to imagine folding back the clouds and the sky like a curtain. You know why?"

Eva shook her head.

"Because I know what we would see. A whole host of angelic beings watching over us."

Eva's first response was to snicker, but she refrained out of respect.

"It sounds wild, but it's true, Eva. And just this minute, I had the most brilliant idea for you to do. What if you took those balloons . . ." She beckoned Eva closer and nodded at the end of her bed. And with a weak voice speaking strong words, she encouraged Eva to do a little project back at the farm. "Do you think you can do that?"

Eva nodded thoughtfully.

"And remember, the future might look a little rickety for us both, but think of it this way. We're all just walking with each other down a hard road to a better place." Then she raised an arm as if she was giving a benediction at a funeral service. "Be strong and courageous, no matter what you face. You are loved and seen and known by God." Then she dropped her hand down onto the bed. The blessing took all Mabel's strength. "You can invite Breezy back now."

"You're going to get better, Mabel. Why are you talking like I'm carrying on some mission without you?" Eva's words were barely audible. "I need you."

"Please let Breezy in, dear."

Eva opened the door for her granddaughter, who came in and sat on the other side of Mabel. She took her friend's hand in her own.

Weakly, Mabel raised her hand in Breezy's direction and offered a vision and blessing for her too, bequeathing her with the task of helping George to overcome his learning disability and learn to read.

"No, Mabel. You can teach him yourself." Breezy shook her head adamantly. "You're going to get better." The young woman looked at her grandmother as if for confirmation.

Eva nodded decisively.

When Mabel yawned again, Breezy gently tucked her friend's hands under the blanket.

"Now you take some of those balloons and do what I told you, Eva. Okay?" Mabel yawned.

Eva untied the arrangement and selected half the balloons to take home as Breezy looked at her quizzically. After Breezy kissed Mabel's cheek, Eva did the same, inhaling her flowery smell of lavender hospital moisturizer. She moved her drink and the nurse buzzer close to her bedside.

Mabel whispered her goodbye as they got close to the door, instructing them to take good care of that George. "I'll see you very soon."

≈

On the drive home, Eva told Breezy about the funeral at the beach, about sending well-wishes for the deceased into the sky and how Mabel thought other things could be sent into the sky as well. "Would you help me, Breezy?" Her voice sounded needy and childlike, much to her chagrin, as if even her body might shrink down to the waifish eighty pounds of her ten-year-old self.

Later, at the kitchen table cluttered with empty mugs and origami papers spread out like a brightly colored peacock tail across the surface, Eva dictated her thoughts to Breezy, who hurriedly scribbled words on pieces of origami paper. Writing smatterings of her own memories to send heavenward seemed too hard, but many of the memories were way too heavy for her to carry anymore. She communicated the thoughts to Breezy with only a few simple words representing the longer story: *Sarah's funeral.* The memories swamped Eva, pulling her away from the kitchen table and back to that day.

Eva driving alone to the church where she met Breezy, Luke, Wallace, and

Rob. The pastor greeting them in a back room, preparing them for the service. Taking their seats in front of her daughter's coffin. Bagpipes.

Breezy's friend reading a letter from Breezy, telling how Sarah was "a little flawed, a little childlike, and a little holy," putting out a cooler on trash day with cold water for the city workers, sometimes even baking them cookies. Their thank-you notes, attached later to the handles of the containers, scribbled on the back of tossed-away envelopes. Finding them in Sarah's personal trunk along with all her special correspondence from close friends and family.

After writing clipped versions of the stories, Eva folded them into what almost looked like paper birds capable of flight and dropped them into a paper bag retrieved by Breezy. They took the bag out to the back porch, where the balloons bobbed in the wind like boxers in a ring, still tied to the shaky wooden deck railing.

Cumulous clouds blew across the sky, partially hiding the sun.

While Eva held the bag, Breezy untied the balloons from the railing and wrapped the ribbon around the top of the bag. The day held ample wind for their project, mussing escaped hairs from Breezy's ponytail and whooshing Eva's blouse as she held the bag. The dogs sat at attention, as if waiting for some sort of reward.

"I need to be the one who releases them." Eva reached for the ribbons. "Mabel said so."

With strong tugs on the balloons and gentle slaps against the bag creating sounds like crackling fire, the wind seemed enthusiastic about carrying away all Eva's pain in the form of sins and regrets and losses.

"Eva, I have some hard news for you." Luke's voice was broken. *"The hospital called. She's taken a turn for the worse."*

After a long moment of reflecting on the contents of the bag, she said, "I can't carry these anymore, God. I send them to you." And she released her hold of the string, letting the contents float away.

The balloons rode the wind toward the blue and cloud-spotted heaven, stirring the leaves on the trees into a round of applause as though congratulating performers leaving a stage. Far above the treetops, the balloons and the bag grew smaller and smaller until only a mere dark speck could be seen.

The women stood in silence. Eva's neck cramped and she looked back down, the mission accomplished. "Would you like to do one more project with me?" Eva asked. "I have plans to finish restoring your mother's old desk and give it away."

"More instructions from Mabel?" Breezy asked.

Eva just smiled.

After changing into appropriate paint-spattered work clothes, the women journeyed out to the barn to complete Eva's requested task. Breezy followed her grandmother's lead, allowing her to give the directions as best she could. The gouges on the dresser's wood still needed a little extra attention, Eva pointed out before directing Breezy to the instructions on the Post-it notes taped above the worktable.

Sand off excess wood putty. Clear the surface of dust. Apply paint or stain.

"Can you blend that can, Breezy? I'll blend this small one." Eva selected a paint color and a tool. *Stirrer, screwdriver, or brush?*

Breezy reached for the screwdriver and popped open a can of paint, then blended the separated layers together, forming one bright color from all the separate hues. Then she handed her grandmother the screwdriver to open her can.

"I want each drawer to be a different color. Orange. Yellow. Green. Bright and lively, like the new owner-to-be." As the afternoon progressed and they moved from drawer to drawer, Breezy opened and blended the individual cans, cleaning her brush in between choosing the next color. Wooden knobs from Eva's old collection waited all lined up on the workbench for the final touches, painted with original designs—a quill pen on one, an open book on another, and an ink bottle on the last.

Though they thought they were fixing up the desk once and for all, someone else might come along in the years following and again carve initials in its surface, making parents decide the desk had been worn a little too hard and needed to be refreshed. That family would repeat the process—stripping and sanding, dusting and painting.

After smoothing out the final lines of the paint on the last drawer, Breezy announced she was wiped out from the day. They collected the equipment to be scrubbed in the work sink and replaced the tops of the paint cans before admiring their handiwork. Once the paint dried and they applied the new knobs, the job would be finished.

≈

The phone rang later that evening as everyone watched David Muir deliver the world news to their living room. Eva knew the purpose of the call even before Breezy picked up the receiver. She knew by the way the air suddenly felt chillier, more like winter air than the last dregs of a summer night, and by the way something bright and warm to her right seemed extinguished.

Breezy took the phone to the dining room but glanced toward her grandmother, her mouth startled in an open position. When she finally spoke in a hushed tone to the person on the other end of the phone, her eyes remained unblinking before dropping shut.

Eva knew.

Breezy hung up the phone and stood wordlessly in the living room doorway as the drone of the television dulled and fell into the background.

George must've known too, as he shot up with sudden alarm, hands lifted protectively to ward off an onslaught of pain.

"That was the hospital." Breezy paused. "Mabel passed away earlier. She just went to sleep and didn't wake up." She moved to hug George, then sat down by her grandmother on the couch.

Outside in the dusky light, the wind moved over the dried grasses in the fields and the slowly wilting trees in the woods. Tears wet Eva's cheeks. She had viewed the woman as a pest, but now felt weighted down under a tragic emptiness. What would she do without the cheery babble and bustling energy of the liveliest and most faithful person ever to crash into her world? Eva folded over herself and wept underneath Breezy's comforting arms.

After a long time of tears, Eva hoisted herself up. "We need to do something. Follow me." She beckoned the others to follow her.

At the back porch, standing on tiptoes, Eva reached for the rope on the ship's bell and rang it hard three times for Mabel. Three times for her friend who found her way home.

George knelt down beside Buck, who seemed to sense his owner's grief. The two commiserated, heads tilted together.

～

The next day as they made plans for the funeral, George made a request. "I'd like to read something at her service, if you think it's all right?" He requested a Bible. "Never could read the thing 'cause of those thees and thous. But Mabel was helping me with some of her favorite verses."

Eva went upstairs and to her memory box where she stashed old pictures, Sarah's and Rob's hair samples, and faded school papers. From the box, she resurrected her childhood Bible. She took it downstairs for George to read at the service. Eva also would face her own fears and say some words there about her friend.

Eighteen

ON THE DAY OF THE service, a dense, cold, damp Massachusetts fog settled over the area. Typical funeral weather. Breezy and Ian seemed to be scheming about something out of earshot of Eva, whispering to each other while stealing glances at her. Isabella had called earlier and Breezy suspiciously took the phone call outside. But really, Eva's heart felt so weary and heavy that anything they might be planning regarding Eva's life mattered little to her at that moment.

During what felt like a long drive to the church, memories of Mabel clattered around inside Eva's head.

Finally, they drove into the parking lot of the small, clapboard-sided New England church that had been Mabel's place of worship for decades.

Isabella pulled in next to the Jeep, Jasmine sitting in the back. A man sat in the passenger seat of her Toyota.

Had the girl brought her own father to the funeral?

Then the car door opened and out came familiar curls on the hunched posture of the man's shoulders as if he read too much.

She gasped. Her mind played tricks on her. It had to be tricks. He was dead. She took a step back. *Was it Wallace?*

Breezy and Ian led Eva around the front of Isabella's car toward the man. Standing by his car door, the man greeted Eva tentatively. "Mother?" He used a loving tone he hadn't used with her since his childhood. "It's me."

Hands rushing to her mouth, she stared and stared, trying to be certain she was seeing the real Rob before making one more embarrassing faux pas.

"Aren't you going to hug your son, Eva?" Ian placed his large hand on the small of her back, nudging her gently toward Rob.

"Is it really you, Rob?" She implored him, tilting her head, unable to handle one more trick of her mind or disappointment.

He stretched out his arms. "It's really me, Mother."

"It's really him, Gram." Breezy encouraged her grandmother forward.

Love, longing, and regret propelled her into his arms. It was Rob, really standing there. Not Wallace, but Rob, looking so much like his father, had come all the way from London. One of the greatest surprises of her life—a piece of her past healing.

They stood in a long embrace, Eva weeping on his shoulder.

Rob spoke quietly in his mother's ear. "I thought you might like a little support."

Breezy gently tugged her grandmother's arm. "There'll be time for catching up later, but let's get inside now."

Eva pulled away and studied his face, the longer hairstyle with the graying temples, the lines etching his brow and the crow's feet around his eyes in the same pattern as his father. The shadow of her younger Rob living just behind his adult face. "You came back to me." A quaver returned to her voice. And without thinking, she buried her face again in his chest, wetting his jacket with her tears of gratitude. "Why?"

Rob pulled out a white handkerchief from his pants pocket and dabbed at his mother's face. "I listened to your voicemail several times, and when I did, I heard a woman I wanted to get to know." He handed her the handkerchief. "Sounds as though you've been through quite an ordeal, Mother. I'm going to work from the States for a while. Breezy needs to get back to school, and I'll stay with you."

"Rob . . ." Eva struggled to fill in the rest of the words while she stroked his cheek, feeling the stubble on his chin. "My son."

He tucked her arm into his and led her inside the church. Greeters handed out bulletins at the door. *The Memorial Service of Mabel Marie*

Maguire read the cover. The greeters nodded, and the Try Again crew somberly marched down the aisle to their place in the front row.

A young man played a somber piece on the piano. Lavender sprays decorated the traditional sanctuary with its arched windows, red-carpeted floor, and wooden pews—already half-full with people. Someone had picked bouquet after bouquet of side-of-the-road wildflowers and set them on windowsills.

Isabella and Jasmine came and greeted the family, squeezing Breezy and Eva with hugs. They took a seat in the second row, rustling through the program.

Eventually, the church filled to capacity. The pianist stopped playing when the pastor stood and stepped forward, dressed in a distinguished dark suit with a white-collared shirt, and welcomed everyone in a deep, formal voice. He prayed for comfort from the Man of Sorrows who was acquainted with grief. Then he stepped aside and the same soloist from Breezy's wedding sang "It Is Well with My Soul," accompanied by a brass section of several French horns, a trombone, and a few trumpets.

Either Jasmine or Isabella sniffled.

When the musicians stopped, Breezy stood, looking very composed in her black skirt and gray sleeveless sweater, as if starring in a production of her own life. She walked to the front and seemed to count to ten, making eye contact with many of the mourners in the pews, as if sharing their grief while offering them comfort.

In the silence, people shuffled their programs, sneezed, and coughed.

Finally, she talked about Mabel's friendship and how she became a second grandmother to her, baking food, checking up on her when she was out late, leaving lights on in her apartment for Breezy to find her way in the dark, taking the trash can out to the street at 5:30 in the morning. "Most important, she brought such cheerfulness to our family—and to my grandmother."

When Breezy finished, George stood and nodded for Eva to go in front of him.

As she walked, Eva studied the red, hooked carpet with worn spots where people had walked and trampled this journey for years, right toward the front without straying to the left or right.

George carried her childhood Bible in one hand, his other hand holding her elbow. Up front, they hunted through the book. Why didn't they mark the place for the reading?

After an extended period of page shuffling, the pastor slipped over. They whispered the passage to him and he turned to the correct page.

George spoke first. "Mabel was helpin' me learn to read. She never made me feel foolish or nothin'. Just treated me like we had all the time in the world. This was her favorite verse and I wanted to read it . . . for her honor." In a stuttering voice, with Eva directing from behind, George read from the book of Isaiah.

The crowd patiently listened while his finger led the way along the page and his tongue sounded out each syllable.

"Your eyes . . . will sssee the . . . King in Hhhis . . . beau-ty and view a land that sssttretches afar." Then he looked over at Mabel's flower-draped casket. "We're sure gonna miss you here. So long, little lady." He blew her a kiss, and Ian came up to steady him and help him to his seat.

Eva's throat tightened from tension, giving her voice the sound of a wobbly metal saw. She clutched Rob's handkerchief tight. But for Mabel's sake, she would swallow her fear of speaking in front of people, drawing on her strong resolve. "Mabel was the kind of friend who knew where you needed to go and gently led you there. She taught me to number my days. When she came into my life, Mabel was a kind person who wanted my friendship, flaws and all. She offered me grace I didn't even know I needed."

Mabel's face peering in her window and the feel of the breeze she made each time she rushed about a room.

For the rest of Eva's life, the air would be still without Mabel. "That's all I'm going to say besides that I'll miss her, and I wish our time together was longer." Then she walked down the steps and back to her place in the pew. When she sat down, her body shook as tears formed a cool path down her cheeks.

THE FORGOTTEN LIFE OF EVA GORDON

The congregation sang "Great Is Thy Faithfulness," with a piano accompaniment. Then the pastor stepped forward and spoke about the pain of separation caused by death. He said death was always an interruption, leaving unfinished business. People leave behind half-written letters, unfinished glasses of milk, books only half read at their bedsides. And it will always be that way because no one knew the day or time of their last breath. "You wake up in the morning, planning to mow the yard, and, instead, you walk into eternity. But Mabel understood for years she was walking a long road into heaven. She lived among us each day as if it was the last time she'd set eyes on us."

At just the point in Eva's life when she was weary from years of plotting and planning how to fix unfixable things, Mabel happened along— this woman willing to wrestle with Eva's past regrets until their remains rested.

After a brief prayer, the musicians split up, some going to the back of the church while some stood at the front. The bulletin called it "Antiphonal Brass." They surrounded the congregation, playing and building a brassy, royal-sounding melody, echoing front to back, back to front, leading and following, alternating like a conversation—or encouragement. They became like human voices and friendships, pushing each other onward and upward. The music built, their notes sounding together. Then with one last effort, they tipped the bells of their instruments to the sky and ended in a loud refrain.

Eva took a last deep breath and the service ended. They had a somber procession over to the cemetery next door, Rob escorting Eva. Afterward, everyone met back in the fellowship hall to share some food. As smoothly as a group of caterers, ladies quickly pulled out sandwich trays, dips, and vegetables. Isabella poured drinks and the brass players passed around appetizers on platters.

The rest of the group spread out to different chairs or tables to eat hunched over Styrofoam plates. At first they talked in quiet, respectful tones. Then they grew more comfortable, echoing each other, front to back, back to front, surrounding the room with voices and laughter, just the way Mabel would've liked it.

≈

When Eva rose in the morning, she found Breezy had started a collection of items on the dining room table. An album, a box of old photos, some paper scissors.

"To make a memory book, Gram. You can keep it near your bedside to jog your thinking when things get muddled. A system of reminders with pictures and memorabilia and snippets of the past."

Eva's mind passed over the good memories that hurt and the bad memories that hurt more, as someday darkness would replace all her memories.

Remarkable and unremarkable days. A schoolyard bully. Fall days in New England, where they sweated and raked rotting leaves, smelling swirling smoke of chimneys from their neighbor's house. Sarah posing for a photo with Rob flexing his muscles. The kids fishing at the end of a Cape Cod dock. Rob closing the door when his father arrived to pick them up to live with him.

"And I want to fill my collection of picture frames with photographs," Eva announced. "I'd like to be surrounded by my family in pictures . . . like other people are surrounded."

Breezy looked around the room, wall by wall, as if confirming the Wards did have a cloud of witnesses reminding them where they came from and who they belonged to, room after room of memories telling their story. She stared off into the distance for a moment.

Maybe she was recalling Eva's house, how it never boasted photos but instead had beautiful but impersonal sketches and oils decorating her walls, depicting scenes she'd never visited. She may have been traveling to Eva's nightstand and envisioning the small vase with rotating fresh flowers from the garden, but no pictures. Her bookshelves, empty of family photo albums, but filled with fiction and nonfiction books with illustrations and photos of other people, unrelated people—gardening books with lavish photographs of peonies and orchids. Biographies of past presidents and first ladies, but no one who shared her blood.

Finally her eyes settled on Eva. "It's about time."

Rob passed through the room several times while they created the book, pointing out pictures he remembered, picking up a couple to examine closely. "Sarah looks so happy in this one." He showed his mother a picture of Sarah on a summer day, the sun like a spotlight behind her hair. Then he went outside to work with Ian, leaving Eva the comfort of being able to see him through the window as he and Ian repaired the porch railing near the back steps. Dressed in work clothes, Rob helped Ian by holding the wood and waiting for new support brackets.

How could gratitude and loss survive together? Who wins the tussle? Her son returned to her but they had lost so many years.

Watching the men work, Eva mulled over a list she would never send to the sky.

Being in the soft arms of her grandmother. Rob and Sarah playing in the first snow of the season. Her dad's cigarette-scorched voice. Sarah's gravelly voice. Rob's determined scowl as he took apart a radio. Wallace's bold laugh when he and Rob tried to create their own comic book. Breezy staring into the face of a hurting student. Reading a novel in a lounge chair on a perfect July day with a box of crackers close at hand. Mabel's whoosh as she rushed around the kitchen. Try Again Farm. The smell of fresh-tilled soil in her garden just before planting. The air just before the arrival of impending thunderstorms. Her wedding ring being put on her finger. Her wedding ring being slipped off her finger.

After a half hour, Breezy and Eva took a much-needed break from making the memory book to check on the guys. Breezy brought out a tray of iced tea and encouraged everyone to sit down under the trees. The group sipped the cold beverage, as bunnies darted around the yard and birds flitted among the branches. For a moment, Eva and Rob seemed to forget together. Fights, losses, anger, and misdeeds all drifted skyward.

"Work's the best medicine for grief," Ian said. "And there's plenty of work to do around here."

"Keep putting me to work, Ian. I'm ready and willing." Rob took a last sip of his tea and set down the glass on a table before rising.

"Appreciate it." Ian stood as well. "If you and your mom want to mulch that garden, I have that big pile over there just waiting." He pointed to what looked like a mountain of mulch to Eva.

Rob glanced at the pile and nodded. "I think we can manage spreading some of that. Right, Mother? I'll shovel, you spread?"

Rob and Eva walked about the yard, piling on mulch to protect the plants from the impending winter. "You've never lived on a farm before, Mother. What do you think about life here?"

"I love the farm . . . and they've given me a place in the barn to work on my refinishing projects." She hesitated. "But lately I'm wondering if I should go somewhere else."

"No." He stopped his work, holding his shovel an arm's length from his side. "Breezy told me about your trips and adventures. You need to stay here and be safe."

Eva placed a reassuring hand on his chest. She thought of the three words she wrote on a piece of paper in her room. "I would go to a safe place, Rob. Would you like to go see it?"

He looked skeptical and alarmed. "Go *where*?"

～

The worded place. Cedarwood Nursing Home. Eva studied the businesses passing by her window, the changing of the yellow traffic lights to full-stop red, the warning of the brake lights ahead triggering an urgent need for action. "I know Breezy's already been talking to the nursing home. I intercepted some of her calls."

Rob nodded his head as if confirming Eva was still the same old Mom who intercepted calls. "I believe Breezy would tell you those calls were *just information gathering*, to know her options. She worried you were going to be unhappy on the farm. But she'd prefer to keep you close. I'm indebted to her. While I've been living the life in London, working during the day and playing my guitar in pubs at night with my band, she's been holding down the fort. I told her I can stay and pull my weight here for a while, if she needs me."

"You play in a band? What instrument?"

"Guitar and vocal."

"You never played guitar when you were younger. What else do you do I don't know about? Are you secretly married?"

Rob let out a laugh so bold and solid, the vibrations bounced around the Jeep like a rock and roll song turned up at full volume, gifting Eva with a sound she hadn't heard in years. "No wife. But I do have a steady girlfriend. Steady is an understatement. We've been together for about ten years."

"Ten years! Why in the world wouldn't you marry the woman?"

He smiled sadly and chewed on the inside of his cheek before he answered. "I guess I'm a little afraid of marriage. Never saw it as an institution offering much well-being to a soul."

Eva dropped her head. "I'm sure I had a role in that one."

On that note, Cedarwood Nursing Home appeared on the right, the sign hanging from a post looking identical to the one waving in the wind in front of Try Again Farm. Rob pulled through the entranceway.

Mature trees spotted the grounds while flowers faded in the garden. Gardeners were pulling up wilting plants and replacing the summer flowers with mums.

Parking by the front door, Rob turned off the engine. Eva remained steadfast, despite the presence of aging people being wheeled about the grounds by staff or family. Some of them appeared to be fading as well. If she moved here to live out her final days, she'd be giving a real and true gift to Breezy and Ian.

"Breezy doesn't want this, Mother. I've spoken to her about this option."

"I haven't made a decision yet. But let's take a look around. Go find a staff member and tell them we want an impromptu tour. Best to catch them unaware and see how they conduct business."

Rob pulled the Jeep keys from the ignition. "See how they care for the inmates?"

"Oh, please don't call them inmates, Rob. I'm just growing accustomed to this idea." She studied a younger woman who was holding open the front door for an older woman coming outside with her walker. The older woman looked to be in a daze, as if unable to comprehend how this happened to her, how her hips suddenly stopped cooperating and her knees locked so many times in one day, leaving her achy and cramped, and her granddaughter, who she once taught to swim in her pond wearing a life vest now had to help her take baby steps out the revolving door. The pair turned around the building and headed to a circular garden, where they found a cement bench to plant themselves. The grandmother stared off into a space above the tree line, seemingly unresponsive.

"The residents," Rob corrected, watching the same woman with her grandmother before exiting the Jeep.

An eternity later, he reappeared at Eva's door with some sort of employee walking behind him, a businesslike smile planted on the woman's lips. "Are you sure you want to look around, Mother?"

Eva again glanced at the two women sitting on the cement bench, her breathing growing rapid and shallow at the thought of what she was agreeing to do. "Yes, I'm sure, Rob."

When Rob and Eva returned to the farm from the nursing home visit, Breezy exploded at the news of where they had been and how Eva had intercepted her calls with the facility. "That's why I missed so many of their messages. You answered my cell phone without telling me? Gram!" She adamantly insisted Eva was loved and wanted on the farm.

Eva smiled. She still had a little control left in her life. "I wanted to go on a visit to determine my own options . . . before it's too late to have a say in the matter."

Breezy recounted her reasons for looking into the nursing home, how her grandmother had been so miserable over the idea of living at the farm, how her running away episodes were frightening, and how she and Ian wrestled with the idea that maybe, just maybe, Eva might be happier in the company of other residents, feel less lonely. "Those are the only reasons I called them."

Eva slipped into a blankness, looking at her granddaughter on occasion without responding to her questions. Breezy giving up, throwing her hands in the air in exasperation. Rob leaning against the kitchen counter, smiling as he watched his niece interacting with his mother. Breezy with her arms defensively crossing her chest. Eva ignoring her granddaughter's questions, until they all decided to stop the arguing and go watch a Red Sox game in the living room, gathering chips and salsa and crackers to eat. Eva in a chair, watching the group rise to cheer at home runs and base hits, sinking with defeat at strikeouts, moving as a single wave whether rejoicing or lamenting. Such an unexpected surprise in Eva's life.

Nineteen

BREEZY STARTED A NEW YEAR of teaching and Rob remained with his mother. When he wasn't working on his computer, he helped Eva with projects in the barn, took walks with her, and chatted over tea.

Rob stayed through Thanksgiving, until plans were solidified. The morning of his overseas flight, Eva tried to etch moments into her memory. The sound of his laughter when Amber scampered for a treat. His expression of love as they talked one last time before he left for his plane. The way he held a thick finger to her lips and shushed her when she tried to one more time express her sorrow for how she treated her family.

"It's over," he said. "I forgave you a long time ago, but I didn't have the ability to deal with your cruelty, so I did it the only way I knew how. I stayed away and put up a wall."

"But am I forgiven?"

"Yes, you're forgiven." Taking both her hands in his own, he said, "You've been a prodigal mother. You might think I came back to you, but you've come back to me. I've just been waiting on the other side of the sea." Then he collected his bag, packed and ready to go by the kitchen door. Arm in arm, he and his mother walked to a waiting cab for his trip to the airport. "I'll be back more often, Mother. I promise."

In the driveway, they embraced in a warm, long-lasting hug. As he turned to get in the cab, she called after him, "I've always loved you, Son."

Later in the day, Ian checked the refinished desk one last time to be sure he'd secured it well in the back of his truck next to Eva's belongings. On the way to their destination, they would drop off the newly finished gift. As they pulled out of Try Again Farm late in the afternoon, a strip of dark clouds lined the otherwise sun-filled sky, offering a type of beauty despite its darkness, inviting orange light to descend and redden just the treetops.

Ian gave the house a nod of approval. "The house is lookin' good. She's lookin' good, Breeze."

Drapes hung in the windows, tied back in graceful curves with decorative rope and trim. Behind the curtains, shadows and shapes of young and old people seemed to dance and eat and talk together into the future—Eva's new, young companions whose timelines intersected with her own.

As if on cue, the clouds burned away, and a strip of sun shot through, beaming down on the house, highlighting her fresh color, lines, gardens, and trimmed shrubbery—so much work done over the past months. The fresh version replaced the old, dilapidated farm with its failing systems, rotting wood, and water-stained ceilings. Eva's imagination at last allowed her to see the farm the way it looked in its youth—the way Ian and George experienced it—likely the way prodigals remain in the mind of God until they return.

As they drove away down the street, Eva turned her head to look back at the house. All those years and decades and lifetimes to live on Try Again Farm, buying a few animals, pruning the trees in the apple orchard, picking the blueberries for pies and jams, canning the fruits and veggies to restock the pantry, watching Breezy and Ian's children—her great-grandchildren—running through the pasture, climbing trees.

On the way to Isabella's house, they passed through Pemberton's main intersection, already beautifully clad in its Christmas attire. Though still November, wreath-shaped lights, candles, and stars hung from wires, looped between telephone poles.

Mabel would have been thrilled. She had loved Christmas and put up her decorations way too early, sometimes before Thanksgiving, and kept them up well into January.

"At least I'm getting ahead on saying my goodbyes," Eva whispered to Mabel.

"When the time comes to release the last smidge of life, Eva, you want to have kissed the most important things goodbye already. Getting old like us involves lots of little deaths to prepare for the big one—like saying goodbye to loved ones, your home, your health. What's more real anyway—death or life? Memories or trips to the grocery store?"

And Mabel slipped out of Eva's memory.

Isabella's Toyota was nowhere in sight at her house when Ian parked his car. He and Breezy hurriedly opened the back and lifted the desk out, carrying it to the back door. Eva had dictated a note to Breezy telling Isabella to write a Broadway hit on her "new" desk. Breezy secured the envelope under a rock, then the couple made their way quickly to the car to sneak away.

Eva smiled with deep pleasure, leaning forward to pat her grand-daughter on the shoulder as they pulled out to the street on the way to their last stop—Cedarwood Nursing Home.

Eva's grandmother sat at her own desk, writing her correspondence. Writing a play would be such an impractical task for someone with so much housecleaning and cooking to do, always keeping in touch with people, real and living people. She never would've dreamed of writing a make-believe story about make-believe people—or of retelling a story differently than it happened. She would've whispered out loud to any who would hear, "Always tell the truth."

Eva rubbed the knobs on her knuckles to ease the cold and tension as they wound their way down wooded, curvy, tree-lined roads to the nursing home.

How she'd miss swimming in the ocean, feeling water washing over the formerly smooth skin of her legs.

Wallace was there at the beach, strolling with her father. Wallace, who hated to go near the ocean, followed by her father, who always wore his long trousers, even in July, and simply rolled up the bottom of the pant legs to keep them from getting wet. They seemed deep in conversation. Eva wanted Wallace to turn and look at her. She had something to say to him.

Breezy stared out the passenger-side window, never turning to face her grandmother. The reflection in the window showed moisture on her cheeks, grief in her eyes.

Wallace and Eva's father stopped in their places and then looked to each other in amazement. They both hurried to Eva. Do they have something to say to her?

"We're here." Ian turned into the driveway. He parked just outside the front door to unpack Eva and her belongings.

"Yes, we're here." Breezy visibly drooped in her seat. "And I feel like a failure."

"You're not a failure, Breeze," said Ian. "You're letting her make her own decision." He opened the back door for Eva, reaching inside for her trembling hand to assist her.

Eva gave his arm a squeeze of appreciation and approval.

Breezy came around the side of the vehicle, her gaze locked on the residents outside in wheelchairs covered with blankets wrapped around their droopy shoulders—Eva's neighbors for the rest of her life.

Eva listened to Wallace saying he was happy to see her. She tried to form the perfect words to reply to him.

Ian shut his car door as a team of men blew straggling leaves into a pile only to have the wind whisk them away to run free one last time. Other groundskeepers planted rootless greenery for the coming holidays, plantings that would look perky for a month or more, then wither, turn brown, and crumble into the earth.

"The greens are imposters," Eva's grandmother said from her writing desk. Then she appeared to be writing down the words: "Just pretending to be truly planted."

"Wallace would like this place. All this nice landscaping." Eva straightened her shoulders.

Breezy led her grandmother to the sidewalk. The brick building wore its holiday dress the same as Pemberton, with different residents displaying wreaths in their windows. The groundskeepers reached for the last of the greens in a wheelbarrow to stick in the ground along the garden walkways. A young whistling nurse wearing a dark wool coat came by, escorting an older gentleman using a walker. She offered the arrivals a friendly wave, encouraging her patient to welcome them.

Breezy's face turned red and splotchy. "I just don't understand why you decided to come here now."

"It's my gift. To *you*." Eva instructed Wallace and her father to wait for a moment, concentrating on Breezy. She wrapped her arms around Breezy when her granddaughter grew weepy.

Ian enfolded them both.

"You don't have to do this, Gram. We can turn around right now and go home, right back to the farm. This isn't how we wanted things to go."

Eva pulled away. "I know. But it's how I want things to go."

"Should we bring the luggage?" Ian prepared to open the back of the Jeep.

"Let's go inside first, Ian. But could you grab my box in the back seat?"

He opened the back door and lifted the box out with his strong arms. The box held her memory book, her framed pictures of family, and her childhood Bible.

Ian hesitated for a few moments to see if she would change her mind, but Eva shooed him off. "Just say the word, Eva, and we're outta here," Ian said. "We mean it. Try Again Farm has a history of taking care of its own. We can work this out at home." He looked so handsome and concerned, standing there with a black winter coat and red plaid scarf tucked beneath the buttons, his hair blown in the wrong direction from his part by the gusty wind, holding Eva's box of books and quilt. "We can get someone to come in and stay with you during the day while we're at work. Or arrange our schedules—"

"No." Eva cut him off. "I'm ready. I made this decision, even though I know you'd keep me at the farm forever. They have a place for me here. I'm not going to complicate your lives."

Wallace and her father were still watching and waiting.

"I'm not going to cause you worry and put pressure on your marriage. You'll visit me, and I'll visit the farm."

And then Eva saw her. Walking with such elegance and beauty, a shin-length skirt encircling her legs, her disease gone, some meat on her body as she stopped and waited for Eva near the front door.

Sarah.

Eva wanted to be alone with her.

Breezy looked in the direction of Eva's gaze, then turned back to her grandmother, not able to see what Eva saw. "You can change your mind anytime."

They finished loading her bags and walked into the front lobby together just as the dinner bell rang—one, two, three times—sounding like a ship's bell on a foggy New England night, announcing Eva's arrival home.

ACKNOWLEDGMENTS

SOMETIMES LATER IN LIFE YOU'RE handed a great gift. This book, dear reader, is mine—an Ebenezer stone.

I count myself one of the fortunate ones to write in a wide circle of community, giving me many people to acknowledge. To my persistent agent, Keely Boeving, thank you for all your hard work on my behalf. To the folks at Kregel—Catherine DeVries, Steve Barclift, Sarah De Mey, Janyre Tromp, Katherine Chappell—I'm so grateful you acquired this quirky story. To Spencer Fuller, thank you for creating a truly lovely cover. Special thanks to my talented editor Christina Tarabochia, who offered wise and winsome edits and insights—and fed my characters when I often left the food unserved on the page.

The Rainier Writers Workshop where I earned my MFA allowed me three years to rub shoulders with talented mentors and writers. Truly a gift. Especially I thank Suzanne Berne and Adrianne Harun, my fiction mentors, for their wise guidance, and Jim Heynen for my thesis reading.

To the Redbud Writers Guild, you ladies buoy me when I feel like throwing in the towel. Thank you for being a faithful community of like-minded writers. I'm grateful we journey together.

A special thanks to Terri Kraus, Margaret Philbrick, Lara Krupicka,

Katherine James, Katherine Clark, and Stephanie Rische for early reads and critiques. Your feedback lives between these pages. And Mary Taylor, who always loved this story as much as me.

Thank you to Chaplain George Ridgeway, USN (R), for your feedback and help with the beach memorial service.

To Bill, no words—only gratitude and love for your unending support and ability to believe when I doubted. And to my large family: Kyle, Robin, Kenzie, Alexandra, Taylor, Lindsay, Jamison, Melanie, Cora, Willie, and Seamus—because of you, truly "the lines have fallen to me in pleasant places."

Soli Deo Gloria.

DISCUSSION QUESTIONS

1. Eva Gordon just wants to go home. She longs for familiarity and the place that holds her memories. Do you feel her longings are understandable? What do you long for in life? Is it a place, a time period, the future, a person? How likely or unlikely are you to have this longing filled?

2. Breezy is a caretaker personality, inviting the hurting and lonely into her world. Is there a downside to having a caretaker personality? Are you a caretaker or a person who needs to be taken care of? Can we be both at the same time?

3. The house is getting a restoration and a second chance. What or who else is getting a second chance in the novel? Do you hope or wish for a second chance in any area of your life? If so, is it possible or impossible? How would you go about getting it?

4. George struggled with reading all his life. How would the lack of this skill affect him or anyone emotionally? Do you know anyone who struggles to read? Practically speaking, in our society, how does illiteracy limit people? What emotions come with illiteracy? How would you recommend solving the problem of illiteracy?

5. Like Breezy, Mabel is a caretaker. Do you know people like Mabel? If you could speak to Mabel, what would you say? Does she remind you of anyone in your own life?

6. Ian feels a devotion to his uncle and a desire to spend his life with Breezy, causing an intersection between his new life and his old

life. Are there places in your life where your past, present, and future intersect?

7. Rob chose to stay far away from his family conflict. How would you label this choice? Is it healthy or unhealthy, or a little of both? Are there people you need to move toward in your life, or people you should distance yourself from?

8. Isabella has a fondness for older people. Why do you think this is? Do you enjoy being with people your own age or people from all age groups? How is it beneficial to be with people outside your age group? Are there ways in your own life you could expand your circle to include people from different age groups?

9. Do you believe Eva made the right decision at the end of the story? Why or why not? If you could say something to encourage Eva, what would you say?

10. Do you believe Eva needed to be healed from her wounds or turn from her ways? Is it possible to need both?

11. If you were Phyllis, how would you handle a friendship with Eva? Would you be her friend? What would you say to Eva?

12. Eva imagines people from her past and the Ward family watching her actions and the house. If you were to imagine people from your past watching you, who would they be and what would they say?

13. Mabel believed in supporting the "lonelies" by attending their funerals. What are some other ways to support lonely people?